EDJU

RW Spryszak

SPUYTEN DUYVIL

NEW YORK CITY

ISBN 978-1-947980-89-1

Cover: By Giorgio de Chirico

"The Enigma of the Arrival and the Afternoon" 1912

Library of Congress Cataloging-in-Publication Data

Names: Spryszak, RW, 1953- author.
Title: Edju / RW Spryszak.
Description: New York City : Spuyten Duyvil, [2019]
Identifiers: LCCN 2018038953 | ISBN 9781947980891
Classification: LCC PS3619.P795 E35 2019 | DDC 813/.6--dc23
LC record available at https://lccn.loc.gov/2018038953

TO LYNNE

1.

If I stood before the glass coffin with the body of the dead saint inside and waited for my miracle, would it come to me?

The chapel veil around her head is yellowing. Becomes a snake. Her face is sunken and plastic. Where the mouth was, a pushed-in pile of blackened lips and catlike teeth. They have put a coating of wax on her body to preserve the miracle of unrotting death. But I think when they poured it, it must have been too hot. It left her gray eyes staring out of dimly burnt sockets. Frozen in a brown edge singe. Still, we believe. A symbol of the deathless death to be admired.

The faithful rosary around her fingers, hands crossed upon her black-cloaked chest. The rust of vivianite like a fashionable blue choker around her neck. Her clothes are dull and soiled. The regalia of an ancient doll found in a moldy basement. The pillows and padding around her are tattered and graying as much as her unconvincing skin.

If I stood before the glass coffin with the body of the dead saint inside and believed and waited long enough for my miracle, would it come to me? Would she grant my wish like a bone you pull at the table? A tasteless fortune cookie signifying nothing. A prayer to the empty sky. The feeble promise of the insincere.

They run from me now, everyone I knew as a boy. They think I am vile and keep their distance. Build walls. Make signals to warn one another I am coming. Or, worse, think of me not at all. They think of me not at all. And if they see me looking they go to each other and whisper. He is back. He has returned. He's looking at you from over there. Run away. Laugh and hide.

I tell myself I may not look. They must not see me looking. I try to do nothing that would alarm them. It has been a long effort. I have rid myself of possessions to be clean. I say nothing and tell all my grief to the dead saint and her daughter.

If I stood before the glass coffin with the body of the dead saint inside and asked for oblivion, and believed and waited long enough for my miracle, would it come to me?

I am followed by men in hats, women in blanched white makeup and familial pearls, old pouting red lips, faces secure in their righteousness. Bad perfume heavy clouding unwashed skin. There was a policeman. Two clowns, one juggling. A man wearing a solemn gold mask and a woman kicking high feet from below her skirt. Babies wrapped in their mothers' arms. Nursemaids. Tappers. Pirates. Painted faces as if it were Carnival again. Foreigners. Released prisoners. Pensioners. Hangers-on. Fat people. Brown people. Men in square brown hats and cripples twirling their crutches as if just magnificent and recently healed.

They wait their turn to stand before the glass coffin with the body of the dead saint inside and ask for their own random oblivion and try to believe and wait long enough for their own miracles to come to them. But they can't get on so long as I stand here.

Beside me is a burlap sack I bought on the mountain. Alice is inside. The dead saint doesn't move. There is no miracle.

8

2.

he set his candles in the red sand. they must be in a line and put just so or the prayer won't work. the curse they come again. but the greens they knock it down, he attempt to remake.

I put money in the can and take five candles from the orange wooden box. They are ivory white and smell of myrrh or the scarcity of ages. Or the trinkets of memory in the damp historic halls. Or perfumed turtles. Or the smooth ink scent of old prayer book paper, crinkling and thin. They have a beautiful scent and it will get better when I light them, if ever that day comes. I must place them standing up inside a box of red sand. And I must space them perfect one to another, the line perfect and straight. It is a careful process. If I do it wrong they will not allow it. Everything depends on the red sand in a barrel.

Hauling Alice from my apartment made my large muscles tired. And now I use these smaller muscles and they quiver as I set the first candle into the sand. I do this knowing it will not work. I will put the second candle in the wrong place or at the improper distance because of my shaking. Not that I am trying to. The monks will come out and say it is wrong like they always do, even if I think I'm doing it right. I cannot go from large to small muscles so fast. The next candle will be wrong as well. And they will come out and tell me it is wrong and I may not light them. Because you can't light them until they are perfect in the red sand. I will look closer at my alignment and my placing and I will only then see what they are talking about. There is only one chance, and I have already lost it.

As I'm doing it, of course, I believe I am putting them in the red sand in perfect order. Or I think I am and maybe one or two are off and I hope they won't see it. But all the time I know it won't be good enough. I do not know why I persist in this effort. I know I cannot do it right but keep trying. I know they will find fault no matter how well I think I've placed the candles. Yet I return and try again.

I finish my row of candles and pull the cord attached to the small brass bell above my head. A monk emerges from behind an ornate carved door and stands beside me. He studies the arrangement. He shakes his head. I can't see his face for the hood. But I've failed again. He pulls the candles out of the red sand and returns them to the box I bought them from. I may try once more or as many times as I'd like, but I will have to buy the candles all over again each time.

I push my hands in my pockets to see if I have money to buy more candles, but my pockets are empty and all my money is gone. I always seem to forget to bring enough. I'm not sure what is happening to me these days.

It is time to return home. There is some money there I think. So, I pull the sack out of the cathedral and walk along the broken sidewalk to my apartment with it.

When I was younger I could carry Alice wherever I went. But these days I drag her here and there. I have become too old and weak over time. The weather always chills me. The church takes all my money. I have sweaters.

3.

I have sweaters and my apartment is simple. I am not like the young men by the river. They live in complex hives across the city while my simple apartment is the essence of quiet. The apex of silence. And the key to simplicity is to have a lack of things. I do not have many things in my apartment. I have a shrine to St. Athwulf beside my bed. But that is no clue. It would reveal nothing to the authorities, as he is forgotten.

I have rid myself of possessions to be clean. I say nothing and tell all my grief to the dead saint and her daughter. I am the pure warrior, untainted by desire.

In contrast to other apartments the authorities will see when they inspect the scenes of crimes, my apartment will offer them few clues. Perhaps none at all. When they break down the door they will find me gone. There will be no telltale trace or mitigating circumstance. No lead will create a trail they can follow. There will be nothing to discern. Nothing to judge. Nothing to use.

There is no television in my apartment. Instead, on the 5th of every October, I bring out my icon of St. Charitina and celebrate her virtue. I am always sure to ask for intercession. How would the police ever know this? And, to this day, this is not a crime.

I have no radio as there is never anything on the radio I want to listen to. I have no books because I do not read. And because I do not read there are no newspapers or magazines here either. Too much knowledge is a trap. You think you know things, and they will catch you. Know too much and you trip yourself up. Under questioning I would not break because I know so little.

I have two cups in case one is dirty.

I have a curtain and a radiator. There is a comfortable chair beside a table. It was while I was sitting in that chair deep in thought when St. Edmund the Martyr appeared. At first, I thought he was only a stain in the wallpaper. But when he spoke I knew he was real.

I have one plate because all you have to do is wipe your plate clean when you finish and it is ready for the next time. I eat out of cans and boxes, so there is only ice in my freezer. But I never use it because water does not need help. I wash with water. When I wash my wrists, I try to remember what St Edmund said to me that day. But it is never of any use. It was too long ago. There were soft shoes in those days. It is not the day of soft shoes anymore.

My kitchen counters are spotless and empty except for the breadbox, which is blue and has a flower on it. It is usually empty. But right now, I do have a loaf of rye bread in there. I better eat it soon or it will go moldy.

I have a couch and a chair and a table by the front window of the apartment. This window faces the street but I have only looked out once.

I have three sweaters. One is green. One is black. And the third is also green. I get cold now that I am older. I do not smoke. I pray. And I can light candles to the memory of St. Gens du Beaucet because he would rather be a hermit than in the world. A penchant for the ideal always rattling around in my pocket, you see.

I do not have to place my candles in an exact row at precise distances in red sand here. Not here in my rooms. I can just light them and sing. And St. Gens taps on my window like a snowflake in the winter because he approves of my frugality and my singing. Still, I know, my poor candles here do not have the same power of those you could buy at the cathedral. But one must make do sometimes. I try to make up in quantity what I have always lacked in quality.

I do not smoke and I do not drink. I get headaches and have five bottles of aspirin in my medicine cabinet. They are next to my shaving cream and bandages, which are just above my statue of St. Iwig.

Many people may wonder, you for example, what I do to pass the time. I could try and explain it but it wouldn't be of much interest to people. Then again, of course, there is always Alice.

I make my food and am sure to have three meals a day but I am not a heavy eater and am not much interested in food anyway. So, soup and bread and water and canned stew is fine. I don't care for fruit except blueberries. But they are too difficult to find and not usually worth the price as they go off and spoil fast in this kind of air.

I sleep in my bed and I shave. I keep washed and take care of my clothes. I have four shirts and five pairs of pants. They are brown and blue. And the sweaters I've already mentioned.

I keep the apartment clean but I worry sometimes about why I have stomach pains. I'm sure it is a virus so I keep the floors clean too and never eat food off it. But I will lay in bed and hold my stomach because it hurts so bad. I do that for hours sometimes until the pain goes away.

I like to have pain. I've noticed that when pain subsides something gets released inside my body that makes me feel good. A kind of bliss that sets in when you feel relief I suppose. So, whenever I am in pain I think – oh, I will feel good when it is over – and it isn't so bad anymore. I especially enjoy waking up with a splitting headache. Because when I take two aspirin I feel good when they start to work. I like the feeling of relief when a long bout of pain is over. It is worth being hurt.

I don't have any pets because they are dirty, but I seem to be always fighting ants in my kitchen. I don't know where they come from but they are not my pets. I once considered waging a full-scale international war against all ants. But after several years I recognized the futility of it. I satisfied myself with the local battle as being as much as one man may be expected to handle.

I don't have a telephone because there is no one to talk to on it. But I do keep a basket of plastic flowers on my kitchen table because they are a light blue plastic. I think they are a wise choice. I do not have to water them. Just dust them. Alice likes them too, I think. But she never speaks because she is dead.

I keep her in a simple sack I bought on The Mountain. At night when I go to sleep I put her in the closet on a shelf so she doesn't attract ants.

No. The authorities could never suspect me. They will never come after me. I am protected by the saints and fight the ants. My life is different from the lives of those down there. Down there by the dead river.

4.

At night the young men and boys begin to appear from the high street and make their way down the rough stairs. They move in a trance down to the formless river that sizzles through our city like an old broken snake. Polluted and dark. Crusted with a hard algae scum. They go down to this river, because that is where they can find the last vestiges of the ancient maze. They come in the dim cold squeak of the late night and early morning. Three AM they come. Out of their own streets and shops and secret, feverish bedrooms. One by one. They are like drug fiends, nervous and worn. Pale and shaking. Tromping down the old stone steps. Passing the abandoned fishing huts and black old shacks. Drawn to the worn down remnants of the Wall that still exists from a thousand years before.

They rub their hands against the old stones of the Wall. They rub their faces into it. Or their whole bodies. It stops their shaking and their moaning. Some lean against it, this monument to a bygone age, and seem to soak in an odd kind of strength from it. They emerge from this covered in the chalk dust of the ages. It calms them. They consider it magical. A talisman. And they are able to relax again after making this contact with the past. The urge satisfied. For the time being.

The entire spectacle frightens the authorities. It has been going on for months and there is some alarm. The government wants to destroy what remains of the old Walls but there are historic principles to consider. That means all talk of these remnants' once-and-for-all-destruction labors on.

These walls that made the Maze are sacred to many. It all comes from the most important time of our history. In the age of the Vikings we were a small country with few people.

The Vikings invaded again and again but we were always too few to fight them. They plundered at will until King Ulf II, known as Ulf the Hermit, built a magnificent maze.

It spanned the entire width and breadth of our country. Overnight ten foot high brick, stone, and old composition concrete. It sprung up like a miasmic weed. The maze broke up the terrain. It created long, winding corridors across open country. Broke up roads and whole villages. Dead ends. False openings. Concentric circles that wound the traveler right back where they started. When the Vikings invaded and attempted to follow their old paths of plunder, they got lost. The maze befuddled them. And while they were wandering aimless we burned their ships. Little by little we killed them by trapping them in blind alleys and throwing rocks from the high walls. After years of constant defeats, they never came again. They held meetings in the great long houses of their terrible lands and said no more of this from these people. It isn't worth the cost. The treasures are poor and the women are ugly anyway. But it was the Maze that did them in.

Over the centuries, of course, need, weather and wind wore down the saving structure of our protection. Farmers cut openings to resume the cultivation of their fields. Towns broke down the maze to reconnect their streets and markets. The rain wore down the rest. All that remained crouched hidden in forgotten places in untouched reaches of the country. Soon enough there were no more Vikings anyway. The killing seed had been routed out of their genetics once and for all.

The maze no longer exists as it was either. It ceased to exist as a function or the thing we thought of it as. It was a thing we saw from a passing car on a country drive. A thing we had picnics beside without remembering what it was for long ago. An ignored thing. The largest of many things taken for granted. Generations came and went without realizing or remembering the reason for the stones. It was something in schoolbooks. Therefore unimportant.

Only in the recent years has this changed. But only after the onset of a terrible plague that raged through the ranks of our young men. This disease seemed to have no cure. Somehow our young men, desperate, found that coming in physical contact with the old stones helps a great deal. It calms their nerves. Helps them focus. Summons their long neglected and waning strength. And stops the horrendous shaking they suffer from.

No one ever understood the nature or cause of these symptoms and maladies. But touching the old maze cured all who seek the remedy. This medicine never fails and seems to have repaired the lives of so many.

It is a great mystery.

But the old walls of the great maze are not for me. I do not have this malady.

I have another.

I have rid myself of possessions to be clean. I say nothing and tell all my grief to the dead saint and her daughter.

5.

I forced myself back to the cathedral of St. Thorfinn. I had to go. It was unfinished business. Like rain when it doesn't fall. Like threats against the state. Like a weak fist.

I return because I know the glass coffin will be returned to the diamond city in two days and I had only prostrated myself before it once. Once is never enough for the saints. They are as jealous as their God. I have to go. But I am weary. I am tired of fighting this thing that I have. This thing that possesses me. The sickness that has ruled my life since there was only a shell of a man in my clothes. The twisted disease of not being able to forget. The curse or remembering everything.

I've tried to talk it out with Alice but it is too late and I know it. I neglected her and sent her away when she did nothing wrong. She did nothing to me. She did not expect to be so dismissed. And, when I look back over the years, I sometimes find it difficult to understand why I did what I did. How could someone as thin and pale and sick refuse the company of one so beautiful?

She was so beautiful. This Nordic maize colored hair and her green eyes. Slender and tall. Graceful and pleasant to look at. A gentle nature too. And a sense of humor. This was the essence of her soul if souls we have.

There was no reason to send her away. No reason to stop our love. Our friendship. That which seemed like the perfect life before us. But I did it. I did it and I did it with a fearsome energy. A fierce heart. And heartless, then, after all.

Now she is in a sack by the window where I keep her during the day. Near the radiator that clinks in the morning cold. And I grieve over it. It would have been better, I think, if I was the one who killed her.

You should understand - I didn't kill her. I am responsible for some terrible things, but not that. When I sent her away she still had her life. She forgot me. Or, I should say, if ever she remembered me it was with scorn and hatred. But no, I didn't kill her. In fact, no one killed her. She died by nature and nothing else. It was years later when I found her and brought her back with me. Because I was sorry, and remain sorry, for the terrible thing I'd done to her for no good reason. This, and much more, is what I seek absolution for. A story for another time. But first things first.

The next day was the last day of the visitation by the saint in the glass coffin. The Holy Woman of Wherever. I forced myself to go. I did not take Alice with me. There was a plan in my head. This time I would set the candles to a perfect line. By leaving her near the radiator I would not have to use my large muscles carrying her through the streets. I would arrive at the cathedral in full strength. Therefore, I would not be shaking and be able to set the candles straight. The monks watch the red sand and guard it with jealousy. Like the saints and their God. Religion is a jealous thing.

It was liberating to do it this way because it was not my usual way of going. I always took her with me and was proud and happy to show her the sights. But I felt, and said to myself, maybe this time I will go alone. She's done nothing wrong and the holiest of all beings sees and hears all. He knows what I've done. She didn't need to accompany me. I left her by the window where it was cool, and cracked the window open just a bit so she could see.

I was determined to make my final apology. Throw myself on the saints and priests and monks and all else available for mercy. From the moment I crossed the threshold from the street into the vestibule I went to my knees. And I stayed on my knees the whole time. I got into line on my knees. I walked on my knees. Hands folded in perfect prayer position, pointed up like the hood of a hangman. All I wanted them to see was the outward, physical showing of my sorrow and penitence. No pride. No ego. And plain clothes. Plain clothes and brown shoes. And no whiskey either. Sober. Sober as an abandoned wrench in the moonlight. Solemn and humbled.

Most people did not bother to notice my dour attire. My studied plainness. I am a simple man, and each of us come to the cathedral out of our own private hells. Those that did notice, and some who pointed at me and smiled, were fakers anyway. Not fit for true blessings, I imagined. Religious for show. Those who do not take the principles of their faith into their lives. Those who scorn others for the color of their coat. Those who put worms on hooks and mix the forbidden fabrics in their shirts. Let them laugh, I said to my imaginary Alice – because she was under the window by the radiator – let them go. They'll get their reward. Faith is all about others getting what they deserve. And I was well practiced in this.

The progress was slow this time. Anyway, slower than before. My knees buckled twice with sharp pains and I almost couldn't support myself. But I managed. I walked on my knees to the foot of the coffin, praying most of the way. Wishing I could go back to the past and try again. To not send Alice away.

Maybe it would be better for me if I had the same malady of those young men by the river and the walls. That would be nothing compared to this. At least they could experience a minute of relief. Get succor and quiet their minds. Once you are in line on your knees, there is no quitting.

I put my hands on the cool glass and stared at the moldering saint inside. I think they'd put on a new coating of wax since the day before. I couldn't be sure. Something was different and new. It stopped me from my earnest prayer and I didn't know where to look.

Then I realized what was different. The daughter of the

saint in the glass coffin was watching me from a door that led to her chambers. The well-known Marta Vansimmerant. She who was the only child of the sainted woman lying there. She who accompanied the glass coffin wherever it went with the sanction of the holy fathers. A daughter of both the saint and the church. Living proof that the Holy Woman of Wherever had been real. Accompanying her mother was her sanctified mission. Dressed in black. Hollow eyes. Old but still young, somehow. She stared at me as I made my effort to pray on my burning knees. The blains. The shooting, arching stab in each one. My offering. My penance.

When I finished my devotions, I struggled to my feet, unhappy. Even resigned. I knew I'd done all I could do. I did not feel relieved of my burden. Like the lightness of confession when transgression is clean and you are free again. No earnest need to repent and make good, in gratitude for the weight being lifted. No. I felt nothing. Achieved nothing. There was no point in trying the candles. I knew my penitence was incomplete. Immature. Tainted. For when I saw her I tried to peel back the fabric from the front of her lean body with my eyes. I tried to visualize her nakedness and the monks could tell. They were watching. My penance was impure. There would be no peace. No help for it at all. I finished the ritual and departed.

Marta Vansimmerant watched me at every step until I was out the door. Her eyes were claws.

6.

If I stood before the window.

No. I did stand before the window. The radiator pipes knocked as the heat went on. It's an ancient sound the others find quaint.

If I stood before the window on my return. I returned from the cathedral of St. Thorfinn of Hamar. It wasn't up for question. I was there. I am there still, in some sense. I don't know why I question myself. I don't know why I say 'if'.

I stood before the window and did not see Alice. The brown sack. Burlap. Sometimes gray. Whatever it was. The sack was gone. Funny how only then did I notice the mud on the carpet and the blood on the doorknob. I saw none of that coming in. Perhaps it wasn't there then. I don't know.

The radiator knocked as the heat went on. Alice always liked the sound of the air going through the pipes. Like a low hum from a motor. Like a fan of endless white noise. Somehow a comfort. Man has conquered the world and there we are with comforting sounds not part of nature that we made. They help us to sleep. She liked that. She liked to curl up inside her sack and listen to the air go. I would put jelly on white crackers and watch her do it. I know.

But she was gone. I left her alone and she was gone.

They took her and I stood before the empty window where a sack used to be full of Alice. I have a headache. Then it is gone. I lose my sense of timing. Is this now or then? Alice is gone and there are clues leading to the conclusion that while I was away someone took her. They were bleeding and had mud on their shoes. I used to be so proud knowing that I would never leave clues for the police if ever they searched my rooms. Now the clues were made by someone else and the police would only laugh at me.

My bedroom is dark. There is one pillow. A green blanket on a single bed. The window. The brick wall of the building next door, across the gangway. No clock. There are no clocks because my apartment is simple. I already explained this once to you. There is a small table and a chest of drawers. I have socks there. I don't recall if I mentioned sweaters.

I know what I own. I know what belongs to me. So, look around, I told myself. Look around and see if there is anything here that doesn't belong to you. I said this to myself as if scolding a child.

I fall on top of my blanket and stare at the ceiling. The ceiling is white with little rosettes spinning in the distance. I must think. I hear music. Then I don't. But I know I must make a plan to save Alice. Clues. There are clues. And I should concentrate, but there are pictures two inches behind my forehead. Terrible pictures of Alice and what they might be doing to her. Whoever they are.

There are evil men in the world who see a dead woman and think this is their chance to violate her. She would never give in to them alive. Not my Alice. But now that she is dead, they think they can do what they want with her body. This is the sickness of the world. I sit up and put my feet on the simple floor. I must get going. There is no telling what they'll do to her. I must save her from it. It's why I took her off the street and put her in the sack in the first place. I must get control of my mind. It floods fast. This is what happens without a bag of Alice by the radiator.

I shouldn't have sent her away all those years ago. Now look what's become of her. There is nothing worse I could have done to her sweet nature and gentle voice. Her green eyes. The rhyming runes she spoke in. The smile. Her dirty feet. A face of gold.

It rumbles around in my head, these cats of light. My skin

crawls. The window opens. There are ants. But also mud on the floor. Leading from the door to the silver painted radiator that clanks when the heat goes on. Footsteps occurred. Footprints they are. They are not mine. What isn't mine is a clue. How did I not see that before?

Brazen and brash like a dried river running right from the world. One, two, three. The thief appeared at night when he knew I was away. Sidebar. High train. Low road. He waited, of course. They watched me to see when I left her unprotected. Someone was watching. Are they still?

The thought of someone watching made me want to dance. I cannot scratch my chest hard enough to stop this itch. I'll sleep on it, says I. Let the mind grow. That's what happens. You figure out things when you sleep, they say. I swallow a yellow tablet and return to the covers I tossed and scrambled on just now. Clothes off to the cool feel. The blank pillow. Salty eyes and tight covers. The sleep of the dead. Let the brain work itself out. The best thinking is the unworking kind. Before you were born you knew nothing. There was nothing for you. This is what death is like. Nothing any more. And sleep is preparation. The ruminating columns of color hopping up and down the scale while the music goes. This is dreaming. And dreaming drives the train. I need to sleep so that the dreams may instruct me.

If I sleep.

If I sleep before the open window there will be risks.

The night passes. There are violins. I know nothing.

I awake to nothing. My open window tells no secrets. There is no breeze of a summer morning. No birdsong on the rooftops or from the worm offering ground. I am used to the sound of traffic on the high road. But there is nothing to hear. No sound of city buses. No cars pushing or trucks hogging. There are no airplanes overhead.

My apartment with no books or radio sits in a dense

pool of no motion. Even the sounds of neighborhood doors or floorboards overhead are missing. There is no crank and groan of small-minded men playing narrow games in faded gray factories.

There was a drum going. I floated out of the room like an antique cartoon, all black and white ink in the film click jerks. A classic wave along the nothing air, sniffing the warm scent of cartoon food. To the seductive snake of a foreign piccolo. Down the door and out the walk. Through the nothing going on to something near the river. Hypnotized, baptized, realized, stigmatized. The Nordic drum amazed.

But, I say to the gathering angels, I have rid myself of possessions to be clean. I say nothing and tell all my grief to the dead saint and her daughter. Does this count for nothing?

7.

The boys were there beneath the crooked stair. The long stair rambling in concrete bits with mouse holes and rain worn streaks. The stinking river dead and still just beyond. Some of them were writhing atop the bits of maze as if making love to the stone, the ancient stone. As if some old woman who held a strange charm for their energy. Available and unmoving. But only stone, after all.

There were dangerous red banners and everyone tried at uniform. Belt buckles. Shoulder straps. Severe heads. The signatures of rank and the markings of cult. A wicked cult that meant harm to someone if only they could find a target. And the speaker, like a marionette. Jerky arms and pleading palms. Strings running up to an invisible hand at the controls. Odd that I could not hear him from my open window for he seemed loud enough. Now the speaker, the marionette, hoarse and wild with fists and sweat and those not making love to the stones listening, rapt.

The whole world was down here by the river. Or at least the whole country. Even the birds and the worms they dug. The life of the city moved down by the greasy river and there were cries to return to glory. Glory as if bored with all the calm. Bored of all the sameness. One last hit of adrenalin before the dotage. This seemed the only reason the old men joined the boys who were rubbing themselves on the remnants of the maze.

There were threats to rebuild the maze, despite what it meant. This was our national honor and the symbol of our history. Their red flags showed a kind of black maze in a white circle too.

There was the marionette. The scarecrow. Waving arms and swearing vengeance on the world that abandoned his country. My country. The country. They'll take this and like it. We will return to our highborn spirit by the grace of these stones. All the cheering was in unison and at no time did the drumming stop.

I rubbed my eyes to rid myself of the scene, but only the colors changed. Blood red, animal shit green, black and hate and spleen. This was not safe. Skinny men eyed me from the side. Who is this – what does he want – why is he not rubbing his body naked against the stones. I realized at once that I'd done a foolish thing. Coming down here without a way to defend myself.

There were two men circling each other at the opening of a tattered red tent. There was a silhouette of a swan painted in chipped green paint on the canvas above them. They were within feet of each other, staring. Leering at each other. With hands on or near the pommels of swords in the scabbards at the sides. When one moved, the other grunted and countered. Neither of them blinked. One would growl the other would grunt. They would raise their voices doing this from time to time. Especially if they felt the other was about to make a move and attack. Sometimes they let out a sharp Hey-hey-hey. To which the other would growl and curse. Always threatening. Always circling. Sometimes in silence, but then growling again if one moved too close to their sword. Sometimes, as they jockeyed around, their noses came within inches of each other. Once in a while one would make a threatening growl and move his hand toward his sword handle. This led the other one to jog step to the side and grunt louder and lean in and threaten to pull out his sword as well. They went quiet and kept circling each other. Threatening each other. Both afraid to break contact lest the other one attack. Caught in an insane dance that was a metaphor for nothing. Round and round.

I stopped a few yards from them. But there was no way

to get inside the tent. I got caught in their dance. They had swords, but I didn't. I had to be twice as careful. We must have made quite a picture. Three men grunting and growling and circling each other. Any new move by either made the others growl and grunt Hey-hey-watch-it even louder.

I began to understand that I could influence their reactions by my moves. I came to this conclusion the longer I danced and threatened and grunted. My grunts and feints and stomps and shoulder jerks, all of my own design, got their attention. All I wanted to do was get inside the tent. But I had to be careful.

I inched toward the tent opening. I stomped as I moved. Landing hard which made the one immediately to my left move back. This, in turn, made the third one grunt and pull back an inch as well. The concert of nations. The Congress of Vienna. Diplomacy. War games. Little by little I maneuvered them out of the way. When I knew I could make a clean break from this rumba I jumped inside. They rattled their swords and grunted Hey and growled louder, but it was too late. I was inside. They resumed their duet. Still audible inside.

The inside of the tent was cool and quiet. A toothless man scratching his matted hair said I wish they'd kill each other already. They're bad for business.

I looked out the opening. They were face to face once more, clutching their sword handles. Grunting away. How long have they been doing that? I asked.

He explained they'd been at it for days. They are there when I close up and go to bed and still there in the morning when I wake up. I kept thinking sooner or later one of them will collapse from exhaustion if nothing else. But the next day comes and there they are again. Like the stars and the moon and the sun. As constant as two doting mothers. They never seem to sleep. I think they'll stay like that forever. What can be done for you?

I got down to business. A sack, I explained. Has anyone been through here carrying a sack? To which he closed his eyes.

What color, he wanted to know. How big? What's inside? I could not answer all his questions. Gray or brown. Big enough. But I never told him the contents.

It's missing, I explained. And important to me. Taken from my rooms just in the night while I was away.

There it is, then. You shouldn't be away, he shook his head. People shouldn't go away. They should stay home. He pointed out the tent. See where it leads? Look at these crazy people. One of those young men rubbed himself against the old stones so hard he started to bleed. What do you call that, because I certainly have no answer. The only thing I saw was the Daughter of the Saint here last night. Her men put something in her car. It might have been a sack.

Marta Vansimmerant. I said her name in my head and it conjured an image in a mirror at the back of the tent. A dark thing with sharp teeth. He saw the image startle me. Oh, don't worry about that, he calmed me. That's just Louisa.

His daughter walked in through a back slit in the tent carrying a bucket. I made to go, but he bade me use the back way to avoid the two outside. They're insane. It's never going to end. Why bother? Look, he pointed at the ground just outside where they were. He showed me how they'd worn the ground down in an almost perfect circle. That's how long they've been at it for God's sake. I have half a mind to blow their brains out. But they're the future, so the others won't allow it.

I slipped through the back as he instructed. On the other side a solid line of men in steel helmets snapped to attention, then broke their discipline. Oh, someone spat, we thought you were someone else. They lit cigarettes and cursed me. Some were shaky, and broke rank to touch the wall and settled their nerves.

8.

I went back up the broken concrete steps to the high street, away from the mass of men and their stinking river. I returned to my apartment and retrieved my pistol. My beautiful Nagant M1895. With a dark brown serrated grip. Slight scent of light oil on the mystery of blue steel. I would kill anyone who got in the way of my bringing Alice back to my radiator with it. And if I was going down to the river again, I wasn't going back unarmed. Not with death so near and helmets everywhere.

I loaded my pistol with its 7.62 mm, Type R and cried. The ammunition was near impossible to find. A harmless bullet, cool to the touch. Ice in the veins. Ice turning molten and cutting through muscle and bone.

It was the gun used by the Bolshevik secret police. The Cheka. And it has been out of production for so long. A muzzle velocity of 900 feet per second. Accurate up to 55 yards when fired with a steady hand. Indestructible, they say. Able to kill fascists even in the worst weather. Never jams, they tell me. I dare not admit these thoughts to the gentle world. I keep them inside like breeding rare animals hidden in basement cages.

Sometimes it was difficult to load a bullet with all the tears in my eyes. Poor Alice, I thought. What are they doing to her, and what is she feeling?

I should have thought about Alice's feelings long ago, when she was alive. If only I hadn't been such a fool. If only I would have laughed when she teased me instead of getting furious with her. Like a little boy. Like a spoiled brat. I'll kill anyone who harms her, I suppose I said aloud to no one. But was I angrier with them or myself? I couldn't tell.

Poor Alice. What she must be thinking, somewhere, wherever you go when it's over.

But she was a strong woman, and I respected that. She carried on with her life, after all. And wouldn't it be funny if she'd forgotten all about me anyway. Here I am loading my Nagant and she doesn't even remember me. What if I'm making too much of my effect on her? Maybe I had no effect. Maybe I tossed her aside and she was sad for twelve seconds and went on with life. What about that? Well alright then. All the more reason to love her.

I imagine she liked horses when she was a girl and was unafraid of the bats living in the stable lofts. Other girls ran and worried the bats would get tangled in their hair like the legends said. But Alice wasn't the type to worry about unproven old tales like that. That was why she looked so beautiful in her high-necked chainmail. And why her mind smelled of the rarest flower on Earth. Funny, I remember thinking as I put the pistol in my belt and made my way out the door, her corpse didn't smell. It never did.

This was my mission. I couldn't stop. I flew out the door. And when I heard the screen door slam behind me and the cash register tinkle I was a child again. I was looking through the tall slanted glass at the shelves of penny candy. Each kind in dishes while the old man with white hair waited feigning patience. It was always so cold inside the store. Newspapers stacked beside the comic books. The short freezer where the ice cream bars and cones were all stuck together. The wall of cigarette packs in beautiful colors behind the high counter. The paperback books on a revolving wire tower. The soft drink bottles stacked in handled cardboard packs beyond. The scowl and spit of the old broken veterans, cursing my youth and sneering at me. I didn't care about the danger of abuse they presented while my parents weren't looking. I could run faster than they could.

I would buy a rubber ball and pitch it against the brick

wall of the school. Paint window frames with fresh mud and dirty sticks. Steal glass bottles from porches and sell them for candy. Then have someone older say, no – you never did that. All my memories invalid. Nothing like that ever happened. I didn't have a Nagant then. Only toy guns. Sometimes I filled them with soda pop so the victim would not only be wet but sticky as well. But that didn't happen either. I sat near the window and yearned to join the boys but always had a fever. No one knew me. I read poetry and dog stories. Shuffled from room to room. Never went inside that store after all. They bought me strange games. Games meant for children twice my age, and I would play with them, alone, making up my own rules. I never minded being alone. It was my favorite thing.

Then, sixty years later, I am a crooked old man in a tall black coat walking on the sidewalk between the snow piles. And the boys make snowballs and throw them at my back. The balls break hard and puff apart, and they laugh and I turn and wave my arms and grunt because I am sick and old. There goes Edju, they scream and laugh. It's Edju, run. They don't know my life. They don't know where I've been. They don't know what I went through to find Alice. I am just a scary old man with a brick face and an angular black coat. A perfect target for snowballs. And laughter. And fear. And derision. Because my mind is gone and I can't speak and they think I am a monster. My arms and my grunting make me Frankenstein's creation in the snow. They are afraid and laugh and run. I go home and heat my leftover soup. Sitting in a rocker with old socks and a wet coat. Unable to speak. It was a useless life. Wasted on gruel.

But it's not the future quite yet. It's now and I have a pistol. And I will kill anyone who stands in the way of finding my sack of Alice. Gray or brown. I can't remember.

9.

Humans sit before their food on a plate. Things they pulled out of the ground. The dirt of ages hanging to the roots. The skin hanging from bones of hapless creatures burned or otherwise fired. And they eat it. They eat it all. In the vastness of the universe there is matter and there is other matter. Compared to the flavor of the sun food is tasteless. But humans push their faces into piles of it and swallow it in sickening gobs through animal maws. Bellies like garbage cans. Then their guts roar and churn and suck out whatever the body can use for itself. A kind of stealing. Killing and stealing and dominance. And when they finish, they deposit odorous bricks of remnant all over the ground. And each human manufactures tons of this through the course of a lifetime. Tens of thousands of people's lifetimes. Millions of people. Billions, since time began. All making countless megatons of this stink and refuse. The world has made the effort to keep your stink off the streets. How will you repay the world for its trouble? So, they say – Each Man Must Justify His Pile.

And then, what human bodies make of poor, pure, simple water.

But I, too, am part of this horror. The horror of eating. The horror of sucking and separating minerals from what is useless. The execution of the cycle. I am also responsible.

I am old fashioned. I shake hands. I tip my hat. If I see a dead woman in the streets, I put her in a sack so the ghouls won't take advantage of her. I try to be positive. Think good thoughts. Help old people. Be kind to little animals. Though I am at war with ants.

It's my one fault. I have been at war with ants since I was a boy. My mission, I used to believe, was to kill every ant on the planet. The failure of this plan is not a matter of desire, but a matter of logistics. I cannot get to Brazil. I cannot stay in Australia long enough. I would take my war quadrant by quadrant across the entire map of the world. But I lack the support of the Congress and the Parliament. I get no backing from the Unicameral Assembly. I cannot get the funding. I use my foot and do what I can.

I will succeed, I swear by the saints who live in the summer mansions in heaven. Because the collective heart of man has a great hunger for killing. We can't turn away. Nor do we want to.

That is why these young men gather down by the river. It is violence that attracts them. And I go among them. Down the weaving steps to the broken quay where they line the river like martinets. Shoulder to shoulder. Skinny. Their faces pocked with pimples. Their voices cracking with the changing of their age. No longer boys. Not yet men. Lost in brute fantasy.

I am not a violent man. I prostrated myself before the statues of all the saints and begged them to help. It did no good. Not ever, in all my life. Despite the sweet scent of holy oil. Forget the animated cleanliness of holy water. The holy sky. The holy walls. The holy chairs. The holy floor. Especially the holy floor. Forget it all. The feet of the statues are set at impossible angles. Nobody can stand that way. The sculptors think we are fools. But I have my Nagant M1895, and I wave it like the firesword of the angel Michael, god of war. I stand beside the stinking river and demand a boat.

You don't have to steal a boat, they laugh. You can just go, they say. But I trust no one now.

I am not a violent man, and all the children know this, I reply. They smirk at me with their sharp angled haircuts and pointy little teeth. Their short pants still brushed with the chalk from the ancient stones they've copulated. Someday their children will pelt me with rocks.

And I would have killed them all if there was no choice, though I am not a violent man. Laughing, they lead me to a rowboat and I put my gun away. They wanted no money. No name on a slip of paper. They seemed glad to let me have the boat. Ten years from now I will still be able to say that their laughter never got to me. They are little fascist children in short pants. Their opinions meant nothing to me. Their laughter meant even less.

I get in.

The boat does not bump into the wood like boats will do because there is no current in the river. The rope that ties the bow to the pier hangs like a wet shirt. There are spider webs hanging from it. The green water is cast with a pallid film. A man at the edge of the dock extends a hand. I give him the pomegranate seeds and he hands over the oars, crossed like spears and I must separate them from the tin foil holding them together. The boys in uniform slap their thighs and know better. No one has tried to cross this river in a hundred years, they taunt. I must follow the daughter of the saint, I shout back. She has stolen something from me.

You will never find her, they laugh louder. Marta Van-simmerant is too smart for you. I ignore them for potatoes. Potato faces. I climb into the boat that does not wobble in the water like boats will do because the river is thick as syrup. I set the oars in their mounts on either side as the laughter carries on. The man with the hand pulls a slender chord of the tie and the rope falls useless. I am free. He puts a foot on the edge of the boat and pushes hard with a strong leg. I am shrouded in fog. The laughter ends. I put the oars in the water to the sound of breaking glass. I dodge the figure skat-er in a death mask. It is all much too depressing. But I row anyway. It is the only answer.

Only then do I wonder if Marta Vansimmerant took Alice back to Rome with her. The glass coffin processional was only in our town for two more days. Have two days past since last I was there? I row hard. Furious. Each time the oars dip in the water there is a faraway sound like bat wings. I am not sure my oars are in water at all. I cannot tell if I am moving. But I must not stop.

If I pull the oars hard.

If I pull the oars hard despite the splinters breaking off into my skin.

If I bleed on the oars, when the pain goes away I will feel good. It's why I enjoy pain.

10.

he is hot to warm in the neck. instant he goes into the fog. oars
crack glass and reveal the wet. far he goes, not far enough.

I row for hours. The landmarks on either side of the river obliterated by the steam. Water drips from lifted oars back into the river below and makes the sound of violins. I am happy. There are veils of fog all around. To push them aside is some kind of sin. My head is down. My shoulders work. My arms tire. On and on I row. The happiness fades.

How does a man go forward when his back is to the future? This is the fundamental problem of rowing. There is an island somewhere far off in the mist. The call of rare birds, unheard for centuries. The creak of the wood. The march of the pods. Broken tines and barrel staves litter the surface of the water now. Perhaps there has been a shipwreck. The island, unseen, biting a passing boat. Lost crew and all, eaten in the foggy dew. Can you smell blood? Does blood have an actual smell? If it is possible, then I can do it. I can do it now. The closer I get to the island, the bigger the odor of blood. I did not pack provisions. I only have a gun used by the Cheka.

This is a moment I need a third hand. One for this oar. One for that oar. One for the gun drawn, or ready between the oars. Or at least near the oars. Near enough to kill whatever creatures are causing the scent of blood to fill the air. To row with one hand on one oar gives the world the usual direction. A man needs two oars when his back is to the future. It's why we do it. What we live for. The way it is and has always been, forevermore amen.

I cannot pray without the face of a saint before me. The words fly away in seven directions without one. They go off with no intent. No purpose. Like water spraying against plastic. The plastic will not relent. The water runs down and the ground sucks it up. One waters the lawn for nothing this way, and it is the same with prayer.

But if I did pray I would ask the celestial assembly to guide the boat or at least be the eyes in the back of my head. And please do not let Marta Vansimmerant leave town until I can cross the river. And please let no one open the bag of Alice. And also food please, as I took none. Also, do not let my gun get useless with the dampness enclosing me. No, says St. Michael of the Arch, not to worry about the gun. It was meant to kill fascists in any weather. Remember? Besides its beauty, that is why you bought it. But he is silent about the other things because I have no painted plaster to beseech and cannot focus. He is the god of war. The angel of no mercy, holding a pike to off a head at the whim of the master. Like the ruin of Job. He is familiar with guns. I need not worry.

But I cannot eat the gun. Nor the bullets. Nor can I eat the residue the firing of the gun will leave in the air and on the ground for the detectives to note and study. I am alone.

There is no island. There never was. There was only weed and wood laying on the dead surface of the water. Perhaps the other side of the river is near.

If I could see it would be different. I could read. I could watch women. Hide my eyes from the sun and worry I am going blind. How is this justice, I ask. I have rid myself of possessions to be clean. I say nothing and tell all my grief to the dead saint and her daughter. Was this never enough?

I am taunted from the shores. Again, and again. I can hear their voices and I wonder, after all my prayers, how is it I am abandoned? How is it the force and face of God is yet denied me? I am ridiculed by beings I can't see.

Who these creatures are I cannot tell. The music they make gives every sign they are insane. Violins do not speak. Cellos do not negotiate. Clarinets do not declare right and wrong in the wars between tuba and oboe. Yet they all are doing the things they may not do. So, they are mad, whoever they are. Yet this music is as haunting as projected swaths of light on gossamer. In the dark. With a cold current of air in a closed space. And an owl. Where this music comes from I cannot tell.

Sooner or later the mouth of God will open below my boat and I will be spit down into the foam. Down the rolling tide. Into the open air. Bow first, crazed and screaming. The bravest children will have arms up. The fearful, who know better, will fall unwilling. Oars will go flying away from my hands, and this will make the watchers onshore happy. And then I will never reach the other shore. Marta Vansimmerant will escape. And Alice, poorest Alice, will be gone from me.

I will not see her lump in the sack again, or hear the gas escaping through her drawstring any more. No more the lilting sound I imagine as the gears of her brain work out the mathematics of decay. How will I fill the space by the radiator? What pile of bones and fabric will I nod to in the morning in hopeful greeting? There will be an empty space there. How will I go on at all? My chest fills with heavy sadness. The boat sinks an inch in the water. It is the opposite of when a man dies and they measure the soul leaving him. It is the addition of the grief, a haunting creature, and part of the air. I've heard of this before.

So, what was the direction my life points to without her? An upward tilt? A slow fade away? An outward shoot? Do they know what they have done to me, stealing her? No. They don't care. They never care. It is a careless world. An unthinking orchestra. Selfish violins, after all.

I row. And I keep rowing. I must. I row for a hundred years because I found her body on the street. Because of the things they will do to her. Because that's the way the world is now. Mean and cruel. Careless and unthinking. Filled with oboes and misdirected by a skeleton in a suit coat, waving a baton. When someone dies there are those who grieve. But as one man cries two doors away two are making love. Next to them someone laughs. There are cats. There is rain. The loved one is dead but the sun returns anyway. It's the cruelty of life itself.

And that the anointed daughter of a canonized saint may do such an evil thing to me seems to tell me something. Perhaps I have wasted all my devotions. All my supplications. All my candle money. No. I cannot believe in the wide white halls of heaven or the dank red caves of hell any more. There is only sleep. Like it was before you were born, so will it be when your eyes close for the last time. What cares remain?

I press on, praying. I cannot not believe. For just when I stop believing it will come true. This is how my luck runs. I will believe and persevere and believe still. Then the moment I quit the clouds will open and the hosts will arrive. And I will be nothing more than a clown with a taffeta collar and big blue shoes, standing in the forsaken rain.

11.

I am desperate. All the images in my head are childish. Brutes and cartoons. Nothing of merit. No meat at all. Silly games. Bad clothes. Worn shoes. The summer heat of corduroy. I grasp at any hint. Any clue. I worry for lack of the potable. Fret for the scarcity of meal. I worm through the dead water as flat as wax.

The journey is a nightmare now. I cannot see the killing ghosts. Third level tricks enshrine my head. And no fast move will end them. In my brain, a memory. It comes from nowhere, pushes through. The fat boss man with debutante feet, sweat pouring from his red-faced heart says sarcasm is not for him today. I wish him dead. I wish maggots fester in his brain. But I must remain modest, or else the gods of travel will unscrew my head. So, I wait and say nothing. He has to live with himself. That is quite enough punishment.

With the scant haven of a faint gift I see a dim light in the distance. An upstairs window of some structure I cannot make out. A bare bulb hanging from a ceiling. Someone painting the walls of the room. It reminds me when I told Alice to leave and never come back. The future is a starship, I said as if a small child. I can't see myself there with you. And she cried. And she tried to return to me. To try harder – but at what I couldn't say. Even I had no idea what I was saying. If she were alive today she would be a fascist, after all. Perhaps she became a fascist because it would be the opposite of me, and anything that was me must have been bad. All I opposed would be virtue in her eyes.

She traveled with the bloated bellies of the world. The fat, swollen-ankled ones who talk with their mouths full and belch without hiding. The ill-mannered blunt cocks with the ill-fitting short pants. The wild talk and shouting jokes of the gun toting masses. Sun glasses. Wide asses. Haters of all politeness. Swearing in front of women. Doing their best to elect maize haired squires of a certain racial stock. Armbands and acne. Hatred and fear. Let the poor suffer and die, we are the ones the world needs.

In her bitter reaction against me anything I stood for she rejected. This was virtue. Anything I embraced must be wrong. And she fell in with men who led her down the beer and leather alleys. Little schooling. No sense of the world. Grunting ugly puking noises if one suggests escargot. Give me beer and grease. Give Alice some too. And so, she allowed her mind to become lazy because it was convenient. Because it was easy. If I worshiped God she would kiss the devil. That I sought justice for the poor meant she turned to eugenics.

I hate Alice.

The bare bulb in the window somewhere on the other shore reminded me of this. When a hand came from amid the paint and pulled the chain the room went dark. And it reminded me that it was I who found her discarded body in the street. It was I who regretted tossing her love away for a thousand years. It was I who gathered her up, careful not to break her, and put her in the sack. It was I who protected her ever since.

I love Alice.

Then the light came back on and I thought of food. It went off I remembered a storybook I read as a child. I didn't want to see it come back on again. I knew that if it did, I would recall something embarrassing that I'd done. And all the reasons they hate me would line up again and ruin my frame of mind.

I looked down so I wouldn't see it. I kept rowing. I even closed my eyes for a while.

My shoulders on fire. My biceps cold. My triceps blue. My back an arching mass of a hundred squid devouring each other. The taste of a guppy in one's stomach.

When the green men pulled my boat to the dock there was the bleating scent of working class onion and stale beer. I'd made the crossing at last.

12.

These were the green men of childhood legend. The ones that frighten babies with sharp sticks. The ones boys run from pointing back to from where they came. Shrieking, it's the Green Man, it's the Green Man. Behind him three other boys stare up at the statued angels all along the roof of the old church.

The kind of green men that are not there but pointed to just the same as they hide behind the statue's wings up there. The green men who slithered between wood door and screen door and hid under manhole covers to grab at your legs. They all wore eternal smiles because they knew they fooled the world. The neighborhood lore of green men in corners and up trees. The ones who did exist, after all, and gloried in the fathers not seeing them. The ones that haunt your dreams and eat pickles on the stoops of abandoned houses. The kind that cackle instead of laugh. But their teeth are so white and their skin is so green you want to like them. You wish you were one of them. You want to know their secrets. To find out how one becomes a Green Man. You want to go with them but they will not let you. The green men of a thousand years of ghost stories. These are the ones who reached far out into the water, somehow, and pulled my boat in. It bumped hard against the pier and the smell of dead fish was in the wood like an omen.

They laughed all the same. All green.

When I got out and stood on the pier the green men were gone. It is a union. A demon gang. One among many gangs we have in my country.

My legs shook. It was as if I'd been at sea, not a river. And for months, not an hour or so. If it was an hour. It could have been more. I was hungry, and I am not a big eater. So maybe it was longer than an hour that I struggled to get across. Maybe it was two. It wasn't a day. But it could have been close to a day. It didn't matter. As soon as I left the pier the fog was gone and the bare light bulb in the window I'd seen was on. Beyond it, as it hung low from its ceiling, I could just make out two lovers entangled on a far bed. Dim and writhing against one another as if each was intent on killing their lover. I saw the woman underneath raise a dagger above the arching back of the man. It glistened in the bare light of the bulb. Yellow and gold and silver like fireworks as it plunged into him from above and behind. I turned away. I had to. It wasn't the act of murder that bothered me. It was that the window was in the nun's quarters beside the cathedral. It was a thought I did not want to consider.

I cast my eyes on the blue cobblestones beneath my shoes and began to walk. And yet...

I stopped to look once more into the window. The woman was standing naked, streaming with her victim's blood and smiling. It was Marta Vansimmerant. There was no mistaking it.

A charge of panic skipped up to my brain from my stomach, ripping my chest open, and cold as it went. Alice, I thought. And may have said her name aloud. This is the woman who took Alice and now this. I didn't want to think about what this meant. My hands went to my throat of their own power. A nervous reaction as I stepped, then walked, then ran to the door of the church. I felt for my gun to be sure it was still in my belt. I put all my nervous strength into opening the door but the knob was tight as if welded in place.

I needed to find another way in and followed the outside wall, trying every door. None would open. I ran to the front of the cathedral and tried the public doors to the sanctuary. Locked. A travesty. These doors were always open. What of someone needed to pray? There are statues of saints inside who could help. Why block someone from them?

It was suspicious. As if the church was changing the rules for whatever reason. Blocking the public from entering the sanctuary was unheard of until now. What about the income from the candles? People die and get sick all the time. Why shut off this income stream? Whatever the reason it must have been drastic.

I continued along the wall, more concerned than ever. What if a cabal of the unclean, led by the trusted daughter of the saint in the glass coffin, had taken over? What if the church itself was in danger? I ran, twisting in the dark. Stumbling over my feet. Scraping my hands along the rough stone wall and drawing little lines of blood where skin ripped off. Irritating little cuts.

This is the way I continued until I came to two slanted storm cellar doors. They were angled against the wall between bushes. I walked through thorns to get to them. They were hidden on purpose. There was thistle and weeds all around. The boughs of the scraggy hedge hung in front like guardians of the maze. If I went around the bushes instead of through them I would have never seen the doors. And they were not locked. I could make out the first step, worn in the middle from a thousand years of steps, but I couldn't make out the next. My eyes were of no use in the blackness so I closed them. Standing on the top step I put a foot out and lowered it until I felt the next step. And this is how I proceeded, eyes tight shut, all the way down into that darkness.

13.

It is so dark I can see the future again. Thirty-seven years from now my winter coat hangs all the way to my ankles. My hands clenched behind my back as I walk, crooked, along the sidewalk. The boys are throwing snowballs again. All the snow is pushed aside so old men may walk. But young boys take advantage of the piles. I should have never gone out. I have this memory of the future under the cathedral trying to find Alice. But I can't help myself. What good seeing the future then? The boys make snowballs and the snowballs hit my back. They puff into powder when they hit me. They leave a white mark. The snow is soft but it hurts me. It hurts my sense of self. My structure. My dignity. They laugh.

I turn. The blood is up. It occupies the small rooms behind my face. My red face only highlights the deep lines time gave me. My face has grown square in my old age. Angular. Like a body sewn together from rotting parts. Someone's forehead. Someone's lips. Like a block of stone on my shoulders. A gray flat cap. My hands shoot into the air at either side of my square head. I turn green with anger and move my hands in small, rough circles and I growl at the boys.

When they see this, they scream and run away. Edju, they scream. Edju is chasing us. One is sobbing. Another feels his heart in his throat. Frightened to the end of their wits, they run, and I am ashamed. I am ashamed for them. Thirty-seven years after this attack one of them will remember what he did and grow sad over it. I wish I could spare him the anxiety but I can't. It will be too late. Thirty-seven years after their attack will be seventy-four years from now. Seventy-four years after crawling through this dark tunnel I will be dead. I will be dead and no one will remember I was here. No one will think about how I opened the angled cellar doors. No one will recall my name. And no one will give a thought to Alice resting in my bag. Either gray or brown. I can't remember.

Do we remember the men who built the great cathedrals? Do we think about the faceless people who worked in factories a hundred years ago? Do we know the names of the people who lived next door to our great grandfathers? All these forgotten names and faces. Forgotten like my trek through this darkness, if ever it becomes known. No. We forget everything for the better of it all. Death is the same sleep there was before we were born.

But one of the boys will recall the time he threw a snowball at Edju and laughed at the feeble, halting old man. The one everyone in the neighborhood said was not all there. Off in the head. The boy will be a man and it will hurt to remember what he did to me. To remember a time when he could be so cruel.

Just as it happens to me, whenever I think about how cruel I was to Alice. My beloved fascist once curled up in a bag by the radiator now lost.

There is a scent of salt in the air. Salt and sweat and unwashed clothes. A blast of warm air comes at me from deep inside the darkness. My hands are on either side, running along the hard walls. The space I am moving through is getting narrow. Narrower and closer with each step. I am sloshing in a thin pool of water, no deeper than the souls of my shoes. But my feet are cold. I feel I must be walking in a stream of mercury.

My search led me through a deep tunnel. Damp and clever. At this point, I imagined, I am under the sanctuary. I believe it will take days to get the smell of fetid water and centuries of wet stone out of my head.

But there was a little yellow light in the not too distant future. Grateful, I crawled where I had to and sloshed in ankle deep liquid when there was no other way. But, in time, I got there. It was not as bad as the river crossing.

It hurt my eyes to enter into that light. That room. I'd grown so used to the dark. It took a while for my full sight to restore itself. But when I could see, I saw the floor strewn with treasures. Shelving overloaded with strange and wonderful things. Boxes atop boxes of ancient items. Here was a cloth with the imprint of someone's face in blood. Dozens of old gold glass tubes with red liquid almost solidified inside. It took a while longer until I realized what I was in the midst of.

Here was the sword of Joan of Arc. There was a living salamander with the bearded face of Jesus, just swallowing a fly. A holy parakeet. The staff of St. Christopher. The ring finger of St. Edward. And so much more. Hundreds of relics. Maybe thousands.

I heard a commotion somewhere beyond the crates and boxes. There was a blue door on the far wall. The one wall the yellow light did not illuminate. It was knocking. Someone was knocking on the blue door. It turned green. Greener with every knock. I took my pistol in my hand and walked toward this door, which was angry red by the time I arrived.

14.

The frantic pounding on my door drew me out of my fog. Whoever was knocking also tried to rattle the knob. Maybe someone spoke my name.

I walked, crooked, toward the noise.

Unhappy voices let out sharp whispers beyond the door. I live just down the street, a hushed whisper came through the wood. What's the matter with you? Why am I here?

Keep your arm still for God's sake, was the answer as I heard it.

I opened the door and three men fell into my kitchen.

One was spitting with a red face. I live on this street. Take me somewhere else, he ordered. The police will find me in a minute.

I recognized him through the smoke coming in from the back stairs. I couldn't tell if the street was on fire or what happened. But I recognized the hurt man as the speaker at the rallies. The one who seemed so mad and wild and angry. A scarecrow of a man with a scar on his right ear that looked like the outline of a spider.

Another man, in a black coat, was holding his arm. Only when they got off the floor did I realize the speaker's arm was in a sling and crunched against his body. I knew the third man. His name was Jürgen. He lives in my building and is part of the loud boys who gather at the river and hate everyone. His face all washed over with sweat. It was he who ushered these other two in and shut the door behind when they regained their footing.

He spoke into the red face of the injured man without so much as a breath separating their faces. Yes, they may come to this street but you'll be here and not in your rooms. And this will be the last place on the entire block they'd check on. Jürgen pointed at me. He's a known drunk. The police have brought him back here many times to keep him off the streets. He would be the last one in this entire neighborhood the police would suspect of harboring you. They will never come in here.

The third man, the dark one, tipped his bowler and introduced himself as Dr. Schultze.

The face of the injured man went back and forth between anger and fear. Resignation and fury. He didn't think this was a good idea. Why don't we just drive away now?

Yes, I thought, his face is clear to me now. The rabble-rouser from the river. Right here in my apartment. The scarecrow, spitting and wheezing and shaking with his bad arm held tight against his chest. Angry as a cornered rat.

We're sure they saw the car we left in. We're going to change cars, Jürgen told him, patting his shoulder. He was doing his best to keep his voice down, for whatever reason. Then we'll leave the city. But not in that car. Not the one parked there. He pointed toward the street beyond the windows above the radiator where Alice nestled.

Wait. Wait, I said, rubbing my eyes. Something was wrong. I looked around for the thumb of St. Drogo or the left shoe of some early Greek martyr from Cappadocia. I was no longer in the reliquary but I didn't know why this was so. I was in my apartment and Alice was in her bag. How was it possible? Did I touch some ancient holy water from ten centuries ago? Brush against the staff of Moses?

The dark man, smoking a cigarette, holding the speaker's arm, spoke in a calm voice. Detached. Stay calm, Wolf. Jürgen is right. We'll leave you here while we leave and get another car. We won't even be one half an hour. Fifteen minutes maybe. Everything will be alright. Just don't move that arm for a while. You dislocated your shoulder. Now that we've got it back in place I want to you to hold it still until I can take a closer look.

Jürgen and the dark doctor with a hat sat their charge on my couch and moved toward the door. Fifteen minutes, the tall man said, finger up in the air beside his ear.

Though he settled into the cushions, the scarecrow seemed nervous and scatterbrained. I don't know where Stablein and Lettle are, he mumbled. They're missing. Everything is up in the air.

I've told you. I'll take care of things, Jürgen was insistent.

You'd better hurry. And you'd better be right about this, he ordered. He seemed ready to launch into some kind of diatribe. But the two were out before he could start one.

I was leaning against the wall beside my lamp, hands in my pockets, eyes half closed. Confused. There was a red door... somewhere. Only when the room went silent did I speak.

What are you people doing in here, I coughed.

The scarecrow looked up from beneath his stringy hair. It hung down onto his forehead like wet, jagged spikes. I'm waiting for a car, I think. There was enough blame in his voice to include Alice and me along with the two men who'd just left.

How did you get in here?

You let us in, he moaned. What's the matter with you? Weren't you here when we came in?

No, I answered. I was underneath the church.

He got off the couch and went to the window overlooking the street. He looked out, standing close beside the frame to stay unseen from the street. They're gone, he scowled.

He returned to the couch with long, heel-first strides, mumbling under his breath. As I watched him, his foul mood turned to complete despair. For a moment he looked as though he was about to cry.

It was an awkward scene. Made even more so because he

wouldn't take his eyes off Alice even though he was in such despair. I took my hands out of my pockets and tried a dozen different poses to make some kind of nondescript impression. I ended up pushing them back in my pockets again. Pointless acrobatics.

The scarecrow crossed his legs and seemed to be searching for something with his one good hand. A pipe appeared in his mouth but was just as soon gone again. His hands still patting at all his pockets.

It's an interesting sack you have there. Burlap? He asked.

Yes. Anyway, I think so.

It's gray when you look at it from one angle, but brown if you turn your head a little.

Yes.

He stopped searching and removed a green tin of mints from a pocket inside his too-small overcoat. What's in the sack, he asked as he tried to open the tin with one hand. He didn't wait for an answer but began to swear at the uselessness of his one good hand. I can't open this damn thing. Here, he lifted it toward me. If you can open it and give me three you may have one.

I took the tin and opened it but told him I didn't want any. I took three white squares out and put them in his good hand, which he held outstretched like a shaking beggar.

There was a tremendous sigh that seemed to come from a deep place inside him, and his voice shuddered. We were alone, he began to tell his story. All alone. None of the rest pitched in. They let us stay out there in the street, alone, easy prey. He turned his face into the cushions. It's over. Over. They betrayed us. A miserable failure. Pathetic. We were there to help the police save the country. They should have joined us. But instead they stood in a firing line and sent a volley into our ranks. I don't know. Someone pulled me down. Now the game is up, and I'm ruined. It's all ruined.

I rubbed my numb face with a careless hand. Well, I said as if speaking to a dead stranger. If it's over then it's over I suppose.

Yes, it is. The sorry little man shook his head, disconsolate. His voice faded as he repeated this again and again. Yes. Yes. Yes, it is. Then he slumped back against my couch and fell asleep.

Watching his face relaxing gave me a strange sense of peace. It was as if he were dead now and the world was calm. It would be so much better if I just killed him right then and there. But I went to my armchair and sat down. I felt the veil of the quiet night cover me like a spring blanket of sod alive with fungus eating worms. Cool and kind. The kind they cover the graves with. I was asleep before I could say my prayers. There was a dream of a small old woman with a cane walking into a snow-covered church. There were bells and the singing of a choir. It was Christmas, 1847. It was snowing. I wasn't born yet.

15.

By the tan gray moon, a pure slice of venom in the blood, what was I and where was the sun? In and out the light goes from me. I am here and am here not. There and somewhere else again. I am twenty. I am seventy. And all is the same as it was. I see the future as plain as a hand in daylight. Then watch it pale in the tan gray moon. A dream inside a dream.

What happened to me I cannot tell. Nor divine the real from the sinister.

If I could but remember in the grip of this fever that I am not here for the salvation of the stones like those young men, but to find what I lost. I squirm in my sleep and it comes to me in the dream; Alice is here. But Alice is not here. Thus, this is a dream and I cannot be back in my apartment. I stir. I rouse myself from this thing of slumber. And it comes to me in the blue cold flash of St. Stefan the Crooked. I am laid low on the floor of my rowboat and never left the river. The smell of fish, dead, pink and silver, all around like prayers. Never left the river. Still in the boat. Never in a reliquary.

No, the boat on the river. This was real. I sat up and was still shrouded by fog or mist or the stale breath of kings. I knew, in my heart and in my spleen. Also, in my kidneys and my lungs. And my veins. I knew I could never catch up to Marta Vansimmerant now. The river was too wide. The shore too elusive. And I had no idea how long I'd been sleeping on top of the musty blanket I didn't know was there. A red and gray tattered thing crawling with lice. Smelling of sweat.

I hadn't eaten in days. Or hours. And I resigned myself to the fact that in family gatherings I was always singled out as the strange one. The statute of limitations running out on everyone but me. Forever seen as the odd one. Even though

I never stole the golden bracelet. I never let my tongue slip in front of people who should not have heard me. I never hurt a soul or dwelled on a slight done to me by others. I would always play the rogue cousin. Burned with this hot iron brand on the day of my birth a hundred years ago. I manned the oars again and began to row. Even though I did not know which shore I was heading to. Or if I were going down or up river and destined for the sea or the mountain streams that fed this fetid stink.

It was difficult, at first, to break through the crust of filth that floated on top of the water. The muck complained and the boat lurched. But I was soon enough on my way. Cobwebs in my head. My right eye blinded from some inner light. And still the hunger. The hunger and the fear that Alice was forever lost.

Somewhere on the river the voice of a child, lost from its home once and for all. Crying and resigned to his fate. A vision of elegant queens of the realm eyeing the new servants' legs and conjuring the zeal of lust. What manner of river is this? I would be the last one to understand. Then there was sun.

There was sun burning off the top of the mist and beating it into clear air like a rug. I could feel the warmth of that wayward orb as it penetrated the haze. And little by little my surroundings came clear. My right eye sharpened and there was no need for a sedative. My hands became strong and sure and I could see that I was at the midpoint of the river's width. This was a relief, though I did not recognize the features of either shore. That was not where I'd departed from. This was not where I imagined I was going.

I applied myself to the function of the oars with the haste of a child opening a present. There was cartoon music in the air. The kind that accompanies great rocks pounding hapless characters into the ground. Saturns and whirling stars around their heads. I was a boy again, wandering the streets of the neighborhood I grew up in. The dark passages through and under broken viaducts. Blank windows of unoccupied houses breathing in the night air. Bonfires with an effigy of a witch in an empty lot I'd never seen before. Strangers offering candy I ran from. Snowballs thrown at the back of a sick old man in the wintertime. He turns to confront us and I see myself sixty years on.

I close my eyes and shake my head and the sun has gone down. There was a tan gray moon, a pure slice of venom in the blood, floating overhead. I reached the other shore. This time it was real. Marta Vansimmerant stood above me on a rise of ground.

Drawing the boat to a sudden pier I retract my oars and tie the nose of the boat to the wood. Pelicans are diving into the water and coming out with old shoes and tires. I stood dripping on the pier. I'd been at sea a long time and my legs were unsteady. Marta Vansimmerant stood above me on a rise of ground, naked and arms open. Climbing up the embankment was a struggle, but her perfume reached out like a muscular ghost that held me close to its face of vapors. Surrounded me. And drew me into the web.

Marta Vansimmerant stood above me on a rise of ground, naked and arms open. A stiletto bauble piercing her left nipple. I've been waiting, she says. She says this in a whisper but her words bounce off the water and are audible for miles. She lays back and beckons. The Daughter of the Saint In The Glass Coffin. Waiting for me.

16.

I buried my face between her breasts. I licked my way down her stomach. I buried my face between her legs. The scent of perfumed lace. Cool skin to the touch. She leaned back and let me do as I wanted. Or as she willed. She stretched herself on the ground, her white hands guiding me to undress, there in the open. Atop the rise above the river. In grass that felt like fur. She opened her legs. Stroked herself. Guided me there.

I explain all as we push to the summoning rip. I have rid myself of possessions to be clean. I say nothing and tell all my grief to the dead saint and you. She does not answer. Only swallows me with her body.

There is a point at which one may say, if a man is made this way, that they do not want this to end. I do remember how it was. You writhe and stroke. You kiss and your bodies pump. Mechanical yet not. Robotic. Sweet and easy. You look into her eyes and you do not want to reach the point of it all. You want to keep writhing and stroking. Let's just do this, you whisper. Yes, all night, she says. Don't finish. You nod and agree, but the words intensify the urge. Certain suggestions are potions. A select few words, spoken as commands in gentle persuasion come to mind. When whispered harsh in your ear they become aphrodisiac. You know the words. Even the daughters of saints know these words. Know these feelings. Yearn for the release and explosion that will come if touched just so. No one is clean from it. Denying it is only the worst of lies.

Her appetite frightens me. I am certain I cannot provide. She is like a giant. Her hunger is mammoth and I cower in fear for my life.

The four corners of the room, high against the ceiling,

begin to ooze a purple foam. Dripping down the wall. You do not remember going inside. Or rather, I. Did the force of our bodies crawl along the ground, open a door, and push inside? There is only one inside now. And Marta coos like a pigeon. Moans like a snake. Is unsatisfied and not yet quenched. Arching her back, slamming herself against me. Devouring me. Fire into me, she commands. We finish in a frenzy. Then lay quiet in predictable half slumber.

How did I manage the courage in the face of this woman? You have my sack, I say as a matter of fact. The burlap one. The one from my apartment. Even after all this, I am thinking of Alice.

It was a mistake to say it. She pulls herself off and away from my motionless impaling and slides to the edge of the bed.

I can't take you away from her? She seems ready to cry.

You know what this is, I tell her. You know why we are doing this. We did this for its own sake. You said. But, in the end, we go our way. You knew that. It was always that way with us. How is it now you want me to stay?

She wipes her eyes and returns to my side. Lifts a leg over my stomach and straddles my hips, sitting on me. Moving herself against me. Making me respond again. So soon.

Alright, she nods. Eyes closed in resignation. This is why we are here. You are right. We do this, then you go away. She is no longer upset. Instead her tongue presses through her lips as she works me. I do not exist. I am only serving.

Through the night and into the next day. I sleep and she mounts me again. She sleeps with legs open and I settle into her. Thirteen times we make love in the span of a day. Until I am dry and she is raw. Then we make love one last time. Gentle, so as not to rip each other apart. I've had enough. She has not.

When we finish, she goes to a closet and opens the door.

My sack of Alice is there. Thrown in, rough and harsh. Careless. More soiled than I remember. Here she is, Marta Vansimmerant says. Go back to her. You will never have this again. I am what you lose. We are taking my mother back to the diamond city tonight. They've finished with the sacrifices and penances. Time to lock mother up again until next year.

Naked, she stands before the chair, allowing me to feast on every inch of her skin with my eyes. This is what you could have, if you wanted it, she taunts me, holding her breasts like sweet animals.

If you were mine, I tell her, we would make love every night of our lives. Every night. What man could resist?

She is not impressed. She is crying blood. But she dresses and leaves. I watch her car pull away from the lot.

I put on my clothes after she is gone. Easy and slow as I am aching and sore as well. I am forced to walk with care, but my search is over. I hoist Alice over my shoulder and close the closet door. I make my way to the front desk where I settle my bill and head back to the stinking river.

17.

My relationship with Alice has never been the same. Not since her corpse had to listen to Marta Vansimmerant and I groaning as we convulsed together. Moans and screams. Urgings and agreements. Educational treatises on the certain functions of specific parts. I didn't think I was subjecting Alice to a kind of torture. She's dead, I told myself. But I was wrong. I, Edju, or so the children will call me. They will scream at my approach in the alley. I, Edju, was wrong. Wrong as a young man. I will continue to be wrong as an old one. As wrong as elephants.

I, Edju, lament. Alice is so silent and cold. But why should it be a surprise? You cannot wind the clock back to the original number. I, Edju, made love to Marta Vansimmerant and that is the end of the world. Will I get a pox? Will I bring it home? I, Edju, smell my clothes. Can Alice smell another woman on me? You cannot turn the clock back to the starting point. Once you use time up it is gone from you. There are limits to its patience.

All things decompose. Physical and spiritual. Hard and soft. The now and the ethereal. Left to the devices of nature all things decay. Why is this not the basis of the theory of everything they search for?

I move down the embankment. Haven't I done that already? Down the embankment beneath the desperate shadow of the vulture above, watching. Alice in hand though things will never be the same. The smell of another woman all over my body.

I, Edju, carrying the ungrateful corpse on my back. The boat is not there. Only the oars. I sit on them and wish hard. They do not fly up like a festering wind. They sit there, squat monsters in their holiness. Holier than thou. Stronger than I,

Edju. I have no choice but to follow the river bank and seek out a bridge. There are no bridges, I think I heard them say. Alice grows heavier on my back. I am a thousand years old and the world is a stinking river to me now.

Atop the mud I go. The first bridge will have to do. Even if it turns into a wall. A wall across a river 800 miles long. The wall of a maze that held back the Vikings and now remits its magic powers to the loins of young thugs. They will turn this country into a police state. But I have rid myself of possessions to be clean. I say nothing and tell all my grief to the dead saint and her daughter. Though having known the look of her naked, it has become more difficult to pray.

I walk on.

18.

The sunlight crept around the curve of the river. It crept around a tree and climbed up the branches. It hung on the leafless arms like a monkey. Made sounds like a cat. Pissed on anything that came too close. Howled so loud the moon broke. Night fights day, and the celestial argument begins again. It happens every morning here. The same war, over and over.

You could learn to accept the river. This I came to see as I walked. As I struggled to find a lasting bridge. That is, you could teach yourself to get used to it. The smoke. The smells. The misty gullies no man trod. The outward outbound ledges of doom jutting up over the horizon like stilted pixies. The fear. The rotting teeth. The mysterious coughing under the blankets at night. Sudden swords poking men to their deaths. The bad films. Pottery shards from another age mistaken for teeth in the sudden summer air. Men drunk with light after a night in the caves. The drums. You could adapt to the rhythms. You could learn the way of things. At least, I found, until it rained. It began to rain. Just to test my theory.

It rained that morning and all the day through. Rain like the spit of dragons. Thunder like the swirl in a vortex, cracking through the trees. Black rain. Dead rain. Sullen patches of rain and unforgiving rain.

The harder it fell the more everything changed. The rain fell so hard it opened graves. The pounding drops cleared the muck away and rode the slime off the rising hillsides. It worked the gruesome soil like a flinty shovel. Picked through the left over skin and the juggled bones of all who'd gone before. Opened sores and exposed what a man had in his stomach when they killed him. Seedlings. Worms. All the bacteria of a lovely summer's gut. Rain washed away secrets and revealed all the lies. You couldn't conceal the future any longer. All the plans, and the results of plans. The failed tries. The furtive attempts. Accidents leading to success and the luck everyone was sure didn't exist. An ambush here. Cold murder there. A garrote beyond.

With Alice by my side I awoke to a morning of detritus flowing over my shoes. The rain already reforming the landscape into thin memory. Eyes and hair from the long ago dead. I hate rainy mornings and this one had lightning. The river made its own weather. But it wasn't the rain or the sick, running feast at my feet that woke me. It was the bell of a nearby chapel. Someone in the tower was ringing the bell.

It was a bothersome thing. Incessant. What good was it doing? I could see the bell going back and forth in the empty window. I hated the chapel. For some reason the rage came up into my chest like a crested wave. If I had the strength and the time I'd take that chapel apart board by board. I'd loosen it from its footings and tumble it all down into the river.

It was all I could do to keep myself from going in there and killing every man inside with the mystery of my blue steel. I grabbed my head in my morning talons in an attempt to squeeze the pain away. But the only answer was to move away. I took up my Alice and trudged along the mud, soaking. The rain falling everywhere but in the river itself. The river remained untouched. There were no telltale ripples, as rain will make on the surface of standing water. No pinpricks rising. The river sucked in the rain like a black hole. Superior to the process. The King of Water. Unmoved by mere rain's paltry effort.

There is no evidence of rain on the river, but I can see myself in its glassy plain. I walk. My image walks. But it is an image of me as an old man. An old man still carrying Alice in a sack, perhaps thirty years on. I have a square head like a Frankenstein's monster. Wide shoulders. Ill-fitting coat.

And I move with a chopping gait. Each shoe thirty pounds at least. I grunt and groan. My skin is green. I am the king of the Green Men and the children run. There are other old men standing just inside the open garage. They laugh when the children run and put their hands on their hips when they speak to me.

You're scaring the little children again, Edju. When are you going to die and leave them alone? They laugh.

It isn't that I'm trying to frighten them, I plead. They are watching too much television and I look like a monster to them. Children see too much but don't see at all. You know how they are.

The children, hiding behind trash cans, begin pelting me with rocks and stones. The smell of dog shit and the mean buzzing hum of a hundred flies, eating it.

19.

The river remembers the rain. Its memory complete with the scent of flowers from a hundred years before. But the reverie has limits. It does not recall my footsteps. It does not recall the sentient days of snowmelt and release. One-legged birds and the flash of gold below the surface, evading you. We've beaten the memory out of it. Slugged it into submission. Buried its remembrance. Disguised it to itself. Burned away the precious pictures of its past with a coating of oil lit by some rogue fire.

And now it refuses to show me a way to cross. To get back to my home. This is vengeance for the neglect and ruin and there is no going back. It hides its bridges from me out of spite. My legs ache and my back pains me. What dead fish are here rest naked at the edge of still water. What air that's here is putrid with sulfur and waste. Old canvas, like in the Mountain. I walk and the fog returns.

Holy saints of the clouds, I whisper low and harsh so as not to disturb those wayfarers watching. Holy saints of the clouds help me find a way across. I promise to build a shrine to Sweet Mary of the Sea if only I could regain my strength. Establish the justice of the monks of the cross. The highbrow of the priest-kings. Canes of the cardinals. I'll eat the shit of wayward nuns. But help me find my way home, I said. I prayed. I begged. And the fog parted and there was a bridge, in answer to my prayers. I fell to my knees in thanks and, in time, forgot all the promises I'd made. No one was writing them down.

It was over now. I saw the ticket booth at the lip of the bridge. It was that easy.

I set Alice on the slick ground and reached into my pocket for my wallet. Two years ago, I bought the ticket that allowed me to enter the game. It sat in my wallet, through filth and sweat and combat and plots, untouched all this time. I had to peel it away from some ancient receipt from some forgotten thing I purchased in another life. I had to get this ticket punched to cross over to my side of the river.

I put this ticket in my teeth so I could pick Alice up and hoist her sack over my shoulder again. The paper tasted metallic and seemed to catch radio waves that made the fillings in my teeth ring. The searing pain only stopped when I took it out of my mouth and held it in my fingers. This was an odd, unexpected property of the ticket no one ever warned me about.

You see what a mad game this is, I told Alice. It's insane. I spat a clot of blood out from my throat and the pain in my head departed with it. The last sixteen steps to the ticket booth were easy. The sick music stopped and I walked free again, like a schoolboy. Fog of war lifting. Unrequited anger dissipated. Alice in the sack, flung over my shoulder. She was as light as an angel.

The wooden shutter creaked open just a crack at first. The yellow-hooded man looked out at me from within the dark guts of the booth. The shutter opened wider. The structure was more like a space carved out of a tree than something built for this particular purpose. But perhaps it only looked that way because it had been there so long and the air was so foul. There was a fugue somewhere. A radio perhaps. The music was a salve to my ears. I hadn't heard any real music in two years. There was no music in my apartment. I lived a clean life with no attachments, after all. Simple lives have no music.

The one inside the hood spoke without moving his lips. So. Going?

Yes, I'm leaving. Here is my ticket.

But he didn't take it. He held his tight arms crossed. In

one hand he held the Crook. In the other the Flail. Just a minute, he said. What's in the bag?

Why do you need to know?

We don't allow smuggling from this side of the river. And nobody leaves without getting the ticket punched. Are you an idiot? Everybody knows this. Open the bag.

What do you mean smuggling from this side of the river? I've just been to the cathedral. I've been to the cathedral hundreds of times. Just the other day in fact. I came to kiss the feet of the plaster Jesus and pray to the dead saint in the coffin. I was just there. I've been there and back to my house many times. A thousand times.

You didn't use this bridge, did you?

No. I used the high road.

Well this isn't the high road. They can manage things on the high road as they like. It's no concern of mine. But this is the bridge and I'm in the booth and I'm holding the Crook and Flail. Open the bag.

I will not. It's none of your business.

We'll see about that, he shouted. The shutter slammed. He made no effort to hide his anger like they taught us all in school. I considered this an egregious flaunting of our lessons as children and the nuns who beat them into us. A knob on a side door of the booth began to jiggle. He was trying to get out of his booth to get at me but he couldn't seem to do it. I heard him cursing behind the door as he shook the knob back and forth in a wild fit. Then it stopped. It sounded as though a key was scratching the doorplate. Like a blind man trying to find the keyhole in the slender darkness in there. I heard him trying to force and turn the key in the lock, but it wouldn't work. Again, the knob jiggled, crazy and fierce. The cursing got louder. Then it stopped.

At once the shutter popped open and the man, who was a skinny fellow, started to climb out of the narrow window.

You see what you've made me do? He was snarling at me, trying to squeeze himself through the slender opening.

I told him it's too small. You won't fit.

But he ignored me and kept struggling. He turned himself at odd angles to find the right fit.

Look never mind, I tried to assure him. There's no live person in the bag.

The ticket agent stopped, somewhat stuck, and cranked his head to one side so he could see the sack. Who said anything about a person?

I tried to persuade him. Why bother with this? I'm only one man and I'm telling you the truth. It's no use you getting out here. It doesn't look like you can anyway. Just stamp my ticket and I'll be on my way.

He tried to twist his torso so he could look into my face as he spoke but he couldn't do it. When he spoke, he was talking to the ground as much as me. It's my neck on the line if you smuggle somebody out, and that doesn't look like just things in there. Not treasures. He pointed as best he could at the sack. That particular bulge looks much like a foot if you ask me.

He waited to see what I would say in response to that, sure that he caught me. But I remained as still as St. Joseph of the Rock. He went back to trying to force himself through the window.

I've got to check out everybody. All there is to it. He grunted and twisted and exhaled to try to make his chest thinner. And being as skinny as he was it was a wonder he couldn't manage.

With him stuck there like that I considered walking away. He could do nothing if I just went on my way past the booth and over the bridge. But I learned my catechism when I was a lad and couldn't do it. I also felt somehow fascinated by the man's struggling. It was like watching a wild animal try to break open a cage. And his anger increased the more he failed.

Can you get back inside and maybe try another key? I was almost laughing.

Don't tell me what to do. I didn't ask for your help. He was gasping for air.

It seems a better answer than crushing yourself trying to get at me from there.

Damn it, he sighed, and began to snake his way back inside his booth. I could hear him mumbling inside as more keys clanged and rattled. From the sound I could tell he was going through a ring of keys. Dozens of keys. They played a music like church bells. Church bells with iron cages in mind.

I heard him spitting his frustration from deep inside the wood. I don't know why you bastards can't just follow the damn rules.

Then he began to mumble and talk to himself still louder. What's in the bag I says. None of your business he says. I'll show you what's my business or not says I. Oh yeah, says he. Could have just opened the bag and shown me there was nobody inside, like a gentleman. Like common sense. But no. No. None of your business he says and then he stands there.

The jangle of a thousand keys never stopped all the while.

We could have avoided all this if he just cooperated a little bit. Just a little bit. But no. None of your damn business, he says.

He was having no luck with the keys.

Damn this all to hell, he shouted at last. From the sound of things, he'd thrown the ring of keys against a wall. His head popped back out, sweating, hood down from his head revealing scars and tufts of red hair. Give me the damn ticket then.

I held out the ticket and his hand appeared from inside

with a small pommel. He stamped the ticket with no force at all, not making much of a mark. But the mark wasn't the point. It didn't matter that a stamp appeared on my ticket. It only mattered that someone stamped it. The ritual was everything. Even I knew that much.

Go on. Get out of here, you coward. You're no gentleman. What do you care if I lose my job? You're a lowlife. Scum is all it is. You're the only real person in the world and the rest of us are just all cartoons to you. We're the junk that orbits around you. I don't have any real concerns in my life. It's all just you in there. What's it like being the center of the universe? He mocked as I put my ticket in a shirt pocket and re-situated the sack over my shoulder.

There was no point in engaging this frustrated old pedant any further. Let him spit and spew, I thought as I turned my back to that side of the river. His opinion doesn't mean anything to me, so what could he say that I should pay attention to? Nothing.

This was my resolution as the agent kept on and on about my lack of character. He bemoaned the end of civility in young people today. On and on as I walked away.

His madness faded behind me as I went. The bridge was clean and devoid of any travelers. A light mist at each end. I heard gunshots overhead but didn't stop.

An alley appeared and there was a sad guitar playing. It was night. I'd only just noticed. I felt that I should have been experiencing a kind of remorse for leaving that side of the river. Some strain of regret like a virus. But I didn't. All I could think of was getting my bearings and finding my way back to my rooms.

I felt Alice shift her weight when I got to the other side. We both relaxed.

There was a voice. If you stopped carrying around that stinking bag they wouldn't run away. The boys wouldn't throw rocks at you in the summer and snowballs in the winter.

It has nothing to do with Alice, I begin to explain. But at the mention of her name the boys close the garage door from overhead. It slams against the concrete. A final sound. Meant to separate them from me. I chastise myself. Never mention her name, I say under my breath. I forgot my own cardinal rule.

20.

On the other side of the bridge the yellow man under the red umbrella sells buckets of grease. Somehow I have money to buy one. I must have forgotten which pocket it was in before. Or the haze that clouded my mind on the other side made me forget. I can't recall. But in any case, I buy one.

I buy one and I sit beside a woman with short dark hair and a severe mouth. She is stunning and beautiful and stern and lithe. I can tell from the first moment that she either hates me or my bucket of grease. Or maybe she is jealous of Alice. I imagine that her name is Assyria. She moves away and sits under a tree that is lit by a harsh light from a bulb I cannot see. I think she mumbles something.

If I had the energy I would explain that I have been a responsible person. That I offer women the equality they seek. That I do not use plastic or paper towels. I wash my own dishes and cups. But what good would it do? She has hard brown shoes that tie. Smaller versions of the kind a man would wear at an informal gallery. And white socks like a man. She is so beautiful.

I eat from the bucket with my fingers. Alice sighing beside me on the curb. The buildings behind me, across the sidewalk, are trim and well kept. Though I have never seen them before they are familiar. Familiar as I am back on my side of the river. Never before this did I realize the great differences between that side and this. It had always been the same city to me before. Now... I doubt I will ever think of my city the same. It is a frightening world over there across the river. Here it is only expensive.

Children holding their father's hands walk down the sidewalk. Returning from the game. Life is normal here. My meal tastes like good meat but fools me. There is no meat in it at all. But it is what we like and I am so hungry.

There are cars honking at each other up toward the intersection. A hundred lit windows spot the sky like sperm diamonds. Funny, a passer-by says, how the river doesn't stink as much in this part of the city. I swallow and lick the glorious savory from my fingers. Perhaps, I tell my fingers, it is because there are no remnants here. There are no young men in uniforms rubbing themselves on worn stones. No mass meetings. No shouting, angry little men contorting themselves in front of the beasts in the crowd. The killers to be. The wild-eyed youths, smug in their strength. Maybe that's why the river doesn't stink here. They are not here to pollute it. And there is no ticket booth on this side. Only a little yellow man beneath a red umbrella selling buckets of gray and brown grease. Like the color of Alice's sack, depending on how the sun hits it.

When I finish, I set the bucket down inside a convenient wire trash barrel. There is one on every corner and there are asters and coneflowers beneath every coiffed tree. The woman with the shoes is long gone. I will never know her name. I lift my sack to my shoulder. I turn my back on the seven evil winds that once plagued me across that river and make my way home. Amid the crowd returning from the game. People sitting on the steps in front of their flats taking in the fresh summer night air. Through a window someone laughs. The small front yards are all in order. There is not so much as a wayward scrap of paper blowing across my path. The houses are not black with soot. There are children. There is music. Conversation. There is a tap on my shoulder.

21.

The kind looking little gentleman in the gray tweed hat. A gray tweed hat and a little red bow tie. A little tie on a little man wearing a red hat. A green tweed necktie. Then it is blue. It all changes before my eyes. And he's smiling. He means no harm. Or the smile is a disguise for the murder he is about to commit. I finger my gun. Ready to blow his little head out from under his orange hat.

He points out a pertinent fact to me in a feeble, tremulous voice. It's an important thing to know. Something I must know before I go any further. Before I take another step. It could all be over if I don't. He points out that there is an arm poking out of the sack. Oh Mister, sir mister, he trilled, there's an arm coming out of your bag.

It was true. Alice's arm found or created a weak spot in the fabric. Somehow the threads were wet and worn. In any case, by whatever means, it was wide enough for her gray, withered arm to poke out. Her hand pointing east.

Mister, oh sir. I think your body is trying to escape your bag. He tipped his hat.

Thank you, said I, and ran into a narrow gangway between two close houses. Until that moment I never thought of what I must have looked like. A man carrying a bag with a clumsy body stuck inside. Walking around in the dark with it over my shoulder, bouncing against my back as I walked. The things you do are never embarrassing when no one sees them. It's only when you get caught in the act. To see yourself with the eyes of someone else cuts all self-deception.

I ran from him down that gangway. And he was old. And kind. And must have seen all the million possible things that could go on in the world. Nothing surprised him. Nothing took him aback. He tipped his hat and disappeared. He disappeared so as not to embarrass me further. Because he knew how it was. There were things he'd been hiding for decades too. Making no judgment of me was an act of a wise man. An older man. The kind children throw snowballs at and he turns like Frankenstein's monster. Waving his helpless hands in front of his face. And the children laugh and flee. He knew better. He sensed my discomfort. He made no issue out of it. Just, mister oh sir, you've an arm sticking out of your bag. And good day to you, sir. I'll be going now. Tip my hat. Pleasant dreams. Disappear.

I put the sack down on the cold concrete walk between the long buildings with the idea of repositioning her. But my personal panic only led me to an acute paralysis. This prospect never presented itself to me before. I never had the occasion to open the sack before this. The last time it was open was when I loaded her into it. When I lifted her from the pavement that night in the rain, dead. Killed. The night I found her. She was still beautiful as I remembered. Older than when last I saw her of course, we are all older now. But still toxic. As toxic as she was when we were children together in the golden age of heroes. When I put her in the sack there was still a luster about her. A sheen. A glow. Even as brutalized as she was. Her green eyes staring out at the garbage cans in the alley. I remembered that night. There was thunder and beer. Paper in the wet wind. Someone walking. Little gravels under their soles. The clock and click of hard heels. Uncomfortable shoes. The way her body felt in my hands. Still soft. Just warm. Thin and lithe like a gazelle.

It was an understandable impulse. The lowlifes do things to dead women they find in the street. Horrible things. Disgusting things. I couldn't let her go through that. I still had feelings for her, all these winding years later.

Things decay, I told myself in the gangway, staring at her thin warped arm. I accept this. I put her in this bag for good reasons. Honorable reasons. No one can blame me for that. Inside. She is inside. Inside this bag. Trying to get out from inside. Her golden hair. Her green eyes. Green yes with silver diamonds exploding in symmetrical patterns near the black centers. I opened the bag. I pulled the drawstring free and opened the bag. We mustn't have your poor arm exposed to the weather, I explained. I was trying to be gentle. The moment I pulled the tied rim of the sack open, her face stared straight up through the mist. The eyes were open. Not green anymore. All black. Black as the worst night of your life. Dark and open. Gaping. Hypnotic. They pulled me in. I reached down and held her head and stared into her dead eyes. She was so beautiful still. But gray. Her maize colored hair matted and dry. And the black eyes.

There were pictures inside. Things just visible. If I strained. If I squinted and stared inside her head. Moving pictures in her head in miniature. Full color pictures. Things I hadn't seen in ages. The night we sat in the basement. The time we walked down the street. I was in those pictures, playing deep in the black holes that used to be her emerald eyes. Sitting in her parlor. Seeing her cry when I broke into her soul and ransacked that hopeful terrain into the stain of the Visigoths. I saw her running to the first open arms. A beer drinking fascist. Just like the scarecrow hiding from the police in my room. The night they brought him there, running from the law. Changing cars. When she cried she ran to the scarecrow.

I had him in my hands. On my furniture. In my rooms. I could have killed him then. I should have. Or I should have killed him thirty years before. When we were children. Then none of this would have happened.

I let her head go. It fell back and bent at the neck. Grotesque. No neck bones left. All disconnected. A doll's head. A doll's head with no sinew or string holding it upright. Folded like an elbow, neck sticking into the air. I thought I heard a bone crack. Her eyes closed.

I reached in and tucked her arm back inside the sack. Set it so that it rested against the weight of her body and would not come loose again. The drawstring tightened again, I looked out to the street. No one there. I put the sack over my shoulder and ran out of the gangway.

Running. Running like a miserable thief. Running so no one would see. Or if they saw they would say I'm running and too busy to talk to. I did not see the cars. I looked into no faces. The path before me was a narrow lane. I knew my way back from here. Running past the dark storefronts. Under the dripping viaducts. And, just as it began to rain, up the stairs two at a time to my door.

Inside and safe. I returned Alice to her favorite spot by the front window. I should rest. I should have said, my mission completed, I have accomplished what I set out to do. I have her home again. I should be happy. Or at least contented.

But I wasn't.

I have a dead body in a sack inside my rooms and the whole place smells like sour melons. Dead rats. For the first time since I found her dead on the street I realized the truth. All this was, everything I granted to her power, meant nothing.

There was a dead body in a burlap sack by the radiator under my front window. The smell of rotten fruit. The buzzing of unsatisfied flies. Vermin scratching at the woodwork in all corners. A Nagant M1895 in my belt. For a brief moment I could not remember why. And neither the imperative of memory or the persistence of habit could save me.

22.

Men in white robes smiling. Innocent with their acolyte boys beside them. One to each man. White robes soon to be purple as the calendar changes. Blood red. But not the bright red of young blood, sealed off from the lost chances of age. Not the bright red blood of paint. Instead the mud red of old blood. Diseased blood, going solid in the vial as you watch. I awake to visions of the blood. Blood is never pure. It is off color and thick. I can see it on the floor. Liquid meat. Base fat.

I can see it on the floor as clear as the cities on the Sun. The majestic great thinkers of the lost ages call them sunspots but you and I know better. These are the hidden cities on the Sun. The masters of the universe. Hiding from our low, common ways. The cities on the Sun. Haven and retreat. They have the technology. They are safe like a rabbit in the weeds. We can only dream. Only imagine. Someday maybe I will take Alice there, if the passport is ready on the day I will die.

But those are white robes in the street. Malicious drums. The high golden banners. It occurs to me I have forgotten the feast day of Our Lady of the Snowstorm. I have another chance. Another chance to atone for all the things I have done to the people who, in turn, abandoned me. The abandonments I deserved. I earned. Everyone off to the university and I alone in the summer city with every face a flat sheet of iron. Unknown and unrecognized. Silence for days on end and I deserved it. I deserve it still. Only if I confess. And here is another chance. The statue of the Great White Lady of the North bobs beneath my window. Her platform held high by six men in white robes turning purple. Soon enough red blood. A parade of righteousness through the streets.

I run to my bedside. The sanctified drawer where I keep my rosary and prayer book. My rosary, my prayer book, my six magic shells. Two fur covered marbles. An old piece of candy once touched by the Angel Gabriel. Fourteen multi-colored stones. I am told they are from the floor of the stable where the Redeemer watched the donkeys eat the afterbirth. My holy drawer, scented with the incense from all the funerals I've attended. Wonderful funerals. A scent I've laid inside on purpose to remind me of the difference between what is holy and what is profane. I must remain faithful. One day, seeing my devotion, the all-powerful residing in the clouds will look down and pity me. This poor mendicant. Cut him some slack.

Fire may destroy or serve. Water may carve rock or ease passage. Medicines save until they kill. But the relics of the saints preserve only one rule. One order and one purpose. To focus the simple mind of the flawed toward the realm of the marvelous. They draw me to their power.

I take the crossed twigs tied into the shape of a cross with twine from my drawer. The Lady of the Snow will bless it and I will eat it and I will be pure. I stand by the window, Alice at my feet, and watch the holy procession march on be-low. There are the golden umbrellas. The ballerinas on imag-inary high wires. The city elders in their top hats and canes. Bearded, gray and important. Welcoming the honor from the diamond city as much as the revenue it means. Children strewing flower petals in the path of the statue itself. Weep-ing old women in a black pack at the back of the line, shuf-fling in hard, block, old woman shoes with thick heels and babushkas. Then, at last, the military band playing a secret song only performed when the Our Lady is on parade. It is a hypnotic melody. Some say written a thousand years ago and only allowed out of its cage in service of such an event as this. It has the effect of myrrh. I am excited beyond my bounds. Adrenalin and expectation balled up in a wad somewhere at the back of my heart.

Alice sighs and complains. It will never work, she reminds me. You always do this and nothing ever happens. I don't know why you bother.

My cross of twigs and twine in my hand, I take my sorry jacket off the hook by the door and run down the stairs in the blue rain.

This time they will see fit to free me from my pain.

23.

I tell myself the holy monk who welcomes me into the procession notices my cross of twigs. I am certain that he admires the careful way I hold them together with a few adept maneuvers of twine. I show it to him, put it closer to his face as we walk and the acolyte's finger cymbals tink around us. I'm sure he saw it. I'm sure he liked what he saw. But as I put it out for him he turns away and ignores it. He ignores me. He smiles at someone else.

Was I too proud? A matter of pride? I know pride is wrong. But he seemed to smile when he glanced at it at first. What did I miss? I thought he admired it. Was admiration wrong in him and he fought against it? Pride and admiration. Some kind of small human connection. I feel dirty and put my cross of twigs in the pocket of my sad jacket.

And it isn't two minutes later I can hear screaming, and the groups ahead of us are changing direction. Us. We. That is to say the monks, the shopkeepers and weavers and cleaning ladies and priests around me. We stop and try to stretch ourselves to see what is happening. There is a force ahead of us. The music stopped. The procession has come to a standstill. People are crying. Then a wave.

A mad wedge of bodies smash into the crowd and knock the feeble over. Feet tromp on the fallen, and this makes some of the runners slip and trip and fall to the street. It's panic. The monk who wanted to hide his smile has lifted his thick robes and is running down a side street escape like a girl trying not to get wet. A side street where there are no lamps and a dog howls like a wolf. The other marchers are fleeing. Running in every direction. I somehow stand my ground. My hands in my jacket pockets. People rushing to my left and right. They tell me, run. They say get out of here. Only at the last minute do I catch sight of the problem.

A line of people push against the members of the holy procession. Just before a club smashes into my head I see the uplifted statue of our Lady of the Snowstorm. Far ahead in a glow of green light. She is tilting and about ready to slide off the platform they use to hold her on high. I am ready for a tremendous porcelain smash. It must not happen. They don't know what they're doing. There will come lightning and the wrath of God for the loss of a holy icon. A terrible crime.

But I don't know the fate of the statue. I black out from the force of the club against my forehead. My last perception before blacking out is of boots walking over me as if I am a holiday.

There are flames when I come to. Fire to the left and right. An open door ahead of me. Heavy fighting behind. I run to the door, hands splayed, arms out ahead. I am a cartoon running wheels beneath my waist. I am inside.

I am inside and the first floor is strewn with paper and dead animals. The smell drives me up the stairs. A long narrow hall with rooms on either side. Closed doors. All closed doors. All shut but one. I go inside.

It is a small room. Coats on hooks along one wall. Schoolbooks. Boots. The children huddle around a solitary nun who, eyes closed, prays. She prays until blood drips from her eyes. The children whimper and cry. Pray with me children, she tells them. The bravest of them get on their knees. I yell for them to get out the back door. To get down the stairs and get out into the back alley. Why, she asks, God will protect us here if we pray. Pray, children pray.

I turn to leave but see the fire has caught the building and the flames are lapping up the side that faces the street. In no time the stairway I came up is impassible from the flames. I return to the room of children.

The nun has them all in three quiet rows, kneeling. Heads

bowed. Hands in perfect prayer points. She kneels facing them. They are saying the rosary. Mumble, rumble, toil and bubble, Amen. Over and over.

Get up and get out, I scream at them. The children flinch but the nun demands they finish their prayers. Some look at me. They are too young to know. They are believers. Believers will be spared. God answers all prayers. They stay at these prayers. Faces down while the flames lick at the wooden hall, approaching fierce and unforgiving.

Get out of here. Out the back way now, I tell them. The nun hushes me and lowers her head, satisfied she has put me in my place. God will protect us. There is nothing we need to do.

I return to the hall. The flames two rooms away. Once more I go in to them and scream at the top of my lungs. I order them. I tell them I will not take no for an answer. Nobody moves. The heat is turning my sweat into smoke. As I reach for one child there is an explosion and I am tossed down the hall toward the back stair.

When I get back to my feet I see the flames entering their little room like a rabid ghost. I can hear their prayers turn to screams.

The flames reach out to me. My coat begins to smolder. My face turns red hot and I can feel blisters bubbling up from the blood. I cover my face and run to the back stair. Three, four, maybe six stairs at a time. I am out and in the alley in seconds. And when I turn, the building collapses on itself and there are no more prayers.

24.

Glass breaks. Wooden boards float by like swans. Men curse. Even women are wrestling each other to the ground. Someone runs past with a knife, stabbing anyone without cause or discrimination. Discrimination would make it alright, I suppose. Like armies where it is alright. This way is just murder.

There are whistles in the night. Where are the police? Where are the firefighters? I struggle down the alley to a side street and he is there.

He is there. Standing in the back of an open-air automobile pointing and waving. Shouting orders and conferring with men in military garb seated all around him. Answering questions. Pointing up and down the street again. Crossing his arms and watching it all. A pillar of fire still as a tall rock while the wind whips around him in every direction. He is calm.

The scarecrow. The hypnotic speaker. The new leader. The man they brought into my rooms that night, running from the police. The funny little man who seemed ready to end it all for himself that night. He spat. He wanted to surrender. He thought his life was over. No one obeyed him, he wept. He sat on my couch waiting for a car. His arm in a sling. Now here he was, ordering his men to attack the ones who broke up the holy procession. The scarecrow. The dictator. The savior of Our Lady.

It is a full-scale war. The fighting is so fast. Arms and fists like windmills. Clubs and sticks again and again and again and again on the same part of the same head, turning bone into mush. Kicking. Merciless damage to one another. Furious. I had toy soldiers once. They were toys and I was a boy.

I played with them every day I could. The toys were men.

The men had names. They had personalities. My toy soldiers. One day I lined them up across the linoleum and, when they were set up, I demanded they speak. I ordered them to come alive. Right then. Come alive or I would break and burn and tear them apart. I screamed into their toy faces. I pounded the floor and cried. I demanded. I ordered. Speak or die. Come alive now. This instant. They did nothing. They were toys. And I took them out into the alley. I took them and made a pile and poured lighter fluid and burned them all. There was a puddle of melted plastic on the cinders. I remember breathing in the fumes and wondering if the smoke was poison. I wondered if the plastic would reconstitute once it was in my lungs. Harden there and kill me. I was in such fear of death from it I ran back to the house and never spoke of it to anyone. Now the men who rub their bodies against the remnants of the ancient maze are killing the men who broke up the march.

I don't remember where I went. I didn't recognize the streets. There was maybe a familiar face here and there but no one whose name I knew. Maybe someone I saw in my building. I don't know. I didn't recognize the storefronts or the voices all around me. Before us, a vacant lot. And in that lot, atop a pile of old chairs and branches and other things I couldn't make out, sat an effigy of a witch.

And the things she sat atop were on fire. And the flames were approaching her. It was not a live person so the children were laughing. If it had been a real person the adults would have been laughing. I know enough to know my people. The flames ate the old chairs and swallowed the wood. They chewed up whatever else was in the pile and soon enough they ate the witch too. There was a lot of shouting one way or another. I didn't wait to see her burning body come crashing down into the vacant lot. I turned and went down a street I didn't remember, past houses I'd never seen before.

It was the stuff of miracles. The cathedral was at the end of the street I didn't know. Above the great holy doors, on a balcony just below the bell towers, two men stood together. Spotlights washed across the edifice of the old cathedral. One of them was the high holy pastor of the cathedral and all its environs. Dressed in red robes, soon to be white. Giving a blessing to another man, whose head bowed but only for a moment. With the magic signs by the grand cleric completed, the man turned and waved to the crowd. A thousand people below.

It was the scarecrow. The speaker. The one from my rooms ready to kill himself. The man Alice turned to because she hated me so much. And all around me cheered until they were hoarse with laughter and glee. The savior of the procession, they called him. All hail. All.

Hail.

25.

I wake on the steps of the cathedral a few years later. It is snowing. The whole world is gray. A man in a pink sombrero hands me a ticket and points to the line of blue men in the yellow shade of the trees.

I don't remember how it happened, but it was soon after the explosion in the rain that sunny day. A little while after the march. The procession. Things started to turn. The scarecrow became The Scarecrow. And his minions became the captains of industry. All with the backing of the church.

I remember genuflecting before the statue of Our Lady That Didn't Tumble and Break. I in a long row of other mourners for ourselves. Self-pitying wretches of the universe. Down on our luck. I don't remember if I had Alice there or not.

But all the talk was of the brave young men in brown short pants and high blonde hair who saved Our Blessed Lady. Or the statue, at least. For as the world knows, as the statue goes, so goeth the Actual Lady of Ours.

We watched as the wine turned into direct blood. And though we celebrated it, we were never allowed to drink it. We sat in awe as the little wafer grew a beard and bones and we ate him and he squealed like a rat as he slithered down us all. This is the magic of the hour. Why we repent. The reason for punching ourselves in the heart. The ransom of our unclean souls.

When you genuflect before the Lady, Our Lady of The Snow, an all-white thing with no cheeks, you become holy. The universe of spirits arrives in a dogcart. It shuttles you into the primroses where men with hanging dicks spit water on you as if you were a marigold on fire. Once or twice and there you are.

And I genuflected before the great statue in the Hall and

something changed. The world went darker and there were dead soldiers on the lawn. Sometimes, for a little while, the power went out and we sat in the dark. There were always gunshots. Men passing through on commandeered buses. The Provisional Government wrote orders and posted them on the sides of candy stores. The Provisional Government orders all citizens to obey the orders of the Provisional Government. There was word of assassination and decay. Someone painted all the steps orange. Then someone else covered the orange with blue.

The post office and the library taken over by somebody's militia. There was occasional mail and no books at all for weeks. Then the water turned off and we dropped our shit into buckets and out the window. Alice complained every day over the lack of order.

There's nothing I can do, I'd tell her. Something is going on but I can't tell what it is.

What is the Church saying, she would ask. But I didn't know how to answer.

What is the Church saying? Every day she asked me this question. Every day I had no answer. I had no answer but she kept insisting I find out. One day I ran into the street and darted through the rubble caused by the artillery. I stepped over the bodies of children cracked open by the shelling. I stepped as careful as I could over shells that sat unexploded in the dust. Within sight of the cathedral I stepped on one and it began to tick. A timing fuse. I ran from it and stumbled on the steps of the Cathedral, falling once or twice on my face. Looking back, a school bus drove by the ticking just at the moment the bomb went off.

The bomb went off and ripped through the yellow bus. But instead of bloody children, armed soldiers poured out. Seventeen, eighteen, twenty-six soldiers. Many were casualties but the ones who were unhurt drew their weapons and scanned the rooftops. It was too late.

Snipers from above pumped bullets at them. Little silver vultures. They were helpless in the open like that. I covered my head with my hands and, as if a miracle, the bullets bounced off my fingers. I knew I couldn't stay in that place or I would get killed for sure. So up I went, weaving as I ran, into the cathedral and out of the fray.

Once inside the father pastor gave me a bowl of rice and told me all I needed to know.

What does the Church say, I asked.

Holy, Holy, Holy, he said. The Lord God of Hosts. Heaven and Earth Fill with Your Glory.

But what does the Church say, I persisted.

Nothing, he replied. It is a building.

No. About all this. I stopped eating and stood up. I stretched both arms out and began pointing in seven hundred directions. To the bombs. To the soldiers. The air. The Police. Dead birds. All this, I said. What does the Church say about all this?

I pointed at different things I imagined were outside the walls. And I kept doing this in silence until he understood my meaning.

The Church says we are praying for our Protectors. But that is all he said and soon left me to finish my meal. It was a long day.

I waited for the shooting to stop and then ran back to my rooms to tell Alice what I learned but she was asleep when I got there.

She was asleep or angry with me and sulking, for she did not respond in any way. And it stayed this way for a long while. Life went back to normal. The shooting stopped. The blood dried up.

But Alice stayed silent.

I haven't yet said what it's like in the morning without

her. The men on either side of me, whose names I can't recall, judge each other by the sound of their machines. A constant rhythm is fine and gets no attention. This is how it is to be. But sporadic feeding, resulting in a scattered release and no rhythm at all draws their scorn.

They will then gather in a dirty corner and criticize me as a bad operator. A useless fellow worker. Stupid. Misguided. Undereducated. No expert. No man. A murderer of innocent children on gleeful summer swings. A baby killer. Less than human. No smarter than the common stone. All because I cannot get my machine to run right. To feed it unsteady. Bothersome. Staccato. Amateur. I hated my job.

I hated my job until it ended. And the men in brown uniforms and short pants broke up the equipment and threw us by the hair into the street.

We will assign your jobs. Line up. They whipped those who did not respond fast enough, even if they had been their supporters all this time. Men with coffee breath whispering, just you wait. The fascists will have this country running like a clock. This is the toughness we've needed for a long time. Now we will be just as illogical as the rest of the world, which is what they understand.

They get out of bed and the springs twang. We eat from bags and return to work and they wink. Now the right people are in charge. You'll see.

These are the first to get beaten or whipped if they aren't fast enough to move to the orders of the men in brown pants. Don't worry, they wave their hands as they bleed from their heads. They know what they're doing.

Seven green wooden tables are set up and the soldiers push us into alphabetized lines.

26.

And so, the moon goes a blue ray from its face to my eyes. I am on the floor and Alice is whistling near the rug. This is what wakes me. But I am in line with the cold air, bundled to keep from freezing, waiting my turn at the little table. The little green table with the little orange man in a military cap asking the names. The names of all that stand before me in the snow. The victors are telling us these things and we do them because this is what we do. Three people ahead of me. To the first in line the man at the table checks a name on a list and says, candlemaker.

The man begins to cry and says but I am a banker and my skills are with numbers. I know nothing of wax and talons.

No talons are of birds, says the second man. And the first man says you see, I told you I know nothing about candles. But it doesn't matter. The man sitting at the table makes a tight, sinister smile with his purple lips in the cold. And he points to the side with a quick thumb. Candlemaker and shut up. Get out. And guards take the unwilling banker away. I do not know what is happening.

But then the second man, who corrected the first man about the parts of birds, is crying. Then the man at the table asks his name and makes a mark. And he says you will paint checkerboard patterns on the sidewalks in front of every bakery. The second man is aghast at this. And this is my job, he asks. Yes, says the little sitting man. We will supply you with paints and brushes and buckets and kneepads and a new apartment. Now get out.

Checkerboard patterns in front of bakeries, he cries. I don't understand. Who decides what I do?

All at once a soldier in a black coat pounds the butt of his rifle against the second man's hip and tells him to be quiet.

Alright then, he picks his derby off the ground. I will paint checkerboards in front of bakeries.

Yes, the soldier sneers. And don't get any paint on the street.

The man in front of me steps up to the table and I am after him. They ask his name and he says it and the man at the table turns some pages and makes a mark. You are a Bible expert now.

But I know nothing of the Bible, he protests. The soldier leans toward him, threatening with his rifle.

You will learn, he tells him. You will talk about Beelzebub and Nabokhov and Lobotomi and Moab. Jezehute and Bingoshell. Zinbibblebub and the Mookiejew. Hardrock and Coco. Mizzi and Kotab. You will learn all the prophets going back to Silas and Markhab, Syphonite and Hraearia. And we will want you to be able to count the children of Yusef. Know his wives Abendinaga, Macondragula, Micha and Picha. Or whatever the hell the last one's called. You will become an expert in the begats. Percadovtan begat Shimmolet who begat Adorinea who begat Fistburn and so on. Anyway, I'm not an expert. You are now an expert. Get out of here and read up on it.

And then it was my turn, one foot in front of the other and he asks my name.

Edju, I say.

He looks up for a moment and repeats it. The one children will taunt when you are feeble?

Yes. That is I. Edju.

The one who, as a child, your father took you to taverns?

It was true, I told him. My father's name was Anselm. When he would pick me up from my mother's house on Saturdays we would go to taverns. I would swirl on the bar stools eating hard-boiled eggs. Then he would sit me down at a club fight and I would watch while he went off with his girlfriend upstairs. Once a boxer's eye grew a bloody welt for two rounds. At last his opponent pounded it square on and it popped and the blood went all over my shirt. The old men laughed behind their cigars and somebody tried to wash it off with whiskey. My father was proud of me that night. Yes, that's me. It is I, Edju. A simple man with few possessions, I said. I hoped that would get me a good job.

You are the bellringer at the church of Saint Bibiana.

Where is the church of Saint Bibiana? I have never heard of it.

She is the patron saint of hangover and headaches.

Yes, I say, and torture victims. And well I know it. I kissed a toe ring once said to belong to her. It had been found in the field after the wolves tore her apart.

Yes, that's her, he said.

Yes, I told him. I know. But I have never heard of this church. Where is it?

Just then the soldier in black slammed the butt of his rifle into my gut. I doubled over onto the cobblestones under the blue moon in the cold. Get your things and report there tomorrow, the soldier screamed.

Get out of here, said the man at the table.

I picked my derby from off the ground and made my way back to my rooms to gather my things. One must do what we tell them for the good of the community. A man's life is nothing compared to the glory of the state. Maybe, I thought, Alice would admire the change of scenery if ever I found the place.

27.

When the man said he was a lawyer from Beijing I knew he was lying. He didn't know the way. I left him standing near the bowling pins on the green that day.

I pulled the sack with all my simple possessions behind me. Meanwhile the sack containing Alice was slung across my shoulders like a dead deer. Alice was a deer I just killed. She played her part well. A deer with a steel helmet shaped like something from a dream some men had of Mars in the days before the Panama Canal was built. A gaudy helmet with arrow wings so that no one would bother us.

I stopped in a simple diner to have coffee and prosciutto for no clear reason. Sitting at the counter with Alice across the top of my shoulders like a dead deer seemed to earn me some respect. People looked at me as if I were somebody. A face they'd seen on TV. Someone they met at a party once. I once thought my trek to find this little country church would be terrible. The idea of the state changing my job, where I live, everything. Then not telling me how to get to St. Bibiana. It is an outrage. But I looked at the horizons all around me and felt the fresh wind and ate an apple and everything was fine. It was a great adventure.

Still, look what the wall rubbers have done to us. They'd come a long way, these boys from down at the stinking river. Now they were responsible men of order and they killed all their enemies. And I sat at the counter ordering an extra piece of pie and everyone watched me. All because of them. They changed the world and the minds in it.

They've given me a job. A place in the line. A bowl in the hand. I have a greater project now. A soldier of the realm in my own right, whether the pie was rhubarb or not. Couples sitting in booths hid their dogs from me. The old regulars slurping coffee were stony quiet.

When I finished I dipped my napkin in my glass of water and started cleaning my plate. Nonchalant like. As if this is what I always do. This is what I do. See me do it? I clean my things. A simple man. You should be this way. Everyone watched.

Tell me, I swaggered my head a little as I spoke and wiped. Tell me. Do you know where I may find the church of St. Bibiana? Confident my manner would garner a respectful reply, I dipped my napkin in my water glass and went on scrubbing. No one answered at first.

The idea came to me that the men at the little green tables did not look like much as I was standing in line. But I remembered that as they began barking orders we all obeyed. You will work as a barber. You will be a mason. It was a lesson learned. I stood on the counter and raised my voice. Tell me where the church of St. Bibiana is. Now.

Just outside Farkeep sir, said a meek waitress.

Yes, just south of the Dune Road.

Farkeep is that little village in Chester County.

Yes sir. Go ten miles down this road and make a left at Route 17. When you see the intersection with Dune Road start looking for a white clap church on your left.

Yes. It will stick out of the weeds like anything. You can't miss it.

They blurted this out all at once. Like toothpaste coming out of a hard pressed tube. I returned to the floor and lit a cigarette. I did not say thank you. My method was flawless like water. All it took was to raise my voice.

You see the times we were living in.

28.

The rings that once spun on a clean mahogany table sang as they twirled. It was a memory I couldn't erase. Everyone back in the diner was glad to see me go. They hated me. They thought I was one of the masters. There was a time this kind of thing mattered to me. It didn't anymore. I moved on.

Those people don't know what they're talking about, an old woman told me by the water spigot. The pipe stuck out of the wooden sidewalk and wasn't connected to anything. It was just a pipe in the middle of a walkway. I couldn't help but wonder where the water came from. She bent over and twisted her mouth toward the sky to drink from it.

Presumably you are drinking ground water, I asked.

Yes of course, she told me, dipping and swallowing after every fourth word. But all ground is dirt. And dirt is the result of total decay and decomposition. Isn't that right? That all makes the quality of this water questionable, doesn't it? So next is you, wondering why I keep drinking it.

I think I nodded. Three or four times. I think that was a good choice.

She stopped drinking long enough to point to a road overgrown with weeds. That's the road to the church you want.

I'm to go down here for several miles, I began.

But she waved me off and put her head under the spigot again, turning her face up with an open mouth to take in more water. The water was a browning yellow. The color of filth. Her mouth, toothless, caressed the water with her splintered lips. Up straight again, she wiped her mouth with her sleeve and started to scream at me. Do what you want. What are you asking my opinion for if you're just going to ignore it. The church you seek is the one they made for the patron saint of headaches. Do you think it's going to be some pleasant, white clapboard country house with tulips and fat women?

Her screaming attracted the soldiers. My impulse was to run. But I bit into my last biscuit instead and chatted with the sergeant at arms as she unwound string from her finger.

Perhaps her advice was reasonable. This I could not tell. But the string she was unwinding seemed to have no end. It occurred to me she must be right about that road. My fear of drawing the attention of the soldiers was all for nothing. One look at my orders and they slapped my back. They treated me as if I were one of them. A fellow traveler. A brother doing his bit for the realm. Part of the new way.

They spoke of dialectics and angora. One wanted to show me his rifle. I made believe I understood them, for it came to me that if they realized I was a phony they might arrest me. I nodded at the mention of the Scarecrow. Yes, he is a great man. The only hope of the country. Brilliant. And his choice of cologne is impeccable. Yes.

At some point I became aware of a thick blue cloud that stunk of sulfur and hazelnuts. The old woman had twirled like a dervish and kicked up the dust. Then, with a snap of her fingers, disappeared in a cloud of blue smoke.

I hate when she does that, the youngest soldier said.

Well, I tried to smile as I hitched up my sacks. I have to get going. New World Order and all.

Yes, yes of course. Good work my man. There's a champion fellow. They saluted and waved as I made my way through the weeds growing straight out of the broken concrete. This was the road she sent me on. Why I took it, instead of the advice from everyone in the diner, I will never know.

The afternoon was a swelter of hornets and the beer was too warm to drink. I could smell the melanoma growing on my shoulders. This always bothered me, ever since I was a boy collecting bottles to sell at the fair. But so far nothing had killed me, so I never thought too long about it. There were pretty purple flowers on the roadside and somewhere far off the sound of workmen.

I was a boy, lost in the confines of suburban dry heat. Fruitless and scared. I cried as loud as I could Mister Oh Mister. Please help me. Mister. Help. The men kept hammering and tried to ignore me but I kept screaming at the top of my powers. I did this until one came down and gave me water. He gave me water. And I would be forever grateful. I wondered if it came from the spigot, just then. I hate passing memories of childhood where I did something stupid.

But now the workmen built something else. Something much different than a house. They were mixing cement and lugging squared stone. They were rebuilding the maze, just as they promised. They started already. The Ancient Walls. The glory of our past. The Scarecrow had kept his promise. Now that he'd crushed the opposition the only fighting was deep in the lost countryside. Scattered groups shooting at tax collectors in zebra pants. Nothing to trouble over. Mop up all that remained. They set to work on the walls of the Maze again.

Everywhere I went from that moment on, regardless of the fields and farms I passed, you could see them. If they weren't building it they were surveying the ground or trying to find the old foundations. Archeology from the mouths of seven international experts. They headed the project. Hidden cameras kept everyone on task - though we didn't know it at that time. My eyes grew heavy thinking about it. But soon enough I saw a structure that was as miserable as the old woman suggested.

No church named for the patron of disgusting pain would ever be white clapboard and ladies who made pie. No apple cakes. No happy canines ripping squirrels apart in the shade of the blossoming spring trees. No.

The church of St. Bibiana was like nothing I had ever seen before. I would sigh and say - home - in the lingering, longing voice of a hungry child. But it was not that kind of place.

29.

It was a geometric thing. Low boxes and a stubbed tower with four windows, one on each side. I could see the bell. The bell. A single bell somewhere amid the angels and the low rolling clouds. The clouds swept across the sky, escaping. Running from this place. A chill escaped from out of my collar. It laughed as it turned the corner. Glad to be rid of my river. Everything was trying to escape.

This was the famous place where the believers came to escape the hounds. The hounds let loose by the hunter of souls. To save oneself it was only necessary to be here. To get down on one's knees and wish for the end of the world. As the ancients did. As your grandparents did. As the true believers taught. But that was ages ago.

Ages and ages in an age in which men believed these things. Believed in cardboard. Believed in plaster and lath. Eyes painted where the sculptor's lack of talent failed to bring the light to the face of the statue. The kind of light only true artists can bring to stone. We cheat like this.

There were streams of pilgrims in the old days. I stood beneath the tower and the low rolling weather. Only then did I remember the pictures in the newspapers. Pictures of thousands touching the hem of Bibiana's robe. The white statue patient and waiting as the flock went by.

All this returned to my memory as I swooned and lost my balance, being too close to the clouds. But the martial orders and sounds of work woke me back to my feet. I didn't falter like an amateur sculptor who can't make eyes or hands. Or the impossible feet of Catholic statues. The shock of a hammer and the whisk of a bricklayer's trowel. All around me in a spinning circle, men clung to ropes and scaled ladders. Pointed at places and struggled to measure. To even. To lay one atop another. Wood. Frame. Brick and mortar. The walls.

They were erecting walls everywhere. Setting them in the old foundations uncovered by the experts. Everywhere along the road and out in the fields. This was how they bolstered the economy. These were the jobs. The unemployment cured. Busy hands and simple minds. The socialists, they tell us, want to share the misery. The capitalists, they won't tell you, want to concentrate the misery on the same people. Generation after generation. Now we build a maze, or rebuild one, as it was in the days we defeated our invaders.

And in the middle of this hive, the stone church dedicated to the patron saint of the insane. The drunkard. The victim.

This was my home. I readjusted Alice on my shoulders and went to the only door in the building. Direct under the steeple.

The door was once painted green but that was long ago, by the look of the patches of paint that remained. I couldn't help think about a door I saw once... was it yesterday? Someone kept knocking until it turned bright red.

I tried the knob but the door was bolted solid. What is it with the locking of churches, I remember muttering into my shirt. There was a time when churches were always unlocked. I made a fist and struck the wood. It splintered under the force of my hand. A barrel of water burst at the staves and dumped the contents on the barren sand. There was a crow. A clock. A cock struck one then the hen chased him away. Above the door turned empty space a small shutter creaked open and a bald headed man appeared. There was a shock of blonde hair in a thick curl coming straight out of the top of his head. He wore thin glasses and smelled of turpentine. He squinted to see me and couldn't.

The door won't open that way, he said, irritated. Knock first. How else am I supposed to know you are here?

The Central Committee of the Provisional Government

sent me, I began.

I know, I know. Amendment Seven. The Provisional Government requires all citizens to follow the orders of the Provisional Government. He seemed proud to say it. To have the ordinance memorized so soon.

Something like that I suppose. They've assigned me the bellringer's position.

The bellringer for the apocalypse?

No. Nothing that grand. Just the bellringer for the church.

That's good. The whole town needs the bell to work again. It's how we tell time, you know. It's been impossible to tell time since they took the clocks away.

Who took the clocks away?

The Provisional Government by order of the Provisional Government.

I didn't know that, I said. So how am I supposed to know if it's time to ring the bells if I don't have a clock?

There's only one bell.

I began again. How am I supposed to ring the bell, then, if I don't…

I wasn't allowed to finish. He pulled himself back inside and slammed the hatch. It looked smaller to me than it did before. I waited for the door before me to open so I could go inside, but nothing happened.

Within a few seconds I became aware of a terrible humming sound behind me. Mechanical. Distant but getting closer. Louder. Grinding. And men shouting, or trying to shout, over the noise.

The thing on the faraway road was just emerging from over the horizon. I could see the men rebuilding the maze at various points around me stop working. They waved their caps and shook their shovels. They made all the movements of men who were cheering something on. But I couldn't hear them for the noise of the thing approaching.

It was a machine with tall metallic arms waving around from a colossal body. And its body seemed more like a gelatinous blob than wrought steel or any metal. But it was iron to be sure. With great black rivets holding it together. It clanked and whirred and pounded from some unseen tangle of ungreased gears somewhere inside. A man in a blue coat was using a whip on its backside, as if it were a living thing he was droving into market. And two iron panels flapped the monster's sides. Rising and falling like futile, clumsy, clanking wings. And with every clank a blue puff of exhaust came out the back end.

A train horn went off in an air pulsing blast. I could see the men at the walls tossing their hats to the sky. Waving their arms like lunatics. The thing went past the church, keeping to the road. It was as big as the church itself. Maybe bigger. There was a driver in a cockpit smoking a cigar and two soldiers sitting behind him firing rifles into the air. But the racket from this monstrosity drowned out the gunfire. I held my hands over my ears but I could feel the sound in my bones, beating in time with my heart. It became me. It was impossible to resist. And I do believe, to this day nothing has ever been the same.

It puffed and cranked and rattled, belching its exhaust behind as it went. In the exhaust fumes and smoke a small boy followed. He kept six ducks on the road with a stick and tried to keep up with the mechanical beast for reasons all his own.

I watched it move like a menacing turtle down the road. And when it disappeared around a bend the men at the walls took a few minutes to retrieve their hats and went back to work.

The church door opened and the man who was once above in the hatch waved me inside. It's all clear now, he said into my ringing ears. What are you waiting for?

30.

They sliced the solemn pastures of the fascist countryside into square blocks. It seemed a pointless order. Right angles. No curves. Nothing round. Hard shapes. Green crop here. Yellow crop there. The birds flew in rigid dementia. I watched the maze grow from the belltower. Their walls separated property and cut through roads. It forced people to go miles out of their way to get across a street. But there was music and everybody ate.

We ate powder and beans. Beans and rinds. Gristle bones. Half fruits. Stoic vegetables poured from square buckets, as all the round ones disappeared.

I settled into my work and tried to ignore Alice's complaints. She had no right to complain. This is what you wanted, I told her. You said – I'll show that Edju for tossing me aside. And you said whatever I believed in, you would hate. And you embraced my enemies because of how I treated you. Now here they are. They rule but you complain.

We had bitter arguments that lasted long into the night. I knew I couldn't win. They would always end in her recriminations and my guilt. If I hadn't told her she could not come on the starship she would have never taken the path she did. I always felt the fool. I consigned myself to drinking the red water that seemed to permeate the countryside.

I cannot explain how I knew it was the top of the hour. It had something to do with that terrible machine I saw when I first arrived. I never saw it again, but from the day it came and went I always seemed to know the time. Either that or I invented the time, and when I struck the hour on my bell that was the hour the rest of the country accepted. But I can't be sure.

I rang my bell from nine in the morning to seven at night.

One strike for every hour. In the time between there was one strike for the half hour during that stretch. And at seven-thirty I sounded one last time and that was my work for the day.

There was a high-backed chair and a small table in the tower where I lived and worked. The rope hung down from the bell high above and dangled in the middle of the room. At first, I kept walking into it, but I got used to it after a few weeks. There was not much else to do and little room to do it in. Rare were the occasions when I could leave the tower. But I had a ring of keys that worked on every door and every hatch. It was passing strange that there were never any services inside the church itself. And the sanctuary was devoid of statues. I never saw a priest. I never saw one person come in to chapel. Nor did I ever see the man who let me in when I first arrived. Yet my food was always left outside my narrow door on a landing.

Below the landing there was a long narrow, wooden staircase. This descended into the vestibule where there were founts of holy water that never dried up. I never knew who brought my food there. There was a knock, and no matter how fast I opened the door there was always food but no one in sight. Leave the door open and there will be no food at all.

It was a meager existence. Bread and rice. Water and pickled beets. Flower petals. An occasional seed. Grease. I had a narrow bed to one side of the tower and a toilet too. But beyond my small table and my high-backed chair where I waited for every hour to come, there was nothing. Alice, in her sack, brooded by the north window. She said she was no longer interested in feeling the sun.

I would sit in my chair for hours, waiting to make the next tolling, and invent scenes of life with Alice still alive. In these versions I never chased her away when we were young. Instead we stayed together, as we intended, from that time to this. Safe in a house with a kitchen garden. In these new versions, even the weather was different.

In my alternate universe we had no children but we remained slim and agile and were passionate lovers. We hunted mushrooms and read manuals. Life was an idyll on a sea of glass. Forever polished with the whetstones of peace and tranquility. The world was in good order. The country never fell apart. The Saints haunted the churches in magnificent display, As I invented and shuffled these alternative worlds around I came to understand that if I had never sent her away, none of this would be happening now. The sickness that pervaded my country was all my fault for lack of Alice.

I do not remember how long I stayed in that tower. I never counted the days. But I do remember my last day there.

31.

My fingers rub along the smooth wood frame around the open window. I think of my old rooms and I wish I was there instead. One Thursday a large red marble appeared on the road in front of the church. It was perfect. Ruby red with a thousand shades of crimson and shine. Thirty feet across at every point. The music it played was much like violins. It was there for days. Then it was gone. We are building fantastic machines.

Men in iron masks dance around the fire and the hammers pound the anvil. The winter was coming. What, I wondered, do I do to stay warm in my belltower when the weather changes? There is no glass in any of the four windows. They are just weeping holes in the walls. There is no fireplace. No radiator. The covers on the bed are only good for cool summer nights. I search for more blankets but find only old newspapers from the time of the plague.

There is a new device in front of the church every other day. In the days between these arrivals I can see the yellow flowers in the field across the way. But when the squat monsters are here I can see them no more. And anyway, the countryside is fading to white and black and shades of gray. Just like the faces of the workers and the trees. I fall asleep worried about the winter. I worry every night.

One morning metallic scraping woke me. There was a series of orange ladders connected at odd angles, spinning like a gyroscope in front of the church. Three men in white coats stood before it with clipboards. Every once in a while, one of them would point at the contraption. The others would nod and everyone wrote something down. But as much as I tried I couldn't discern what they were observing. The ladders just kept going around and around without any difference in motion or speed. Their spinning filled the air with static electricity. Touching anything metal inside my tower caused a painful spark. I don't know why.

Another morning there was a vehicle that seemed to be a kind of truck with a long flatbed behind it. But it wasn't a flatbed on twelve wheels at all. It was a floor made from doors that opened of their own power. Each time they opened someone yelled ah-hah and a stout man with a cane ran over to shut the door again. The action became a sick game the doors were playing on the man, who was crying and exhausted. I couldn't continue watching because observing seemed like complicity to me. If I didn't see it, I reasoned, it wouldn't upset me. It wouldn't exist. If I stay busy with my bells it was no concern of mine.

But after all what could I have done? The young men who once rubbed themselves against the old stones were in command of the whole country. I didn't recognize anything. My country got itself ripped away and replaced with red marbles the size of tractors.

And then it happened.

I suppose I should have guessed it was coming. Life had been too quiet. Too predictable. Too sedate in my tower. I rang the bells and ate food. When not engaged with my duties I sat staring out the windows. I could see the maze growing at every view. I'd grown accustomed to my routine. Even Alice's silence no longer bothered me. She could do what she wants, I told myself. I've been thinking of her all along and this is the thanks I get. I even got to the point where I didn't miss going to the cathedral back home. I no longer thought about lining up the candles in the red sand. No longer frustrated that I was never able to place them in a perfect line. It didn't matter anymore. My job as the bellringer took all my time and energy. What more, I asked, could I want?

This is the condition of complacency that the gods watch for. The minute you obtain wisdom you doom all hope of peace.

32.

I am the worst of all men. Don't talk to me about your loneliness. I am one alone all my life until my last day at the tower.

It began with someone calling my name. I heard it from the road as I sat in my high-backed chair. I admit I was nervous that day for reasons I dare not explain. I admit I sat rigid. Back straight, plastered against the reeds and leather strips used to make the chair. I admit my body was stiff, locked into some kind of agitated yet linear paralysis. But I am sure – as I was sure then – that my state of mind that day had nothing to do with it. I heard someone calling my name. And that was all there was to it.

I went to the open-air window that faced the road. That same road where all the fantastic monster equipment was every other day. It was an automatic thing. Something I didn't have to think twice about. That's the window you go to when the strange machines arrive in front of the church. The window you use when someone calls your name.

Instead of the kind of contraption I'd become used to seeing, there was only a yellow box. Big enough for a child to sit in. Strapped closed shut with heavy paper tape. Brown tape. The serious kind. And from inside this I heard my name. Edju, it called. Edju, and nothing more. It was a muffled call. The clarity confounded by the cardboard and tape. It wouldn't stop calling me. I had the impression that everything around me was getting angry at the noise. The walls. The door. The bell. The air. The trees. The road itself. The workmen in the distance. The voice calling over and over was annoying to everything and everyone who heard it. I felt compelled to go down there and stop it before the whole world was angry with me.

Something touched my sleeve before I left the tower. Something didn't want me to go. Telling me to stay inside the tower. I had the feeling at that moment, but I ignored it. I raced down the winding wooden stairs and flew out to the road where the box was. Or, at least, where I thought it was.

It wasn't there at all. Gone. And, being gone, no one called my name

And my bell, high over my head, of its own accord, tolled one.

I turned back to the church and saw the bell swinging in the tower. But how? There was no one inside and I was the bellringer. I was numb for a moment, transfixed at the impossible sight.

Then the bell struck two.

Of course. Noon. It was noon and I was not at my station. I ran back to the door and tried to open it. Locked. Jiggling the great brass handle did nothing.

The bell struck three.

I reached for my ring of keys at my side. At least they were still attached to my belt. At least I hadn't been stupid enough to allow myself to forget it. I bent over to see better and find the right key.

Four.

I was sure I had the right one and slid it into the keyhole. I turned and nothing happened. I turned it again and tried the handle at the same time. No. That wasn't the way. You unlock first and then turn the handle.

Five.

I couldn't turn the key. It was the wrong key. I pulled it out and cursed the devil. I went through them one at a time.

Six.

The key I wanted had a copper tint. Old copper. Greenish, gray and black. I found two such keys. I didn't know what the other one could be for, but I slipped one in the door and tried to turn. The wrong key.

Seven.

This is when I noticed the sweat falling into my eyes. What was happening? How is this happening? I am the bellringer. I found and slid the other key with the same coloration into the lock and turned.

Eight.

There was a satisfying click as the lock released. The right key to be certain. I moved the handle and it turned easy in my fingers. I let the ring of keys go. They jangled at my side as I swung the door open. In time to hear the bell clear as anything.

Nine.

I jumped at the stairs and took them two, sometimes three at a time. And stumbled. Searing pain in the toes I stubbed. A solid crack of bone just below my knee from the wooden edge. For a moment I thought I would faint. Pass out from the pain.

Ten.

It was as if someone took a hammer to my lower leg but I couldn't spare the luxury of suffering. I regained my footing and limped, somehow pulling myself – or willing myself – up the stairs and to the landing.

Eleven.

Once on the landing I turned the knob on the door to my room and pulled but something was holding it in place. I did not have the strength to fight against it. My leg was bleeding through my breeches. I put both hands on the door and yanked.

Twelve.

The door let loose. It swung open. I almost fell backwards onto the stairs, a tumble that could have killed me to be sure. I jumped into my room and saw the rope. Swaying. No one there. No one in the room at all. Something had just let go of the rope. The bell swung but there was no more tolling. Only iron and rope rubbing on ancient wood. It creaked to a stop, and hung lifeless over my head, taunting me. The rope still swaying ever so slight.

I heard my name called from the road.

33.

A tall man was calling for me from the road. He had a white egg in his right hand and a short ice pick in his left. At his feet was a large red bowl. Plastic. Filled with more eggs. He leaned against a fence that before this I never noticed was there. And he asked me, without raising his voice, would I like one of his eggs?

I couldn't muster an answer, nor did he wait for one. He made a hole in the top of his egg with the little pick and put the egg against his lips. He threw his head back and sucked the insides out. He made a horrendous show out of it. An ugly sound. When he finished sucking the insides of the raw egg out he tossed the shell into the grass. There were already two empty shells there.

Would you like an egg Edju, he repeated.

No thank you, said I. But how did you know my name?

He bent down and took another egg from his bowl. Everybody knows Edju the Bellringer. You are our bellringer. An important man around here. How do we tell the time around here without you? You tell us when to go to work and when to go to sleep. The entire countryside is beholden to you.

I do not toll my bell at every hour, I reminded him. How do you tell time when I am not ringing?

I don't know, he said, picking a hole in the new egg. Perhaps we don't.

He sucked this egg, licked his lips, tossed the shell onto the pile, and asked me if I wanted one again.

No thank you, I told him.

I'd long ago stopped trying to assign a pattern to all the things that were happening to me. The bell ringing of its own accord. A tall man sucking eggs and calling my name below my belltower. It was like that feeling when a strong memory overwhelms you. Even though I knew I never lived through any of this before.

No. A book. When I was a vagabond on the Square I put together enough money to eat for once but bought a book instead. Something by an obscure Spanish author. That's where I'd seen this before. Only this was a seven-foot tall man and not a wild little coquette. At least from the look of his clothes.

He sucked down yet another egg. Head back, elbow out. I returned to my high-backed chair made of reeds and wood and leather strips. He kept calling my name. I worked to ignore him, though he said it over and over. It became a game we played. He stayed at it all day and into the night. Somehow, he never got tired though I was facing a numb kind of exhaustion.

Edju, he kept saying. Even Edju sir. Like calling a workman down a ladder. It was a struggle to not answer. The central eye grew more tired than the other two, waiting for the load to fall.

The petty dragons and heartfelt strangers. These are the signs you will meet along the way, denoting something. Thirty years working in one hole is not a recommendation for one's character. I am no good as a man. Everyone I once knew has abandoned me. The more success you have, the quicker your friends despise you. This is all the lesson a child needs in the world. I learned it all too late.

Edju sir. Edju, he called.

34.

By now you know that despite everything that happened, I survived. It is a kind of spoiler for you I suppose. Because not surviving all this would be so strange, considering I am writing this. If I had not survived my story and was writing this it would be a kind of news.

I would forgive you for thinking I got killed in this story. Killed or rendered damaged and disfigured. It's a forgivable assumption.

The days and nights in the tower jerked across the screen like sick children. Moping and shuffling. And every day the maze grew larger. Taller. More complete. There were ceremonies when a section got finished. And there was another, more insidious event. Sometimes if another section wasn't finished fast enough they took those men away. It wasn't something that happened every time. Just sometimes. I noted the times in a journal I began. Punishment. There were consequences for not working hard enough in this world.

I supposed that if they did such a thing on a regular basis they would run out of workers. Or, I should say 'we' would run out of workers, since everyone speaks in the 'we' viewpoint now. The tall man who eats his eggs below my tower windows told me so. Also, his name was Jacinto. It was a name I felt I could trust.

At any rate there were times the men who finished ahead of another group got buttons. Or even fed. But those who lost this strange race were sometimes loaded onto trucks at gunpoint. I would watch as they sat waiting in those trucks. The soldiers would give each of them a stone, which they had to hold in their laps and talk to. I saw one man dragged out of the truck and beaten when he refused to talk his. Of course, I do not know where they went. It sounded like it might have been a carnival.

Then there was nothing. Silence for the longest time. The wind was cold. There were fewer ants in my belltower. A hat blew across the lane. Something was different. I thought, at first, it might have been the Mountain calling again.

35.

Our flag is red with a golden maze emblazoned across its entire field. The fascists have come a long way from the days when it was just a little black maze in a white circle.

After days of silence and no motion, I often hear shooting from the cluster of houses that make up the town. But it is not the usual firing squads we've all become used to. This is an exchange of fire. Different calibers. And you can tell by the anger behind the shooting. People are setting traps for each other out there. Ambushes. I keep my Nagant close. No work had been done on the maze at all. Not for days. I kept cautious and watchful.

What I haven't yet said is that the stairway changed since I first arrived. In the beginning I thought nothing of the warping. A natural thing, I said. Who knows how old this place is, so anything is possible. But the laminates began to separate and buckle. And small shoots of woody growth began to fire out from the broken seams. These spawned tiny leaves. The tiny leaves grew into large leaves.

The railing shrank in diameter and began to twist. Soon it was nothing more than a few thick vines twisted together. Small flowers, colored yellow and periwinkle, grew out. They were pretty and smelled like wine. But their stems brandished deep red thorns and the railing became impossible to use.

Every day when I opened my door to retrieve my meals there was something different. I decided to stay where I was and never risk using the staircase again. But I was not the only one who must have thought this, because every once in a while, my meals did not arrive. I went hungry. And there was shooting every night.

And when, at last, I counted three days without food I knew I had to chance it. I stood in my doorway and studied the overgrown tangle the stairs had become. I would have to climb down backwards in places. Jumping from this height was not an option. The growth, whatever it was, would need careful negotiation. It swayed in the wind, though I couldn't tell where the wind was coming from as I was still inside the tower. But it swayed. Or maybe it was breathing. I heard a kind of moan and wondered if it was alive. But the moan turned into my name and I recognized the voice coming from beneath one of my windows. It was Jacinto.

Edju sir, he was calling. Oh mister oh sir.

I closed my door and ran to the window that faced the road, as that was his usual place. He held an egg to the sky in his left hand and the red plastic bowl with more eggs against his chest with the right.

I can't get up there anymore Mr. Edju sir. The stairs are overgrown and I'm sure they won't support me. I'm almost seven feet tall, you know. And I'm too heavy for it anymore. Would you like me to throw you an egg or two?

You mean you've been the one feeding me all this time? Why yes sir. Of course. Who else?

I had at least a dozen questions to ask him. Who was it that employed him? How has he been able to avoid me seeing him inside the tower when I tried to catch him? What is all the gunfire in the town about? And more. But none of that mattered. I stuck two hands out the window and down toward him and said, yes please throw me an egg. I'm hungry.

He didn't have to toss it far because he was so tall and I caught it with ease.

Do you want a pick to make a hole?

I shouted no it's alright as I pulled back inside to get a cup. I cracked the egg against the rim and let the gelatinous insides pour into it. I don't recall where I put the empty shell pieces, but I had two hands on the cup and poured it down my throat in seconds.

He called up and said, do you want another?

I caught a second one and repeated the process while he went on talking.

I don't know what will become of this job of mine now. There's never anyone in the commissary to make anybody's food anymore. I can't find my boss and I haven't gotten a paycheck in three weeks. I'm thinking of starting a bicycle shop with the money I inherited from my Uncle James. He had a powder manufacturing plant before he got killed. So, I don't know what will happen to you. Has anybody talked to you about your job?

I wiped a bit of uncooked clear egg white from my face with an oily rag as I stood in the window listening. No. You're the only one I've spoken with since they brought me here, I said.

Well, have they paid you in the last three weeks?

I shrugged my shoulders. I've never gotten a paycheck. Ever.

Oh, he said. He said it as if he'd stumbled onto a secret he wasn't supposed to know. He shook his head and set his red bowl on the ground. So, I guess if I leave you'll just starve or something?

I didn't have an answer.

He rubbed his chin and shook his head. I don't know Mr. Edju. Were I you I'd get out now while no one is looking. There is no telling when the fighting's going to stop. And my mother and I are both sure that's why everything has gone to rags around here. Were I you, I'd get out of there.

And such is the world. I may tell my neighbor he is a Great Man. I may offer him a stick of gum, and praise him for being that Great Man. But it will do no good. He forgets my praise and my gum and dumps his garbage on me all the same. No one can see the future. Who would have guessed that I would yearn for the return of the summer days of monstrous devices in the road?

36.

I lower the sack of Alice, slow and careful, from the window. Jacinto's arms are long and it is easy for him to take her and set her on the ground. Gentle and kind. I make a good search around my quarters to see if there is anything else I need to take. But I forgot, I am a simple man and have few possessions. It was right to leave. I had even missed the last few hours and forgot to toll the bell in all that time. And no one came to complain. The countryside is solemn and blue.

I have developed sores. Jacinto says they are the kind of sores undertakers get from handling the dead. I have never heard of them, but he says a name for the disease. I do not recognize it. Jacinto says there is no known cure. That they are not a threat to my life but once you have them they are permanent. Jacinto says he knows about this because his father had them. I am left to wonder if putting Alice's arm back in the sack so many weeks ago began the incubation of this disease. I have only touched her twice since I found her dead. Jacinto says they may go away if I get enough sun. It is yet another reason to leave the tower.

Jacinto says there is fighting everywhere. The new government is under attack from rebels who don't like the fascists anymore. But Jacinto says the rebels can't win. Every time they are on the verge of a victory the fascists rub their bodies up against the old stones. Doing this gives them superhuman strength. Bullets do no harm. They get brilliant ideas and no longer need to eat for days. Jacinto says the power in the rubble only works for them. Jacinto says it is all in the head, though. Jacinto says there is no special power in the stones. Jacinto says it is all sympathetic magic.

I am weary of all the things Jacinto says.

He keeps talking and I don't listen anymore. I must negotiate my way down the staircase that has turned into a twisted vine. It is breathing and has grown pustules that spawn spiders. As I put my foot out on it to begin my descent, it complains about my dirty shoes.

I can't help it, I say, I have to get down. All the while Jacinto is outside the tower going on about the politics. I am not interested in the politics. I am a simple man and have few possessions. I used to have sweaters.

I tell the vine I must grab a branch now and then so I don't fall. What do I care if you fall? You are nothing to me, it moans. I'm not responsible for anybody but me.

That's all well and good, I answer as I slide down the thick central trunk. But that's why you'll never be President.

The young spiders stop scrambling and look at me when I say this. They have never heard the vine chastised in such a manner before. I begin to wonder if I've made a mistake. Perhaps, I think, I shouldn't get the vine angry with me until I am off of it.

As I inch down I feel it vibrate and rumble. Do you put too much cream in your coffee? Answer with care, it warns.

Answer with care indeed. No matter if I answer yes or no, how do I know what is the right answer? So, I tell the truth. I don't drink coffee.

Good answer, it chuckles. The only possible answer. The best answer. Alright. You may pass. Continue on.

I complete the rest of my descent in peace and quiet. Except for Jacinto saying this and that outside the tower. Now that I am nearer the door below than the window above, his voice comes through the keyhole.

In a matter of seconds, I am on the floor. Untroubled and unhurt but for a few thorns in my hands. I brush them out and they leave no telltale sign. There is no need to take one last look at my bell tower. I am glad to be free of the work and I am more a cautious than a sentimental man. I am simple, and do not own much.

37.

*C**ast in silence on he goes. to saints he speaks. but others poke*
his praying head.

The shadows have eyes. And gleaming teeth, yellow with sin. Ill at ease with the light. A child's nightmare brought forth in a cup.

All I want to do now is get back to my rooms. My two bowls. A bed I understand. The government seems to have fallen and no one is watching anymore. I want to kneel on bleeding legs before the shrine of Saint Polycarp of Smyrna. Holy stabbings and locks of hair dripping sweet toxic blood from my shoulders in the quiet of my sanctum. A rose of thorns around my head like the boy itself. Extrapolating the flagellating acolyte

I am wary since the news of the fighting and the sudden shots. And these shadows want only to include you in their game. They seek the livery and the stone like a rocket. It doesn't matter if you desire this inclusion or not. Their imperative is gold in the teeth and the sizzle of electrum. It is unstoppable, irresistible, and smells of oversweet cologne. These dark rings cannot imagine a life outside of their signposts and debris. The power is always near. It watches from the shade. You cannot escape it. One must never get too comfortable. There are enough eyes to fill the spontaneous road.

Jacinto, Alice and I are the new serving in their dinners.

Jacinto is near to tears. I have nowhere to go, he says, whimpering. Since the boss doesn't come around and there's no food left, like I said.

I'm permitting you to come then, says I. But keep to your own side of the road. You are too tall. As tall he was. Seven feet, he said once long ago beneath my window, all owed to his diet. And did I want an egg?

No, I put a finger to my lips. What is that sound?

We stop. I set Alice down and Jacinto leans into the wind. There is a rustling in the leaves, dead on the roadside since the last freeze. I crumble some to dust with my foot, fascinated by the multicolored powder they make. Gold and red and most of it brown. Some yellow.

Someone is watching, Jacinto says, still leaning. I would know that sound anywhere.

And I have been suspicious of the same. But we are twelve steps closer to the town that once depended on my timekeeping. Three quarter. Full stop. Treble o'clock. But there are no moving parts. No swaying bodies. It is treeless, and all the houses are white. They are white until they blur blue in the stark sun that pierces through the dead mantle sky.

Where is everyone, I ask.

He quits his leaning and does not answer. Instead he shrugs his shoulders and says I have a lantern in my cellar if you want to stop for it. But if we are going to your rooms I wouldn't tarry too long here. I can hear the watching.

They gaze at us through a green crystal propped upon a chalklike rock that was once a cornerstone of the old walls. Soldiers at the ready.

We're no threat to them, I complain.

If you are not them, you are the other. It's in the Constitution now. Didn't you know? Jacinto's voice is getting deeper as he speaks. I pick Alice off the ground and Jacinto holds an egg in his hand. He tilts his head back and breaks the egg with his thumb and fingers. Breaking it in half as if a master chef in a bowl. The clear pus and the yellow-orange ball slither into him like snakes. It is getting close to midnight. And at midnight all will be shadow and the world will be theirs.

Jacinto bids us to his house. We should stay until dawn and not travel the night, he warns. I take my finger away from my lips and follow him. But before we go in it is obvious to me that we have also entered the maze. In the dim I can't make out the directions and hitches to the walls. It had been a clear path from the crumbling church into town. But now, from his porch, I can't tell the way forward. I point at the high walls on three sides of us and begin to speak. But before I can make the first sound Jacinto pulls Alice and me into his foyer where the butler takes my coat.

We stay the night there. His voice is commanding and square. Someone hands me a cup of water.

There are bright lights down a yellow hall. Unoccupied niches in the walls, making a long and empty hallway. He sees me studying the empty shelves.

You are wondering where the saints are, no doubt.

Yes, I hand the bag with Alice to a footman in a red lacquered coat. The niches are rather sudden in their emptiness.

We don't know, he stares at the empty spaces as well. I can see his face turn away from me as if to hide his crying. He becomes almost inaudible. We do not know. A rippling sigh escapes his throat. It came from deep in his chest as if the inside man wants to cry but the outside man refuses.

He is facing away as he explains. His voice is calm and careful now. Wanting to savor every detail. To massage every nuance. And to make sure I can hear him over the hammering that starts somewhere upstairs.

I suppose I must have done something sinful. I have always loved the church. That church was where my parents conceived me. It was where I was born and baptized. I suckled the statue Mary's nipple when my mother ran away. I have been so careful to do the right things. Make the right propitiations. Place my coins in the correct slots. Light the right candles. Sift the red sand. Make sure I touch my left shoulder first. Never let anyone see my privates. I thought I was doing everything right. And that, in exchange, God would protect me. He said so. And the priest said it too. But it didn't work. I woke up one night and the doors were slamming back and forth in the wind and all the saints were gone. I was careless. So, I went back to the church. The boss said, yes there is work you can do. He said, a new bellringer is going to arrive and he will need to eat. Do this in penance and perhaps God will return the saints to you.

Did you have many, I asked.

I had Columba and the Witch of Exeter.

This astonished me. I'd seen the statue of the Witch but only ever heard rumors of the statue of St. Columba. There are only three known of Columba, I said. And you had one of them?

Yes. It was a long-standing prized possession in this family. My father brought it back from Jakarta in the last century. Some say it came there with the original Portuguese explorers to reach those shores. I must have done something sinful.

I'd heard one of those statues sold for almost half a million dollars at auction.

Yes. And the patina on mine was original to the final percent. At auction I think it would have been worth at least 700,000.

We settled in a nook beside an orange lamp and talked into the early morning about the rarity of certain relics. The value of statues. The hierarchy of saints. Celestial cells where the holiest of dead hermits make their final rest. The hammering upstairs receded beneath our awareness. It melted to nothing as we shared our love of these things.

They are building a catapult anyway, he said at one point. Deep in the smallest hours, ticking unheard in the immortal steam. It is of no interest to me.

38.

Jacinto and I will make excellent friends, I told myself as we went to sleep near dawn. So long as he obeys and remembers that he is still a servant.

I promise to let him choose two or three of my saints to fill his plundered niches. I have plenty, I tell him, and you shouldn't have these empty cubbies all along the hall. There's something untoward about it. I have plenty of saints in my apartment. He seems to relish the idea. The bare niches have only fed his nascent loneliness. It is the least I can do.

After a day of rest, we set out the following morning with full gear and Alice. He filled his red bowl with more eggs. We stepped out, confident in the morning cool. That one moment before sunrise when the houses and trees are a hundred shades of blue. And only blue is the world. All that was missing was birdsong. I fear they have all gone missing. Fed up with the fighting, returning to their primordial manners and secret trees. Secret trees where no mere human can find them. It's the price we pay for our way of life. Nature being a zero sum game.

But to make our way away from the church we must play the maze. It has us going along a wide curving wall that cuts some houses in two. Jacinto pointed as he explained. Inside that one you must walk three miles back that way to get from the kitchen to the dining room. They eat their meals cold now, he says. And milk spoils in the glass from room to room.

This is the new world, I shrug.

People can get used to anything, he shrugs me back.

Curving along we make our way down the street. Three dead ends and a porcelain cave filled with music. This is how we defeated the invaders generations ago. Our little island in the middle of the North Sea. Windswept heather and thistle.

Cod at every meal. Six hours to cross the street because of a wall. It is our heritage, and the fascists played it to full effect.

But what is this fighting, I ask again. Unsteady with the occasional flare and pump of automatic weapons unseen beyond the rooftops. Is it ambush? Who is there?

There has been a backlash, he rubs his nose. The blue shirts have pushed some too hard. Others never liked it, especially the red shirts. But it's the orange shirts who are fighting back. Well, he corrected himself, orange and yellow shirts. Plus, a little green. And a smattering of white. But by and large orange. And yellow. Shirts.

I have no idea what he's talking about. He forgets he is a servant, and I order him to carry Alice as he is twice as big as I am, younger, and a servant. He shoulders her with the ease of the stronger youth and I am jealous. There are no complaints forthcoming from the woman whose honor I have saved. It is ingratitude on her part to the highest degree.

I am thinking of ancient torture devices when I notice that Jacinto does not see the string. All he saw in the road was a banana. This was an exotic and unheard of thing to him. There has not been such a thing in the country since the rebellion, he drooled. A rare relic and treat. He saw the banana. I saw the banana tied to the string.

And before I could warn him, he and Alice, banana and all were pulled to the side of a lean-to. I followed, in concern, to help him. But the provisional government surrounded us. Soldiers in stark gray necks with tacit underpinnings. Unconventional weapons the size of mighty hammers. And all these weapons clicked and cocked and pushed into our faces.

39.

They put each of us in solitary confinement. Jacinto's room was long and narrow. Mine was a white cubicle. Alice's reminded me of a dank basement when they threw her in. Then, after three days of bread and water, the interrogations began. And, they warned us, if your stories do not add up or you all begin to say different lies, you will all die.

Jacinto was the one they concentrated on first. They left Alice and me alone while they took him away every day, sometimes twice a day.

He seemed to take it all on with bravery at first. The first few times they brought him back to his cell he made no sound to give me a clue how he was doing. But then, in the middle of one night, I heard them dragging him back from the interrogation room. I could tell they dragged him because of the sound his shoes made scuffing along the floor. He was whimpering. Mumbling something to himself. Asking for eggs and bananas, and also asking them to call someone named Fortunato.

They threw him back in and slammed the door. He wept aloud like a child then. Called out for a blanket. Wanted to die. Do me the kindness of killing me, he said over and over. One of the jailers returned with a ball peen hammer and struck the metal door of his cell a dozen times with it until our ears rang. Someone from the entrance to the cell block screamed at him to shut up or they would kill him on the spot. I could hear him trying to muffle his sobs. I didn't want to imagine what they put him through. I knew it was waiting for me.

But what could they want, I wondered. I did all they ordered me to do. And when order fell apart I only wanted to go home. There was no way I thought they could construe this as a crime. I tried to pray to whatever saints I could think of, to help me face what was coming. But without their crooked little porcelain faces to pray to I found it impossible. One doesn't pray to a wall or to the air. One needs a figurine. A representation to help one focus.

I was going to ask for a statuette with the hope they could bring one to my cell. I reasoned, the provisional government supported the church and the church supported them. I recalled the procession when the fascists broke up an attack on the relics we paraded. There were camps on the verandas, or so I thought I saw once. Camps on the savannas. Camps in pockets of the maze. And if I showed my need for prayer, I felt, they would see I was a loyal son of the church. They would spare me then, I tried to convince myself.

But, in the end, it wouldn't do. I whispered to another prisoner, who brought my bread every day, of this idea.

His whisper was a rasp because they'd cut his throat with ammonia razors to rid him of a virus. No. No my fellow worker, no. Others have tried. It won't work. They view it as a sign of weakness now. Many say there has been a rift between the Scarecrow and the diamond city.

I wanted him to stop talking. My hand went to my throat as I imagined his pain. I was sorry I asked. Sorry to have mentioned it. I wanted to apologize for making him talk for so long. But I couldn't stop him. And he didn't want to stop. Even if every word he spoke made me more and more mindful of the torture I was putting him through.

I don't know what the truth is. But proclaiming the faith here gets you nothing. Nothing, fellow worker. Do you understand? They see it as a weakness or, worse for you then, a ploy. If they think you are having them on they will wait until everyone is asleep and come into your cell and beat you. No. Don't do it. Pray to your patrons without the use of a form. To ask for a statuette would go bad for you.

There were things I could have said in reply. Things I wanted to explain. But instead of engaging him I thanked him. I pulled my bowl of bread in through the hand latch at the bottom of my cell door. I didn't want to hear his horrible voice any longer. It was making me queasy. It gave me a taste for cold apples, where you eat them with a sharp knife like a vagabond in the trees. Reminded me of green fields where the wind blows so hard it bends the blades of grass silver. Made me think of a candy store in my youth and all the banana caramels burning in the fire that killed the owner. How they made everything of wood in my childhood. Wood and canvas and scratchy shingles that glistened in the light. And how the flies massed on the dog shit in the alley. I sat there eating my bread as an entire array of memories flooded my mind and made me cry.

Why did I ever leave my grandfather's backyard? Those were the happy days. Summer songs and gentle breezes. My grandmother standing at the gate, clapping her hands and taunting the black lady as she walked by. Jigaboo, jigaboo, my grandmother danced. I was too young to know my grandmother was a fascist even then. I try not to think of that. I like to remember her blind and her hands along the wall not knowing where she is. It was her punishment. I never minded.

But those days. I remember. The processions with our white prayer books and shimmering blue beads. Flags and marching bands and pledges of loyalty to the King. Tables of pastries set out in the sun on the sidewalk. The cranky old men. Cigarette smoke everywhere. And a vision of myself, forty years from now. Crooked and lame. The boys throwing stones and names at my head. There is Edju. There is Edju.

Edju, came the voice. My door swung open and three men in uniform stood smiling and drooling at the prospect of my torture. Edju. Stand up and come with us.

I took my last bite of bread and they handcuffed my wrists to one another at my front. One of the men had a stick with a hook and he grabbed the chain of my handcuffs with it. They pulled me out of my cell with a rough yank that snapped my head back to my shoulders. I almost passed out. Or did I for a moment? For the next thing I knew they threw me into a chair beside a table with three blue cups in front of me. These cups were upside down, rims to the table.

A woman in a clean white shirt leaned into the bright light that made my face hot and smiled with yellowing teeth. Watch, she said. Which cup has the pea?

She began to move the cups around in dodging, crazy motions. Half circles, doubling back. Short jerks with the cup in her left hand to distract me from her moving the position of the cup in her right.

Then, as if by a strict and predetermined system, she exchanged the inside cup with an outside cup. The other outside with the new outside. The middle with the old outside. The new middle with the new outside. Back and forth. Around and around until my eyes hurt and my head spun. At some point I tried to remember if she ever showed me which one had the pea in the first place. I couldn't remember if she did or not. Not knowing where the pea started, all this motion was pointless to me. I stopped watching the cups and concentrated on her face.

Maybe her eyes would reveal which one had the pea. What if her eyes never stopped watching the cup with the pea? What if, when she finished, she looked right at the cup for the briefest of moments before looking up? I watched her face. I watched her eyes. I tried to ask Saint Odilia for guidance and patience. But without her little painted face it was useless. And I worried trying to do this would only hurt my concentration in the end.

Looking back, I don't know how I managed to even think

of such a thing under such duress. A part of me, no matter how threatened, always seems to remain detached. This before me is a matter of fact. Carry on regardless. Even though the rest of me may be in full panic, there is a strain of this inside me.

After what seemed like twenty minutes of her shuffling and misdirection she stopped. Her eyes were on the cup to my right for the length of a blink of an eye. This was what I saw before she looked into my face and smiled crazy in the night.

Well? Her satisfaction was so heavy in the air it made me doubt even my mother's name. Where is the pea?

There was hesitation in my hands. There was the consequence of being wrong, after all. What would happen, what would they do to me, if I am wrong? Or for that matter what would they do if my guess was correct? I knew she looked at the blue cup to my right. It was a theory. It was the only thing I could think of. The only weapon left to me. There were men chuckling in the dark behind me. Also behind her. Someone's silver tooth sparkled in the dark.

I lifted my tied hands above the rim of the table and touched the cup on my right.

Her body pulled away from the table with the fierce anger of a mad cat. An arm swept across the top of the other cups and knocked over the one I'd pointed to. There on the table sat the pea. Except it wasn't a pea, it was a yellow kernel of corn.

I thought for a moment that I would lose on a technicality. They wanted me to find a pea, not a kernel of corn. My heart stopped and my chest went tight and heavy. I could feel my neck break out in sweat and my breathing went insane.

But she began to cry and the men who brought me there stood me up. Get up, they ordered, and sounded low and disappointed.

The door kicked open and the light of the hall blinded me. They took me back to my cell and threw me in.

I could hear them complaining bitter and long about me. I could hear the woman in tears. There was a gunshot. I assumed they killed the woman. I never saw or heard her again.

40.

I had many opportunities to ponder my past during the days and nights I spent in that cell. They left me alone after the cup game and only fed me through a notch from then on.

I wasn't always as I am today. I am pious now. I am quiet. A man of few possessions and simple wants. I live in quiet fear and this is good enough for me. When I was a young man I was brash and careless. I did not attend to my relationships. People's feelings did not interest me. I was full of myself. If people did not bend to my will I discarded them. And I kept doing this until, in the end, I was the one discarded by so many.

Those nights alone pouring tequila down my throat. The orange bile it called up from deep inside as I wallowed. The green fairy and the golden brew. Sitting alone in the hot summer night, deep night of the severe predawn morning. Unable to sleep. No one to talk to. People had fixed ideas about the person I was. They built these ideas on the knowledge they had of me as a young man. And no one allowed that I may have changed. You change. A man changes. But if the rest of the world has this idea of who you are and of what you do, it is of no use.

So, I studied the ancient arts. Took off on rectangular tangents. Transcendental meanderings. Holy bridges to the cosmos. And in exchange wasted what could have been the most productive years of my life. These are the things I thought about, locked up and unbothered in my cell, as I heard them try to question Alice.

They dragged her out of her cell and pulled her bag into the interrogation room. There was screaming and demands. Certain slaps of wooden slats against dull burlap. But she never broke. She never gave us away. Never admitted anything.

As I pondered her unshaken bravery in the face of their threats I realized how much I still felt for her.

And every day they dragged her out of her cell, cursing at her, I loved her more.

These red jails and down they went to the edge of the water. Drop the fish in the belly and the algae taint is the perfume. It didn't matter what they did to her. Down these narrow halls (and they were all narrow). Cross-lit lines blaring out of sudden doors as they took her under the lamp. Slam the doors and you will never see your family again. They asked her to cut the cards but she refused. Demanded she play word association but she kept silent.

A hundred questions unanswered. So. You wish to remain silent? She never answered. What is your name? No sound. Where are you going? Who are you with? What are your orders? What year did you graduate?

Nothing to no one. Nothing. Repeated again and again.

I didn't understand why they never figured out that she was dead. I know that, for me, I see what she was once. It was possible, I supposed, that the chief interrogator had become enamored of her wit and charm. He saw only the wax hair and emeralds for eyes of the past. Not what she is now, in reality. Not with her rows of rabbit teeth locked inside receding gums. Not with that lingering stink of the body gasses that let go when the heart quits altogether. Now there were only true black holes swallowing whole suns where eyes used to be. I imagined, in my midnight silences, what our life could have been. An ugly man becomes appealing when he walks beside a beautiful woman. Maybe the jailers felt touched by glory.

Back and forth across the aisles they dragged her. They pulled and slid her across the floor with no regard for her delicate condition. They went in on her at all hours. Blared music just outside her door. Had an old woman stand in the hall and call her name a hundred thousand times. I know they broke sticks on her body, because I heard them swatting at her. This was always followed by the loss of the switch. Then came the cursing, accompanied by someone throwing the useless weapon out the window.

She never said. She never admitted. She never broke.

One day, after they'd dragged her sliding across the cement floor and closed her door on her, they cried. Two grown men cried and admitted they could not reach her. Admitted she'd beaten them. One, I heard the next day, blew his brains out over his failure. The other became an acrobat in the circus. Alice beat them all.

It was not too long after this that they released us.

I was the same as I was when they first arrested me. Jacinto seemed a foot shorter somehow. But the sack that held Alice was clean and emitted a healthy glow in the summer sun like pastries on a table.

The angry soldiers kicked open dirt in their anger. They returned our possessions to us and led us to the swing door. And as he unlocked the gate the man in the clown face mocking tedium and remorse warned me in a whisper.

That girl in your bag is a holy relic. I would take care. If the churchmen take notice, your life will be in danger. He swung the gate and began to sing a nursery rhyme I'd never heard.

I put Alice on my shoulders high. Jacinto began to sob. Somehow, I still had my Nagant. How they missed it I will never understand.

The gun. The fact that Alice is dead and their blind stubbornness trying to frighten her. The hidden pea game, which they lost even though it was corn. And the one man they broke, Jacinto, who had nothing to say that they needed to hear. I admit that I grieved for the fate of my country, since by all evidence it appeared to be ruled by stupid men.

The road was yellow before us in the glaze. We walked. I should have been mad with joy over our release. But the words of the clownman clawed my head like a lust filled talon. The girl in your bag is a holy relic.

41.

We three lumber into what remains of the town. Even I don't recognize it, says Jacinto. There are no old people, he says. There used to be but they are all dead now. You, he points, are the oldest man in the world.

And all the young people in the market look upon me with suspicion now. I either have the color of the old belltower or the stink of the jail on me. I am certain they can sense one or the other. If only I knew which was more acceptable. I raise my collar to cover my neck until I can construct the proper hierarchy. But the stares of the young people make me nervous. Perhaps, I think, my collar isn't high enough. Or the color of my shirt is wrong. Or the shape and size of Alice's sack isn't proper. Their eyes stroke me with one corrosive gaze. My stomach is of fish swimming in the filthy water of my guts.

I no longer know what is in their world, since they imprisoned me for so long. Long enough, at least, to miss the killing of the old people. Their appearance is all so strange to me now. I can no longer recognize who is in power. Not like before, where I could guess who they were. Do they mean to be frightening? Or are they just projecting hardness because they are so vulnerable? Is it because they are, in fact, cruel? Or is it armor to protect weaknesses? I do not know what they've done to my world. It has the ringing flare of epitaph.

They've changed the language and the boundaries of beauty. Nothing, I lament, has ever been the same since they found the power in the stones of the long ago maze.

We walk past wooden bins of unrecognizable fruits. Colors of bread that should not exist. I don't know what I'm going to eat or what I'm going to say when I am hungry. I look in corners. On I go. Childish. Desperate. Unattached to anyone but Jacinto. And he is quivering, poor company.

The woman following us always stays the same distance away. She never seems to get closer. Jacinto notices her as well.

If I stop, she stops. She stops and looks at the sky, which no one can see for the canopies and the bare hanging light bulbs from wires. The wires crisscross the air over our heads. The bulbs all painted red. One imagines the sultry glow they give at night when the market turns purple and deadly. We shouldn't stay here, Jacinto sniffles. He wipes his nose with the back of his hand. It will be dark soon enough.

If I move toward this woman she steps back. If I turn to catch her gazing she averts her head. But I know she is looking at me. There is something familiar in the way she limps. I note her position on the map in my head with a violet flower. I move it along the streets as she comes. So, I call her Hazel.

42.

By midnight she was crouching along the pier. Deep in the morning, birds flew around her head waiting for worms. But it hadn't rained so they were only dreaming. Jacinto took it the worst, being near tears every time he saw movement behind us. This woman I called Hazel followed us all through the night.

Once or twice I determined to turn about and walk towards her but she was a mind reader. Every time I made this move she disappeared. When this became clear to me I tapped Jacinto on his elbow and mentioned it.

Maybe we should just keep walking towards her then, he quivered. Then she'll stay disappeared.

It was an intriguing idea at first. But the more I thought about it the less possible it seemed. If I turn to walk towards her and she disappears, I asked, how will I know where I'm supposed to keep walking?

You walk where she should be. To the place we last saw her and then just keep going.

But that's not where we want to go. I am trying to get back to my apartment. You'll be safe there.

In your apartment?

Yes. You'll be safe. It'll be safe there for us. We can wait out the troubles. I have some bread, I think. Or anyway things in cans that should still be good.

What if she follows us there?

Well, I thought for a while. Maybe she's just hungry.

She frightens me.

Oh, come on, I gave him a nudge on the arm. You are seven feet tall. Anyway, you used to be. What are you afraid of?

He didn't answer. He didn't answer and I shouldn't have asked. The second I finished the question all the things he feared in his life flowed into his mind's eye. He began to tremble. Whatever they did to him back there changed him forever. Or perhaps he needed eggs. I couldn't tell. Neither of us could recall when he last had his red bowl.

Come along, I tried to comfort him. It'll be alright. She can't harm us. It's obvious she doesn't want us to get close. She keeps disappearing every time we turn around and try to walk toward her. She won't allow herself to get close to us. So why be afraid of her?

What if she has a gun? He was gripping his shirt as if it were a hide he was trying to rip off his chest. As if it was an alien creature enveloping him. As if he was suffocating. As if it was squeezing the air out of his chest.

I pulled out my Nagant M1895 and pointed it to the dark sky. This is what they used to kill the Czar, I said. I don't know if she has a gun, but I do. And the Dark Monks of the Blood Whip dragged crystal blue rosaries over it and sprinkled it with holy water. This means I hit what I aim at, and I kill what I hit. St. Gabriel Possenti himself watches over the path of my holy bullets.

His long, boney hands shook like water. Snot trickled down from his nose. He had to work at breathing. His voice trembled more than before. How can we be sure?

I looked in the direction we last saw this Hazel. Her beady head was just over the hood of a dark blue automobile. I could see her fingers on either side of her face. Her short hair unbothered by the sudden wind. Watch, I said, and aimed the gun direct between her eyes.

The gun popped. I'd forgotten the satisfaction of that sound. The full throat. The sure fire. The kick of the beast controlled in my hands. The noise suppression common to that model.

But she must have ducked down below the car the moment she saw me square the weapon in her direction. The bullet pocked the vehicle with a beautiful hole. But I knew I missed her.

See? He cried.

From somewhere along the barbed wire in the distance flashes of light sparkled at us. Small and angry. Something like bees bit into the ground around us. It was all soundless but for the thud.

Run for cover, I screamed. Someone's shooting at us.

I pulled Alice by the rope that tied her sack and the three of us dove behind a low wall that was riddled with holes. Honeycombed from past firefights. Bullets pinged along this wall, seeking skin. They made sharp little pellets from the stone and mortar and tossed them around our ears. I tried to judge the spaces between the firing and would pop up above the wall long enough to let off a few shots in return.

More fire came from a window of a burned out farmhouse behind us. But this aimed at whoever it was that was shooting at us.

It didn't take long for me to understand what was happening.

Jacinto, I tried to keep my voice down but stay loud enough to overcome the gunfire. The gunfire that now passed over our heads from both directions. Ahead and behind. No one is shooting at us, I said. We've blundered into a firefight.

Whose side are we on, he cried, his hands over his ears and his knees to his chin.

I grabbed him by the collar. If I didn't have my Nagant in the other hand I would have tried to slap him back to his senses. Listen to me. Jacinto. Listen to me.

I had to put my face an inch away from his. Only when he smelled my breath did he dare to open his eyes. Jacinto. Do you see that rain barrel at the corner of the farmhouse? I pointed with the gun.

He didn't bother to look but nodded his head anyway.

You grab Alice and run behind it. I will stay here and cover you. Understand? When you go, I will rise up and start firing back at them.

Somewhere a grenade went off. We stayed unharmed but felt the wind of it blow against our hair.

Do you understand me?

His eyes shut tight but he nodded.

Grab the sack and go when I say.

It took a while for him to find the top of the sack twisted and tied with heavy rope. But when he found it, I took the extra length of the rope and tied it around his wrist. He understood what I was doing and did not complain.

I slapped him on the shoulder and screamed for him to go. The moment he and Alice darted away from the wall I rose up to my knees and started firing. The bold Nagant sparking in the direction of our attackers. No wonder war is so beloved, I thought. I emptied the weapon in their direction. It is odd, somehow, that there is often a lot of fire exchanged in battle yet nobody ever seems to get hit. Nobody seems to get hit until there is some catastrophic reckoning, and then dozens get hit all at once. And a man you thought was beside you firing has gone quiet by your side. Firing a gun is like fucking a ghost.

I ducked below the low wall when the firing from the other side came my way. I let them pour their fire at me. I let them release their anger and their fear and their hatred at me for trying to kill them. They pelted the stones with their bullets. I counted four hundred and seven of them before they eased up.

When it was obvious to me they went quiet I crawled on all fours toward the barrel. Either they were reloading or didn't see me. Or the fire from the farmhouse covered me. I don't know. All I do know is that I'd joined Jacinto and Alice and we were all unharmed.

From the barrel we could get up into a crouch and run behind the house. And then once behind the house we could run as normal, and as fast, as we could. We ran for a long time. In minutes, the dragon roar of the firefight behind us receded into memory.

We dove into a clump of tall grass alongside one of the new walls of the Great Maze. Here we rested. Worked our unwilling chests to calm down and regain our wind.

I could not see the end of the maze wall in either direction. The night and the low smoke from the campfires of the transients down in the gully masked my view. It didn't seem to matter, so when we'd recovered I took one direction and held to it.

We walked close to half a mile down the fresh wall. Our hands running alongside it as we went, turning out fingers white as if with loose chalk. After that distance the wall ended in an abrupt point. We turned around the corner this made and saw an open field ahead of his. I recognized it as a field I played in as a boy. It was concrete then and nestled between the buildings of a church and a school. The concrete and the buildings were gone. But I still recognized the air. I knew we were on the path back to my rooms, and not far.

I looked behind us once without real reason. Hazel was there, bounding between hedges, trying not to reveal herself to me. I did not tell Jacinto.

43.

The center eye grows more tired, faster, than the other two. Waiting for the load to fall. The petty dragons and the heartfelt strangers you meet at roadside blend together. They make a blue swirl of beans and ribbons. You long to be young again but it will not kick. Thirsty years in the same hole does not make for a positive recommendation. We moved with purpose but avoided the river. Where the walls of the new maze descended into the river, they built the wall all the way down to the river's bottom. But they used iron bars beneath the surface so that the water went through unimpeded. This also assured that no human could use this part of the wall as an underpass. There was to be no cheating of the direction the maze sent the traveler. This was their message to the people. The depth of their urge to control was deeper than any natural river we owned within our borders.

And the closer we got to my city the more angled the walls became. I could see the spires of the churches and hear the bleating of the sheep on the front lawns. But no matter which direction we chose we never got there. It was in a dead end at the end of a false passage where we decided to rest the night. No closer to our target than we seemed to be that morning. And Hazel's head kept peering around the corner at us. We could not shake her.

I made a fire with the dried carcass of a rat and started a pot of water for our coffee.

Rats aren't noted for their high temperature, Jacinto said. He stared into the glow of the embers glowing in with the dead animal's fur. Much better to use wood, Jacinto said.

Yes, I answered, staring into the rat's swollen black eyes. But there are no trees in this alcove. They've divided the countryside into the strangest compartments.

It was the intended effect, after all. The same one the ancients had when they used the original maze to confound and defeat the invaders in the days of old. We had been hypnotized by the monotony. Hypnotized by the endless tangle of corridors and sudden openings, everything leading nowhere. We sat before the glowing rat exhausted. Half asleep. Jacinto's hands were going all over his body. Patting and digging into pockets.

What are you looking for, I asked.

I don't know. I felt I should have something. Somewhere.

If the circumstances were different I would not know what he meant. But I did. There is a memory of something. You can't pin it down. It has a tangible reflection in your brain, but you couldn't explain it. Like nostalgia for a time yet to be. Or a remnant of something you once held. There can be no name put to it. You could never describe it to anyone should they ask. But it was something. Something that happened, and it was good. You liked it, but you can't get what it was. Something like a drum, but not a drum at all. Something like a face, but no one you can remember. No one you know. Or perhaps you knew them once, but they're lost to you now. Someone you should have never let get away.

You want to remember. It is just there, on the edge, but it won't allow you to touch it. It won't allow you to own it again. Yes. I knew what Jacinto meant. I experienced the same things many times in the last year. Well - perhaps 'many times' is not accurate. Three times, to be exact. I felt this way three times in the last year. Four, counting this one while Jacinto searched his pockets for something that wasn't there. I wish I could remember what I was trying to recall. But it is of no use.

Rats aren't noted for giving off a lot of useful heat, I mumbled. Jacinto didn't hear me. He stopped searching and sprawled on his back against the Earth. And the Earth spun beneath the deceiving stars. It took the better part of an hour to get the water to a point where I could make coffee. By then the rat was ash, Jacinto was snoring, and Hazel was still peering around the corner like an elf.

I drank all the coffee myself. If Jacinto wakes up, I told myself, and complains, I'll tell him to go to hell. And what did he mean by going to sleep without us deciding who would stand watch that night? Since he forced me to be the one, I deserved the coffee. It was a perfect argument with geographic logic. But he never woke up all that night for me to use it. I knew that, by morning, I would forget its brilliance. Another great thought, wasted.

Hazel disappeared behind the wall for a while. I assumed she was sleeping. The thought occurred that this would be the perfect time to investigate who she was. To find out what she thought she was doing. But I didn't do it. I should have, but I didn't. Part of me was afraid. Another part didn't care. And half of me was too tired.

I fought off sleep all that night. The monstrous birds passed overhead and either didn't see us or were looking for someone else. There were distant sounds somewhere beyond our walls. Like trains or engines. Rumbles and earthquakes. I listened for a long time before I recognized them as gunfire and bursting shells. There was a war on, still. Someone was out there, challenging the fascists who rebuilt the maze. The rough men who held us captive were coming up against resistance. I wanted to know who was fighting them. I imagined these forces to be heroes, fighting for freedom and a return to the quieter times. But if they were the same forces that tried to break up the holy processions, I thought of them as the enemy. I no longer knew what to think. I was not part of the life of my own country. This was no longer the same place I'd lived in all these years. Somewhere along the way everything, and everybody, changed. I was certain it had something to do with the horrible things I did to people in my youth.

The doctor told me that I mustn't think of my younger days as a guilty sentence. The harsh way I acted to people. The stupid things I believed. The shoddy way I treated all my friends, now gone. Sending Alice away when we were just on the verge of promising our lives to one another. I should not view these mistakes and vices as a final decree of my low value. He said I should look on them as things I learned from. Things I changed, in time. Things I did when I was immature and silly. Underdeveloped. A child. That people who continue to dwell on these things were wrong to do it. And the people who kept reminding me of them and torturing me with them, were not my friends but people to avoid.

I knew, in my heart at the time that he was right. But I couldn't do what he said. The guilt was too much like the walls of a maze. Whitewashed and new. With Hazel once again peering around the corner.

I picked up a stone and hurled it in her direction. It fell short, but she retreated behind the corner just the same. The top of the walls around us that formed the dead end began to turn dim blue at that moment. The sun was returning. It would soon be time to resume our search for a way back to my city. But I was so tired. So tired. The center eye wanted to stay closed. The other two were difficult to keep open. I roused Jacinto. Even before he was full awake he complained I saved him from something white. I did not reply. I do not answer the charges laid by other people's dreams.

44.

These were all the wrong turns. We weren't getting anywhere. The spires and the watchtowers of my city got
farther away the closer we got. An illusion. Like the coming
sandstorm seems an approaching mountain complete with
goats on ledges. The hope of getting home replaced by the
unmistakable scent of the country. There was nothing falling
to concrete. There were no car horns. There was only the
smell of hay and yarrow. Milkweed and long grasses where
the locusts hid before they attacked. These are not smells discovered amid the spires and the armed parapets of a frightened city. These were the smells of youth and rancid vigor.
The conclusion was inescapable. These were all the wrong
turns. The maze was winning.

What is the psychology of the maze? A maze. Amaze.
Amazed. What is the ticking inside a human brain that re-
jects the idea of retracing one's steps? Why, once a man has
gone so many miles through the breathing hallways, is turning back never an option? Why?

This, I supposed, was the exact intent of the ancients
when they built the old maze. When they built the old maze
to befuddle and unnerve the invaders into surrender. How
brilliant and wise they were, knowing this is how the mind
works, even so long ago. Knowing how little human nature
would change – if there was any change at all - over the centuries.

But I long as I go...

If I could escape. A step, a step.

If I could escape and free myself. Another dragging step.

If I could free myself and escape from the pointed daggers. The pointed daggers that flow from Hazel's eyes as she
follows us. She doesn't approve, and I can tell. No matter

what I do I'm wrong. She slams empty boxes against the concrete. She shuts metal doors when I'm not looking. Trying to scare me. Make me jump. Mess with my heart rate. Frighten me with the unexpected. Agitate me. Bring me down to her mud. Making war whoops.

I do my best not to react. Act like I think nothing of it. Tried to be nonchalant. Didn't want to give her the satisfaction of knowing her noises worked. Made me jump or get me angry. Ruined my demeanor. Threw me off my game. I kept looking forward. Forward down the lanes and aisles of the never-ending maze. Thirty-foot high walls and all ways of climbing over removed wherever you go. But in this I outsmarted myself. My pretended aloofness only served to enrage her anger all the more. She started writing notes and describing her observations to the police. I acted unafraid. But we quickened our pace.

For a while I thought we'd outran her. But on the fourth morning after leaving the prison I awoke to see her and Jacinto making angry love. And, in the most unthinkable way, they were doing their work on each other behind Alice. Behind Alice, all crumpled and gray in her bag.

Two feelings twined inside like medicinal snakes around a flaming sword. On the one hand their proximity to my Alice irritated me more than anything I could imagine. But there is always the futile magnetism that occurs when one watches two others in the grasp. Pumping at each other. Their eyes closed and the entire wider world reduced to a pinpoint of attention. Spasms of reward for the move that guarantees the species. All around them obliterated in the darkness infused with rose water behind their eyelids. Only he. Only she. The rest of us are nothing.

I wanted to run there and drag Alice by the rope and save her from having to be a prisoner of their motion. I also wanted to watch until their zeal crossed over that point and lost control. Hazel was beautiful. I had never noticed it before. And Jacinto was all muscle and tone. All seven feet of him and brown.

I did nothing. I watched. I sat with my back against the impenetrable wall and drooled from the apple juicing between my lips. I watched. I observed.

I observed that the act of mammal coupling is all the same every time. A twist or a variation here or there, to be sure. But it is service to the imperative, in the end, in every case. We are foolish to think anything has never been tried. Foolish to think we invent a new angle. A new pose. There is nothing new in the world. Those seeking a unified theory of things should consider the functions in the body. The different uses all in one place. Why did the stringent powers and forces of adaptation do it this way? An overlooked compendium, no doubt.

Yes, the art of watching other people making love often sends me to philosophy. It's calculated activations that get the goods. The ordained process. You can't deny it. Done as entertainment in some orders of the species. And despite all clean intentions, unstoppable.

The sounds from Hazel's mouth. The color to her face. The crying eyes and closing brows. She lets you. She lets you. She lets you. I wish Alice were still alive, but I snap back to purpose at the thought of her. The reason I saved her from the streets was to keep her from the degrading acts that may happen. As I once explained, they do things to dead women in the streets. Mine was a noble cause.

I walked away while they reached their mutual falling. I am the pure warrior.

They cannot touch me. They may not pierce me with the common knives of mere nature. I saved Alice. This makes me near a saint.

Someday they will have parades and feast days for me,

perhaps. With this in my future, I sat against a different part of the wall. One that didn't face their meanderings. One that couldn't hear their explosions. I sat there and consoled myself. Maybe now this Hazel will leave us alone.

45.

never awake or fallen. not finite. not finished. just going he goes. and not by the fine fit of the mooring dark dragon moon.

I thought I would never see it again. The thought of it made my hands sweat. My stomach seizes. It embarrassed me to think of it. This cult. But instead of the dark looming towers of my city, now ages behind us, was the Mountain. The Mountain I'd left so many years ago. Unmistakable in the green haze the collective gases the dead made.

This is where I went as a young man. A fine march in my step and a sword in my hand. Good-bye all I knew. Alice not even considered. The rest of my life unaware of this episode. I escaped it down a cold alleyway to the sounds of crying guitars and mournful singers. The music came from open draped windows in the night. Songs of what I lost by coming here in the first place. My reputation. My friends. Everything gone so I could chase the eternal verity.

It was the epitome of a man-made structure. Started years ago and built-on with considerable ardor ever since. From outside it seems the most unworkable thing. A ridiculous notion. An impossible scheme. But once you are in it, climbing it, engaged in the contest, it possesses you, this Mountain. And I could see it looming high over the thirty-foot walls of the new maze.

Its nature is that of a black hole. Not even light can escape. And we who were only nearby were also sucked into it. It's collection of the long dead and those soon to join. All the halls and byways of the maze seemed to lead there now. To get anywhere one must pass the Mountain.

Jacinto never saw it before. What are they doing, he asked. More a gasp than a question. We stood and watched the hundreds of living men climbing the artificial structure. Faceless ants upon a distant, unrecognizable shore. Everyone striving for the top. Clamoring over one another. Here and there the flash of swords. Angry cries. Fighting and running everywhere. Crawling over the bodies that lost the game.

They are trying to get to the top, I said, shaking my head at the merciless stupidity of it all.

Are they fighting, Hazel wanted to know.

They are. They are killing one another if they have to.

To reach the summit, she kept asking.

Yes.

Our eyes followed the long trail of streaming men toward the top in unison. Our heads tilting up to aid our view. But we could not see the top of the Mountain for the clouds. A smoky mess made of that ugly haze formed by the putrid gas and stink of decay.

What happens at the top, Jacinto squinted. He put a hand over his eyes to fight the glare but it did no good.

I don't know, I told them. I have never seen it.

Have you been on the Mountain?

Yes, I was sad to confess.

It's just a poem, Hazel made a nervous laugh. Something said that means something else. Isn't it? It isn't there for real, is it?

It is a Mountain, I explained. A Mountain made of all the bodies of the men who fell along the way. It was just a hill once. Those who think it is a symbol for something are the ones who die the easiest. It is real. I pointed at the sack that Alice was resting in. All I got out of it was this sack. Sometimes it is brown.

Is that where you found Alice, Hazel wanted to know.

I began to harbor a distinct hatred for this woman. But since she and Jacinto became lovers I put up with her for his sake. I didn't like her voice. I didn't like her squat legs. Her tight curls. Her glasses. Her pudgy fingers.

No, I replied. I found Alice on the street. She was dead. I put her in the sack. The sack I already had. It has been a long time since I was up there. I was young. It was one of the things that helped me put Alice behind me. But it is a cult. And it embarrasses me to admit I was in it.

We walked without much purpose. There was no way to change direction except to retrace our steps. The walls on either side of us drew closer together. Like a funnel toward the horror. The lane we used led nowhere else but to the base of the Mountain. We moved slow as we talked. Or they asked, and I answered.

It was before the love of the Saints, I told them. The calming love of all the Saints and the touch of clean, holy relics. It was a long time ago.

The closer we got the easier it was to hear the racket from the side of the Mountain facing us. It was much higher than I remembered. It was years ago and men had labored on it since. Broadening and rising the breadth and girth of the thing. Killing and piling the dead ever higher.

I believe it was only half as high the last time I was here, I told them.

We walked out from between the walls into an open, irregular plain. It was a great expanse with the Mountain square in the middle. And all around the structure were at least a dozen entrances back into the maze.

We need to pick one and get back to the city, I told them. But I could see the light dance in Jacinto's eyes.

So, you climb your way up to the top and you win, is that it, he wanted to know.

That is the theory, I said. But Jacinto, I pointed at the squirming men running swords through each other. I let the screams from the fighters punctuate my words. Jacinto, I stressed. This is not some kind of metaphor. This is a Mountain made of flesh. The bones and skin and innards of hundreds of thousands of people. If you burrow down to the core you will find nothing but the dead from times past. There is no ground in it. The mud slope you see is human slime. The residue of decayed flesh.

We could see men slipping on this unsteady surface. What confused Jacinto was that the Mountain had been there for so long. It had taken on such a massive bulk. And it was complex like a natural mountain. There were ridges and shoulders. We could see areas where no living people were. He pointed at what seemed to be trees.

But what are those?

Fungus, I told him. It only grows here. There is no name for it.

Jacinto smiled. You get a sword and try to get to the summit?

That's it.

Who thought of this, Hazel squeaked. She was sounding more and more like a pig the longer she was with our company.

No one knows. The legend is that a man once stood on a pile of rocks and threatened everyone who passed him. They say he killed six men at his feet before someone avenged one of the deaths. Then it was vendetta. Everything came from this. But no one knows if that is truth or fable. If there is a difference.

Jacinto could not keep himself together. He bolted from us toward the thing. Toward the ground station where they sell the swords to all those who want to try.

I called after him. Hazel ran his way, imploring him to come back.

I squared Alice higher on my back and ran to stop them all before it was too late. Only then did I remember how strong the cult was. How tempting. So absurd it was unstoppable.

The miraculous bird flew over the Mountain of Flesh wrapped in a fiery aura. Wings stretched full inside a blurring halo. Over the poison mist. Over the running fungus trees. Far below the hand heart of the prodigal sun.

I never wanted to come back here. I can no longer race the passion. The miraculous bird appears to speak to those below. Jacinto, sword already in hand, lifts his face to it to listen. It is too late.

46.

The first man we passed lay wounded in the muck. There was blood on his shirt. And the smell of the blood made Jacinto hold his eyes shut.

You will have to kill him, I said. Run your sword through his neck and finish him.

Jacinto was ready to cry. But I persisted.

These are the rules of the cult. He's dying can't you see? You put him out of his misery and then you go through his possessions and take what you can. If you don't kill him now you will have to fight him later.

I don't understand.

Jacinto, I pleaded. There are no restaurants here. No stores. You kill or you are killed. But if you are the one left standing you take whatever supplies your kill has on him and keep going. He put both hands on the sword handle and made to drive it into him.

But a heavy man came barreling down behind the wounded one. Jacinto's reaction was good. He saw the man charging and held his weapon back in case this one attacked. As Jacinto watched him approach the wounded man moaned out loud and begged us to save him. There was a moment of confusion. Jacinto pointed his sword at the running attacker, but he raced by without seeing us. Before we could all turn around we heard a metallic clang and a rustic thud in the belly of the air. When we looked we saw the burly man had run square into another man and the two tumbled down the squishing muck. Each one trying to kill the other. It was the first fight Jacinto and Hazel ever saw. I, to be sure, had seen this kind of thing hundreds of times.

The man at our feet squirmed in agony. I took the sword from Jacinto's hands and sliced the poor soul's neck open, and he was at peace. I pointed at the carcass. Go through his pockets and his knapsack there. Take everything of use. Take the knapsack too. Do you see the helmet on the ground beside his head? Take it. If you're going to do this you need to pick up anything you can use wherever you find it.

He took what few things the kill offered and we resumed our climb. All the while I was whispering. You shouldn't do this. If not for me you'd be dead already. You will never reach the summit. No one ever does. No one knows what happens there. It is a stupid, stupid game.

He wouldn't listen. I could see the fear in every motion of his body. But his face displayed nothing but the fascination and lure of the thing.

The second fight we passed was in its last throes when we got there. It was a bitter struggle. When we came up to them both men were stuck clean through with each other's sword. Standing, leaning against each other in a death dance. Both sword points sticking out each backside. Blood poured out everywhere, but neither one would go down. One was spitting into the other's face, and the other was trying to choke him with a broad, wet hand.

These two are dead men, I said. Their fate is sealed. It's obvious. You wait until they fall and when they are dead, you can get what you can off them. I pointed at the one trying to choke the other. That one has a nice pair of shin guards you can use when he croaks.

But so long as they were alive they kept fighting. There was a punch to the face. In response, the other attempted to bite off an ear. And all the while each kept twisting their sword inside the other. Making tunnels. Trying to skewer each other. But they were both losing strength and blood and life force at an astonishing rate.

And yet even when they finally tumbled over and rolled away they kept trying to hit and spit and kick at each other.

When the rolling stopped and they finally came to rest they lay together in a tangle. A confused, intertwined, bleeding mass. Groaning and swearing and still trying to do damage to one another.

You see the depth of it, I asked. Neither of these men have any hope of reaching the summit. But they are killing one another. One kills because the other tried to kill him. They agreed to kill one another. That's the way it is.

It's madness, he whispered. Killing is approved here.

It's required here. Men consider it an honorable profession. They leave house and home and kin to come here and murder one another. And the elders praise them for it. Write songs about their glory. Erect statues of them back in their home town. Tell little boys to be just like them. Just like that, I pointed. Smeared guts and all.

Jacinto's mouth hung open. Mesmerized.

I slapped him on the arm as the two men continued to die together. You'll never make it. While you're focused on these two, I said, anyone could come over that ridge and take your head off. I put my finger in his face. You need to pay attention.

I don't want any of their things, he said. His face was green.

Well then that's your second mistake. But if that's what you feel, let's keep climbing. See how far you get before you run out of supply or someone runs you through.

By the time he got to where a third fight had taken place, it was already over. One of the two lay dead and the winner was resting on his elbows over him. He was breathing fast, but his sword popped up at Jacinto when he saw us, ready to defend himself.

It tempted him. This man was in a vulnerable position. Jacinto thought about making his first kill. I could read it in his eyes. The rain became a torrent. He stood over him for a long time before he dropped the sword and turned away.

He was going back down the Mountain. He'd come to his senses. This wasn't the place for him. I thought, as we descended, this big, tall man lasted only ten minutes. I was part of this madness for almost two years. It scared me how quick everything I'd learned came back in a flash. Just being on the lowest part of it again after all these years.

I heard Alice's voice, sad and weak, from inside the bag. It began to rain.

47.

In my lucid moments I knew she wasn't talking, in reality. Dead people can't talk. They cannot intercede on your behalf through the hierarchy of Saints. They can't appeal to the last true arbiter in the clouds. They don't watch what you are doing. They don't get angry when you don't go to their grave and kneel down in the grass. They are not there. They don't shake their heads at your mischief. Or cry in their sleeves when they catch you doing the things you never tell anyone about. They are dead. Dead people can't do anything anymore. Because they are dead. In my lucid moments I know this.

As we stepped off the Mountain the shells of eaten turtles crunched under our feet. And the rain washed bones and eyes out of the ground from long ago. I was lucid in that way. Lucid enough to see Jacinto, holding Hazel side by side as they walked, shaking from what he'd seen on the Mountain. Lucid enough to begin to consider which of the twelve or so openings back into the maze we should take. Lucid enough to piss my pants. I have earned my sentence to be alone. Alone in rooms. Alone in fields. In doorways and beneath transoms. On trains and in wagons. On the tower and the lookout. From horizon to sea as the brazen moon flows. Alone in majestic cement. I've worked for this condition.

Days and nights send us down alleys and into dead ends. All through our struggle to find our way through this maze Jacinto and Hazel make love when it turns dark and we rest after small meals. Every night. Every night.

It holds no magic for me. I don't watch anymore. It is a disgusting thing. Dirty and unclean. To do it in the grass. With ants and worms trekking so close to an eager anus. And to what end? To oooh and aaah like bulbous fish. They think they come in contact with the heavenly meaning of all the sentient holy cosmos on high, amen. They work at it to exhaustion and collapse on each other. We eat little and are weak. When they finish they are more exhausted than contented. And to what end?

We walk along the outdoor corridors and all this time we pass only four or eight other travelers, also lost. I speak with them. We trade information. What is ahead. What is behind. Where are there doors? Is the whole maze finished? Don't go north when you get to the notched wall. Look for this marker to tell you that lane is a dead end. Don't go into the blue house to find the kitchen. The wall goes straight through the building and you will not get there.

I study the stars to see if I can get some bearings. Keep tabs on what little provisions we have. Make sure we move in an efficient manner.

But they saunter along discussing the moves they intend to try on each other that evening. If you touch this while doing that... If you can once in a while give a pinch behind this... If only we could find a chair... Oh, you like that? On and on. A clinical forum for their paltry moves. Paltry compared to the vastness of the universe they think they go one with. Every day that goes by Hazel disgusts me more and more. She wants me to watch. I saw her looking at me once while they were in the middle of their work. She smiled at me. She waved. She wanted me to watch. I folded my arms and turned away. That was my answer. And I have been against her ever since.

I am a simple man with few possessions. I am a pure warrior who is not corrupted by the flesh. If not for me our expedition would get nowhere. I am stoic in my solitude. Days pass without saying anything. Sometimes I dream of Marta Vansimmerant's hand stroking by naked back but I never admit this. When that thought comes to me I bruise myself. I sit by Alice and wait for quiet and sense. And for the lovers to stir.

The world is vicious. Venal. Animalistic. We are animals. I don't think too long on the state of my country and my surroundings. If I did, I know I would find myself hoping the fascists are winning their fight.

But so far no one we have met seems to have any news. No one knows how the fight is going. And no one wants to tip their hand about whom they are for.

It is a temporary thing with me. I know, deep inside, that I could only be a fascist if I were the dictator. Only if I were the leader. The Scarecrow. Otherwise I will side with democracy. There's no use denying it. It's a fact.

48.

Somewhere we pass beneath emerald starlight as the dragon breeze plays on the mind like drums. Jacinto and Hazel are always together now. Their lovemaking is blue in my hand. Red in my eyes. Don't they know that I can hear them, here in the dark? They wake me out of deep sleep. I sit near Alice with a wet cigarette. White paper stained brown by the sweat. By the rain. By the passing of the age.

What kind of Saints do you have, Jacinto asks in daylight.

(It is daylight. It is day. Day. Morning. Morning and he is chewing from the last bowl of roses in our provisions. He eats the flowers and Hazel chews the stems. I pray for a thorn to cut her throat and kill her).

What do you mean, I ask. Elbow out. Eyes half closed.

You said, he reminded me, you'll let me have a few Saints for my empty niches. Remember?

Of course, I frown. The thorns, I note, are having no effect on her digestive system. She seems to enjoy them. The hotter the better. She does not die.

So, which Saints do you have?

I said I would look. That I can't remember. I've answered this way seven times since we left the church. Every time I answer he is happy and excited. Why change my answer?

His enthusiasm scours me like diamonds, and I keep close to Alice. I have taken to holding my old scapular tight in one palm to protect me as we walk. I whisper Saints Boris and Gleb, protect me from the vile notions of the world. If only I had a green votive candle in a box made of sandalwood. I would hold it in my lap while I whisper deep devotions to Saint Dwynwen and her lover. I could pray Jacinto and Hazel away. Then I would not have to wish harm on them. But I have no candle. And Alice has been silent for a long time now. The oily stains seeping through her sack bother me. But the prospect of finding a new sack is slim in these times of uncertainty.

Then, for two days, bedeviled by a fog, it was clear we'd become lost. The solemn brass bell around my neck allowed them to follow me and keep pace. Like a cow in the field. The fog, I think, would offer cover.

I think of the many ways to get rid of her. Perhaps killing her is too severe. If I could find a gulley I could push her down and say it was an accident. This would not be killing, it would only be a lie. The best time to kill someone is while they are singing. Eyes closed. Concentrating on the tone. The correct lyric said right. The nuance of note and word. Mouth open and mind focused. They never hear the cat feet when they are singing. They never sense the burst of the opening door. They feel only the chilling air it lets in, just before the knife. The gun. The fingers at the throat. The best time to kill someone is when he or she is singing.

49.

The explosions came up with the sun on that panoramic morning. Kicking up a cloud of red dust on the horizon. We assumed it was fighting. But going a mile or two down the morning corridor brought us to a wide field. Parts of all the surrounding walls are all knocked down and the view was open like rum. And in that field stood a multicolored army in somewhat order. They stood at attention. Detonations brought down whole sections of walls in the distance.

So, Jacinto said. They are doing what the Vikings could not. Dismantling the maze wholesale and opening up the country for maneuver again.

You can tell the rebels because they have no uniforms, Hazel pointed with a smile. The Resistance. The citizen army out to topple the Scarecrow. The lovers embraced when she said this. It was a promising thing to say but at just that moment the idea of the doing of sex disgusted me beyond reason. I vowed then and there never to do it again, should the opportunity ever present itself.

Over the last few weeks, though, life had become so tedious and stifling. I had the urge to abandon our journey. I would abandon Alice, walk away from everything, and join that army down there. But I didn't do it and I don't understand why. Something about finishing what I'd started. Plus, the possibility of getting killed for ideas. There was nothing more absurd than getting killed over an idea.

I determined not to go down there. I would join neither rebel or Scarecrow. I picked up a walking stick from the detritus that we always had to step over. I turned my collar and resumed our walk. Three steps and I realized I was alone.

Jacinto and Hazel ran down the embankment. They were down there, waving their arms. Stroking hands and kissing

rifles. Though inside I felt a need to attach myself to the soldiers and officers down there too – a visceral blain of fire – I
held back.

The times are uncertain. No one knows how the last wind
will blow. I wouldn't want to be on film. I wouldn't want anyone to know what I favored. I wouldn't want to have to answer, should these fellows lose the game to the black hand
that would rule us still. No one knows the true strength of
the Scarecrow. I began to look for cameras.

I looked for cameras and worried about the growing stain
on Alice's sack. I waited for the other two to finish their ablutions in the fountain of men below so we could get on.
I rearranged my belt. Combed my hair. Stuck gum on the
underside of tree leaves. Thought about why my piss had
no scent at all. Wondering if that, coupled with the strong
shooting pains in my liver, meant harm was coming to me. It
was a pastime. Soon enough they returned. They looked like
children. And we resumed.

The bush, on fire, speaks. Riddles me at the start, then
makes ashes with harsher truths. To get my eternal guidance
from burning foliage. This quest, promised to me as good as
land. A lot of passports and questions I have not. The work
will make you holy. This is why sometimes I tell myself I will
give Jacinto all my possessions. Be glad and give it all away.
Give it all to him and let him go. Let them both go. And I
will return to the country to live in these same hills, alone.
He can take what relics I have and fill his walls. There is too
much talk of walls. I rejoice in the smashing of them. We can
see the hills now that the maze is coming down. And there
in the hills, when I return, I will eat thistle and shit prayers.
I will live there until the solar wind erodes the moon like the
desert wind carves the rocks.

We walk on. They are quiet like penitents having gotten
their requirements for absolution. Bless me father under my

chin. We walk.

Feet in shoes. Shuffle step beyond the ever explosions freeing the countryside. The forklift smashes the Scarecrow against the wall. We watch the life flow out of his face and thighs in the poetry of blood. Blood from somewhere behind his chest.

We used to go in circles. Now that the maze is dying, our line is straight again. I see the dungeon spires and windows of my city. Alice heaves a heaven's worth of sighs. See how much she knows me mind?

This is why I should have never let her go.

50.

Returning home was much like sin. Hazel looked up at the building I'd lived in from the street and was near tears. I saw it through her eyes. It was a ruin now, from all the fighting. But there was still a light on in the window behind the same plain curtain I always kept. Warmth to me. Shame to them. I saw her shudder. I saw Jacinto's hand rub her shoulder with care. I said there's no shame in showing the same series of sure solemn scents so many stories up. She smiled.

Hot stairs like urine in the bowl and the squeak of the feral. A radio played the national anthem in scratchy time. Someone with a cigar sang the words in a bathroom. Though we could tell by the sound of his voice that he wasn't naked. A cat spat and the blue tinge mold up in the high corner gave off an odor of old wood and honey. We reached the landing and my door, unlocked, stood part way open to the world.

Better to have come up the back, I admitted. I hadn't yet realized the back porch had blown away like so many sticks. I pushed the door open onto the green carpet. There was a television going and three hungry children sitting in a cardboard box. Dirty faces and the smell of dead beetles. The radiator was missing, and absentminded pipes jutted out from the floor like periscopes. It was a warm day so the water ran in the sink. I did not recognize the place.

Are you sure this is your apartment, Jacinto cocked his head like a true dog seeking reason.

I am home, I sighed. I knew that the fighting would jumble everything up. I had a feeling. Logic, after all. It stood to reason. People took what shelter they could and someone saw this place was empty and moved in. They put three children in a box and found a television. That's how the empire of the air got started. I didn't have the heart to trouble the children further.

Perhaps I will just get some of my possessions and we'll go, I nodded.

Nothing was the same. A withered old man in suspenders sat in an unmoving rocking chair under an empty birdcage in the kitchen sun. He pointed at the wall and tried to speak, but he couldn't form a full word. He made the same noise again and again. Everything sounded a jumble and he seemed convinced he was imparting something important. We stood by the children and wondered. A woman with sagging arms emerged out of the bedroom and brushed past us. Without looking at us, she lifted the box of children and took them into the bathroom. The water was running in the tub and there she dumped them. They came out like dirty carrots, rolling out and plunking into the water.

I went into what was once my bedroom. I'd forgotten how small it was. But the chest of drawers and the boxes at the bottom of my narrow closet were gone. I shook my head when I saw Jacinto watching me. They're all gone, I frowned. Everything is gone. Maybe sold for filament or something.

Filament?

Whatever they use to keep warm, I shrugged.

Filament isn't something you use to keep warm. You mean something else. And anyway, it's summer. Jacinto's lower lip began to quiver.

We've been gone a long time.

I'm sure that's the lie you want me to believe.

I recognized there would be no consoling him. The old man in the rocking chair began to roll a cigarette with shaking hands. Tobacco going all over his pants.

I'm sorry, I said. I don't know what to say.

The truth is you never had any statues. Isn't that so? The truth is you just wanted us to help you get home and now you're going to abandon us. You never had an, statues. Never.

Jacinto, I began. Don't be ridiculous.

You lied to us, he began to cry.

The sight of a green seven-foot tall young egg eater sobbing was the strangest thing I'd seen in the last seven years of my life. Everything else that ever happened to me seemed normal next to his convulsions. But I put this out of my mind as it worried me he couldn't stop himself after a while.

The old man tried to lick the slight glue on the edge of his roll but couldn't locate it. His tongue shook and vibrated pink and useless against his stained fingers. Jacinto was crying so deep his chest shuddered like a seven year old. I never noticed the dark orange circles around Hazel's dead eyes. And the three children splashed in the tub in pain, screaming, trying to escape. I heard the woman who brought them there singing to herself as they flailed around in the water. I'd seen enough.

I picked Alice up and threw her sack over my shoulder like the holy giver of food and made for the door. This was no longer my apartment, Jacinto and Hazel were no longer my friends, and I had no idea who the old man was. I told myself I need to understand. Times have changed. Things would be different now. They had to be. So much has gone on. The country is falling apart or had fallen apart and now the work of rebuilding would begin. The People's Army was routing the fascists. The maze was coming down. All the dull young men who drew strength from the old stones were dead now, or in hiding, having lost.

The idea of a television set in the room where I took my favored silence day after day was an insult I could not bear. This used to be the room in which I watched Alice rest so careful and quiet.

This was the end for me. I walked out the door and took to the stairs.

At the bottom stood three men in black coats and white

collars. Black leather gloves. Black shirts under black suits. One bounced back and forth from heels to toes with his hands behind his back, whistling. A second blocked the door with his bulk. He saw me but averted his eyes as soon as I looked down at him. And the third was pushing his glove up to see the time on his watch.

I took one step and realized there was a fourth, standing on the landing above and staring right at me. A black lacquered truncheon gleamed in his hand. It caught the light from the lone bulb dangling on a cord running seven floors from the top. The bulb flickered. It was an omen or a signal. The three men below had come up the stairs and seized me. When I struggled, just by reflex, the fourth one came down from above to join them.

If I saw the arch.

If I saw the arch the truncheon took.

If I saw the arch the truncheon took in a wide angle and landing just above my eye, would it save me? Would the shock of pain lead to the relief of no pain after? I love the feeling when pain subsides. I live for it. It is like a chemical thing. You are in pain and then in pain not. The bliss of relief that comes makes the pain worthwhile. Because it only comes after pain, and never without it first.

51.

My life before, in sepia warmth, even colored the trees of my youth. The urge to climb. The houses and the happy storefronts. They welcomed a little boy with money in his hand calling Mr. Harold, Mr. Harold. It was a land of trusted strangers and the sun never killed anyone. Even in times past those, my later youth, in ochre browns and settled tans. The buff drab of life in higher tones than henna surrounded me with warm blood and singular rhymes. My life, when compared to the ticking wheels and gears of hate and grinding sameness, was a study in amber. Graced by pools of chestnut faces and sorrel hands that always helped and were kind.

When I awoke to the deathlike blue steel of the inner sanctum, I could manage nothing beyond silence. It was black and hard with no soft hue in any corner. It was their robes, colored by the indigo night that seeped in through razor windows. It was the hint of cobalt that made my throat go dry. Even that which was white, or seen to be white, was only a stark silver gray meant to deceive.

And came the voice from the central blue man seated so far above he seemed to be God itself. Born as if from within the livid air. Part of the howl. A brother to the wind. Protected by legions of owls and staring ravens. And all perched on twisted statues between the jury's bobbing, faceless heads. Heads in hoods. Robed and dark. It was a calm voice. Calm as if this harsh room was only azure and not the obvious doom that dripped on my fingers from every corner. Azure, so don't worry. Calm as if my growing dread was as imaginary as the second moon. Only in my head like the names of lost children in a box. His tone was an orange bolt to the heart of black water. A hazardous calm. A fawning calm. A threatening calm. A why be anxious, we are only here to help you calm.

A shrouded arm raised the dagger finger at my eyes. And the heavy face within his Gaelic hood spoke words I could not hear. He spoke my language but the air inside the sanctum was thick with the clouds of funereal incense. Or my ears went useless. Or I could not focus on him. My skill for focus flit around inside my head like a sick moth and I could not hold it to aim it. I couldn't make out his words. Not even one or two, here and there.

Above me, above us all, there were doors on every wall. There was no way to get to these doors. They hung high on the walls of the sanctum as if ornaments or a flaw in design. Hung without purpose or access. I didn't notice them until they began to open and angry faces leaned into the sanctum and spat at me. These doors opened and closed, and opened and closed, until my face became covered in spit. I could not clean myself for my tied hands. When they finished spitting, they tried to throw tiny seeds at my eyes.

I imagined the speaker at my side a prosecutor, for he pointed at me as he ducked away from the spit and seeds. He spoke in muffled eloquence about the nature of my crimes. The judges, sitting regal and still on the high bench, nodded behind poised hands. Fingertips to fingertips. I heard the man speak, but still could not make out the words. There was a low, dreaded hum from some unseen device. And the sweet metallic odor of truck exhaust overtook the holy spice that once ruled the air.

No matter how I strained, I could not hear the charges. I could not understand the arguments. I could not hear one true word.

I did hear the gavel pound me out of the room, and three men in armored gloves took me. These were disease-free men, luckier than the rest of us. Kept that way by design.

Trained for this special duty and protected from the gobs of spit that clung to my shirt and my face.

I remember an anteroom and then three winding hallways. Two doors. Seven courtyards. A series of steps going four up and two down for what felt like miles but I'm sure was only minutes.

There was the smell of sewer water. Old dogs. The matted hair of street rats. Then roses and lavender. Spearmint and thyme. And back into the darkness again. There was a church bell. A vision of six angels. Somewhere a door opened – but only for a moment – and I heard a choir. This door shut at a particular crescendo. There were military orders shouted outside. We stepped into a bright courtyard where others, tied in the same manner I was, stood crying.

This was far from the days of hickory and brown. This murderous sun cut through our faces. Cancer knives, slicing a hole in our bodies for an invader to make his home in the crevice and kill us. Slow and steady.

51.

I think they sang the day in. The river dreams rifling along. Still uncertain. My crime, in the end, unknown. I sat beside my sack of Alice, her brown stain growing like a menace, on the stone floor. Back against the low wood rail. My fellow prisoners stinking like dishrags from the fungus and low light.

They untie our hands to eat but put them behind us again when we've finished. There was no council for us. No advice. No notice. No word. And no one except a few even knew their crimes.

A vague face whispered to me from the side of his mouth. The others, he said, all worked or fought for the fascists. Which battalion were you in?

I was in no battalion, I whispered back with sweat above my lips.

Perhaps you said the word that means the thing for which there is a word you may not say.

No. I don't think so. I've been pretty quiet for the most part.

At which point he flopped to his belly and began to rock on it like a fish just pulled out of the water. I recognized the symptoms.

In time, as I traveled among my fellow inmates, I realized that things were not as simple as I at first imagined. Their stories and observations fed the missing information into my brain. Soon the situation, though muddled, came clear to me.

The fascists did not rule long, though long enough to rebuild most of the ancient maze. Their regime was harsh and uncompromising, which led to revolt. But it was not just the People's Army that plagued the Scarecrow and his minions. The Agrarian Front mobilized a force beneath a yellow flag out in the rural south. The unions, organized in several towns and cities, presented a mosaic of armed forces. These were somewhat allied but autonomous. Of late they'd splintered into fiefdoms run by warlords. The national army was no more. Gun battles erupted inside barracks and at border checkpoints. Soldiers who once trained together killed each other as they joined opposing factions. There was no national army. There had been no national army for some time. There were even different councils around the country. Each one declared itself the official government. Each one denouncing the other six at any given moment. Street gangs mobilized quick strike units to attack random targets just for fun. There were serial killers who belonged to no one but their own depraved notions. Foreigners getting rich selling arms. Frightened citizens attempted to form their own militias throughout the countryside. Escapees streamed into makeshift boats to leave the country once and for all. People sold their children. Ate their dogs. Used their houses for firewood. Made love to statues. Wrote jagged memoirs. Painted over masterpieces hung at museums in full view of adoring crowds until everything was just blocks of white in ornate frames.

There were spies everywhere. Spies from other countries and spies from other factions. Books burned. Clowns outlawed in several counties. Proclamations went up on the sides of buildings and then torn down within the hour. There were gun battles in the zoos. Many churches became armed fortresses. Madmen tossed hot tar on innocent pedestrians from the rooftops. The clouds lowered. Lights kept dim. People got knifed in the alley for their jackets. There were incidents of cannibalism reported from the last remaining forests. People wore too much perfume, too much cologne. And once, ten different groups took over the same newscast at the television station. Each time a new group took over the telecast they reported contradictory stories. And their victims, the previous newscasters, bled to death on live TV. It was democracy at its top.

Then who is it that holds us, I asked several times during my research, but few were willing to speculate.

As near as I could make out the controlling faction that kept us prisoner were old landowners. Remnants of the old aristocracy. Monarchists. They crowned the last descendant of the old royal family at the cathedral of St. Philomena. There were disagreements within the church about the legitimacy of the whole thing. There were fights between priests and a harsh schism ripping the church apart as well.

The whole country had gone insane. There were voices on the radio claiming this or that group was warehousing children to sell as slaves. Spit spewing commentators warned of ambushes about to spring from abandoned department stores. News reports from pirate stations detailed a new conspiracy every week. Jews. Catholics. Terrorists. Shoeshine boys. Radical gardeners. Ancient secret societies of necromancers. And always the reports of beings, half-worm and half-human, forming militias in the mountains.

And the brown stain on Alice's sack kept growing. It boggled my mind. It was disproportionate to any living material left inside the bag. I did not know what to make of it. All I knew was that I had to get out. I had to find a way to escape. I didn't know where I would escape to. But leaving the country did not seem as traitorous an idea to me as it might have just a few years ago.

The red ink on the tattoo had long since faded. The fat man with the spider web emerging from his navel, who complained as I forced him to do it, was dead a long time now. What was I holding onto anymore? My friends abandoned me when I was a young man. I ran from my family when they attempted to eat my brains. Now the country I lived in was spooning out its own liver and was feeding it to foreign maggots for money. And the only one left to me, my long dead Alice, was the last friend I had.

There were islands in the sea where things like this never happened. I resolved at that moment to find one.

52.

Whenever I wanted to escape there was always the peaceful enclosure of the blood hedges. There was always safety behind the concrete. This was in the younger days with the sound of wood falling to the street. I don't want to fight. I don't want to engage the thousands of caring people now trying to beat the country to death. This is a failed experiment. No one is happy. Everyone hates one another. No one will compromise. The cheerleaders get rich and the pile of victims grows. And they say, let them kill each other, all the fewer thugs on the street. I help no one. I want to find a place to hide.

Long ago there were toys strewn across a linoleum floor. Games on the park bench. Dances across the sidewalk. Now they dodge the bullets of the privileged ones every night about seven. This is when the various spawns come out to fight for freedom. Or power. Or neither. But fighting for fighting's sake. No one remembers the reason anymore.

Just in the last few days as I sat naked in the communal cell I heard the guns going and the mill churning the bones. The lost idea. The forgotten promises. The country it once was, now just killing and blood sport everywhere you go. No one wears a jacket on the bases anymore. The game takes forever. There is no refuge. There is only crawling to avoid the shelling.

One night without food we heard the machine return. The machine I think I saw when I rang the bell at St. Bibiana. Clanking and clanging with iron wings. Great tangled arms throwing firebombs and spewing teeth across the meadow. Biting at those who returned fire.

Someone propped himself on a ledge by our lone iron bar window and gave the account. It was coming to rescue us.

Our jailers were going to die. Soon routed. It was unstoppable. Bullets bounced off its apron and fell meaningless to the dirt. Then I saw a group crouching behind a broken house and aim a tube at the war machine's innards. One strike and the beast reeled. When they loaded again it limped along the road. The second missile hit the eye and we all heard a great roar of pain as if from a drunken rhinoceros squirming. Caught in the drying last mud of Pompeii. Our announcer climbed down, tears in his eyes. The battle over. The hope of rescue lost to us. The hulk lay burning. No better than a dead beetle. Men climbing out of all possible orifices, broken and on fire. Gunned down in the rain as they tried to surrender. There was no surrender in our country anymore. They executed each operator they caught alive and served them to the fish.

How the fascists cried. How they mourned their soup and cupped the last straw in their shaking hands, resigned. I didn't feel anything. Or rather I felt nothing, on a positive note. I'd received my excommunication. Emulated. Eradicated. Eager to escape from every hole I saw

There were six men digging a tunnel. They used spoons and old leather quivers that once held arrows and there were also cups and saucers. They started under a table. And when the guards moved the table they started a new tunnel under the sink. The guards turned the water off. Then they scraped at the walls. But the guards pulled them out of the cell by the hair and shot them in their necks for trophies.

I spent a sad day mourning the loss of skin. But I was just as determined to leave. To find a way.

In the meantime, I gathered bits of food I found on the floor and what I found I kept in my pocket. The idea of a feast appealed to me. If, I reasoned, I was patient enough someday I could fill a table with the crumbs and morsels. I managed to squirrel a lot away by sheer vigilance. And sometimes even steal from the fingers of the dying.

After a few weeks our teeth began to rot. The men turned on each other to cut off arms and limbs to eat raw in the sun while the guards laughed. The priests prayed over us and no one spoke again. I don't know why everyone avoided me. But Alice's sack had turned all brown and soiled and was difficult to move for being so wet.

In the end I sat isolated in a corner, the rest of the men huddled along the far wall staring and pointing at me. Holding their noses and complaining to the guards. They insulted Alice every chance they got and I swore I would kill any one of them who came near her. And it was this way until the night of the halo.

It started as a faraway rumble that seemed to come from outside. But I soon realized it was coming from inside Alice's sack. The sack I got on the Mountain so many lifetimes ago. I did not realize that a light was coming from it until I saw it reflect on the faces of the others. Yellow light on their grimy faces as they cowered along their wall. Shaking. Pointing. Gasping at my sack.

At first, I wondered if there was a light shining through the lone window. But I could see it was a dark night out there. No. I came to understand the light was emanating from inside Alice's sack. It glowed gold like the shine on the wet back of a walrus that had just emerged from the sea. Proud and bright and unforgiving.

The commotion attracted the guards. They stared at the strange light from their watch holes above us. I heard them shouting for a priest to come and see. In seconds I heard the priest on the other side of the door. He was peering in through the slot at the bottom where they slid the food through on our good days. I worried he was dirtying his ferraiolo on the filthy floor. Still, at that time, I cared for the dignity of the cloth. Somehow.

Then the halo appeared. Strong and bright surrounding Alice like bathwater in the air. Pointed spikes and golden rings. All shimmering in the cold cellar air and casting light on everything. The priest got to his feet. He shouted orders and, in a minute, I heard the keys rattle. The door spewed open and guards with lances and helmets rushed in. The Holy Order. Red and gold and purple and holy.

They seized Alice. They took me by both arms. They dragged us both out of there in a flurry of curses and stomping boots.

Following the fast swishing priest down narrow halls lit by torches, we came at last to a carved door. This the priest unlocked and opened wide. They tossed Alice and me inside. I fell, face first against a small pile of crosses and beads and broken statuettes. Then the door slammed and there was silence. We were alone.

It only took a few minutes before I understood where I was.

Long ago I crossed a river to find Alice when she disappeared from me. Somehow, I was here again. The same room. The same cellar. The same reliquary I'd entered years ago, searching. Searching to save her. I was beneath the old sanctuary I once invaded and explored. So long ago. The one with the green door. The green door that was turning red as they knocked. Redder with every separate pound. Louder. Louder and redder until I had to cover my ears and close my eyes to keep them from stealing my sight and my hearing.

53.

I got lost to the lamplight for a while. The faint crystalline glow from the eternal sand of the St. Marcus miracle. The one where the fish filled the nets and the little village never went hungry again. The one that spawned a shipping industry and made everyone in the village stinking rich. Here amid the reminders of the marvelous. The deep green bird and the mitigating swords. Why put one's trust in fascists? They only change into puddles of burnt leather in the end. They're all the same. Always. They eat their own and shit venom until nothing can grow in the putrid dirt they defile.

I wasn't hungry. When the knocking at the door stopped it opened with ease and a party of monks or holy men hurried over to my sack. They made to seize it, or open it, or in some other way take it up, and I raised my voice. You may not.

A hand came from the sand shadow and caressed my shoulder. A magical mind trick meant to calm me. Meant to make me forget to protect what is mine. And what is mine is not the property of the church. I don't even know which church you are, I shouted.

But the hand clutching me like a claw with red painted nails went to my cheek and touched me gentle as blue water. I looked.

Marta Vansimmerant had returned to me dressed in red velvet and steeped in the stink of white roses.

White roses for the dead in us, I asked her.

She put a finger to her lips with one hand and clutched her breast with the other. She let out a fearsome moan of pleasure and closed her eyes.

She had not considered that making love was abhorrent to me now. It disgusted me. I hated the animal intent. The stupid way it looked. The silly faces turned up and mouths open, panting. Wretched behavior. Uncivilized. Reminiscent of the zoo. Of monkeys playing with themselves. It made otherwise intelligent people make dumb animal sounds. It turned conversation into a checklist of automation. She did not consider that these were my thoughts. That I was the pure warrior now. The chaste knight of the realm. She thought another round of making love to her, or at her, would make me forget the sack. Make me not care what the monks were doing. But she was wrong.

I stood and turned on my feet, pulling the ties and bunched end of the sack out of their beady little hands. They gasped and pulled back. Marta stood, incredulous, behind her smokescreen.

None of you have any business with this. This is mine. You will not have it.

Don't be so dramatic, Marta laughed. Her laughter put a lie to what I thought was her shock at my reaction. But she wasn't shocked at all. It was as if she expected my reaction. Planned for it, in fact. She laughed. Laughed like children on a playground when I could not get up from the snow. When my legs crossed on the ice and I broke them in the fall and they laughed as I struggled. I sat in my room by the window and watched them play for weeks after that. And when I returned to my life nothing was the same. My sister weighed seven hundred pounds and grunted like a walrus. Her offspring spinning at her hips like jellyfish. The laugh. Marta knew. She must have read the report card and studied the films. Laughter would enrage me. Unnerve me. Pull down my reserve and my resolve. I let go of the sack as an old priest came forward from among the monks.

My son be still. We have reason to believe we have seen a miracle today. We must look inside this bag to please ourselves that this was not a trick. We need to know if you are some gypsy magician from overseas come to take away our jobs and our women. Won't you let us look?

Marta laughed again. This time without joy. Not so much as a smile. A laugh from a dead forest. The laugh of hate. The laugh of victory. I'd heard it so many times before. When I lay half dead with the pox and my schoolmates taunted me in the classroom. Surrounded me in the boy's room and poked their fingers into my pockmarks. And me, crying and pleading for release like a frail, wet bird. Please don't hurt me, don't hurt me. I hated myself for twenty years after I broke down in their teasing circle. Marta laughed and I crumpled to the damp floor of the cold cellar.

The monks lifted the sack in their eight hands and the priest held a cross over it. He put the cross back into his belt and the monks lifted the sack into the air. They held Alice high over their heads as they swayed out the door chanting the Salve Regina. In the meantime, Marta Vansimmerant could not restrain herself from chuckling behind me.

What's the matter with you, she spat as they floated away, chanting through the bending halls. Have they castrated you?

Before I could answer she repeated the word, castrated. It seemed to give her some kind of pleasure. One eyebrow went up and her eyes saw nothing in the room as they focused somewhere behind me. Her eyes concentrated on an image she'd conjured up in the distance. Then she tore herself from it and stared at the space between my eyes. You had a perfect chance. You still do. Your girl is out of the room. What is the matter with you?

It is unclean, I buttoned my collar. I am tired of seeing women who can only appear as objects of sex and debauchery.

I am what I am, she pointed at me. You think women don't enjoy it?

188

I'm sure they do not. And this is what makes them holy.

She threw her head back and laughed the green out of her lungs. I went to the floor again, demoralized. She knew how to take my feet out from under me.

You are a naïve little boy. How many women have you had?

It took me a few seconds to count them. But I held up a hand without showing a number. A few. But if you count them all you would have a finger or two unused on this hand. I was proud to say it. It was so against the usual boast men make. I think it made her fall in love with me. But I knew that must never happen.

And I was one of them, she cooed.

Yes.

And that one, she pointed out the hall where the monks had taken Alice. You slept with that one as well?

No, I answered straight and plain. I never made love to Alice. Never. I never touched her that way. Not once.

I never said that to anyone before. On hearing this she backed out of the room in a straight line, never taking her eyes off of me. She moved as if she were sitting on a wheeled pallet that carted her away smooth and easy. No hint of walking. Floating instead. I can't explain her expression, but it seemed as though some realization came to her. How is it, she may have wondered, this woman I never made love to has become the one light I protect above all others.

Marta Vansimmerant will never understand. It's because the window had an eye.

54.

he long time from five candle in the red sand. now he count the holy. all the holy one more time and the sand is frozen in a snap of weather.

There was an amulet in the shape of a cross decorated with fine enamel like a jigsaw. The enamel set inside golden lines that divided red from blue and green from white. There was something about it. It reminded me of the gravesite. I stopped by a roadside long ago on a trip to the woods. Just past being a boy and only a young Edju as I was. There was an old cemetery on the edge of a riverbank, high on a bluff. A headstone from one hundred years before spoke the name of a little girl underneath. She was born and died and her years were only seven. I can't recall her name but she stayed with me forever. I sat beside the grave for three reasons I can't summon anymore. The air went quiet. I heard the river far below. There is always a river, you will notice. No wind. Just a breeze so slight and scented with flowers of some mint behaviors. I could not move away and a friend said maybe I knew the little girl in a past life. This was how sweet the minutes. My friends wanted to go. But I couldn't get up. No standing. No noise. I was overcome with peace in every direction. No half-truths. This little girl one hundred years dead was my talisman. How could a child this dead hurt you? But we left. I looked out the window of the car and watched. The grave sunk into the horizon until a thousand trees blocked the space between her and me. It is a terrible sin I can't remember her name. This is why people abandon me. I am no good at important things and forget them. They take it as an insult and leave.

This cross reminded me of the little grave. Because the air

was as sweet when I found it cold in the dust on the floor. Unused. Attached to no prayer. Abandoned too. And wherever I went inside that reliquary I took it with me.

I got myself into the habit of returning to the green door in my ritual of waiting. And every time I stood beside it I thought I heard someone coming at first. It would be them, bringing Alice back to me in a madrigal mist. The final return of the lost love. The elephant outside the room. Gloves. Spears. Arrows in the gloaming. They would bring her back to the fluting of medieval minstrels and tell me we could go on our way.

It was a mathematical formula. Sympathetic magic. Every time I stood by the door, I imagined, I was hurrying the process. Pushing events through the seam of time to a desired conclusion. No sleeping aides required. My being close to this door would force time itself to skid through space. My body the event horizon. My being near the door would lend me the power to change the whole manner of time. I cannot now explain how I came to those conclusions. It was more wish than magic, I suppose.

But a little at a time I became used to not having Alice there. No apron. No sweet voice and golden hair. No seeping brown spot like old oil to worry me. I talked to myself. Lips going. Mumble or go mad, I said. So, I said things and answered them. All this without reservation. So, I speak as if in deep conversation with scholars. Sometimes I voice opposition to myself and cut down the fault in the argument against me. The famous men of the capital city interview me and all can see. Our guest tonight is Edju. Edju is here and we welcome him to our show. I discuss the scarcity of relics in the world like a true bystander. Present my case for sudden learning. Denounce the sun. It is all exceeding sublime. I educate on the nuance of the important issues of the day. The meaning of the civil war just going. The significance of mazes. The metaphor of flags.

Sometimes I evolve theories on the things at a distance moving in unison. Though millions of miles apart they act in concert as if not from this common world. And I refuse to stop the process of thought. There is a great danger in not thinking far enough. Suicide is the incompletion of a thought. Telltale stupidity rampant in the land. Obvious the user has not taken the idea far enough. Allowed his bias and then quit.

And by these methods Alice's absence became a poem to me. And, so, easier on my nerves.

I occupied my time like a responsible man of simple tastes and few possessions. Methodical and forthright. A man with sweaters. After all, I told myself as I surveyed my surroundings, there were bones to count and boxes to sort. I was, at that time, still thinking of myself as a follower of the church. I am bound to duty, then.

I found a pad of paper and a dip pen. Blotters stacked in a corner and a barrel of ink. I did not take them for relics though, looking back, I should have. With these tools I began an inventory of the sacred shards around me. How proud they will be of my work. How grateful.

There were suspicious bits of clothing. Tattered scapulars. Teeth in boxes marked with names written in faded ink. Molding rosary beads. The molars of this or that saint. The buckteeth of an evangelist in the wilderness. I counted the withered flowers and strands of rope. Rope in a hundred different colors and length and material. There were hair clippings. Half-moons of holy fingernails trimmed from the dead hands of holy men and women from a thousand years ago. Curls and locks taped and pasted to disintegrating paper and hardened board. Brooches. Pins. Rings. Coin-sized lambs and fish formed from cut glass colored to mimic dead rainbows. Mottled gems. Ancient things of no possible use from

Visigoth monks and Ostrogoth nuns. Forty seven pieces of the True Cross, from splinters to while planks.

When I completed my list, I scanned the inventory for forty-seven mistakes. Any kind of omissions. And when satisfied I stood by the door with my amulet in the shape of a cross and waited for them to return. I sought their approval. I admit it.

But the woman who had been watching me all this time did not approve. She scoffed at me from behind a Byzantine chest studded with jewels. She spat from a toothless mouth with her hands on her fat hips, chewing the air.

55.

I jumped, expecting I was alone. But there she was behind the altar stones, sweater and jowls. Head cocked. Brown smile, laughing at me. I gripped my studded cross when she spoke.

Shame has an end to it, she said. One day the sun will explode and all the shame there is in the world will fly away with it. Fly away into space along with the great minds. All history. All the things that were ever built. And the wars. And the gods. There won't be anyone left to remember. Everything you did. The great things accomplished. All the little cheats and vile sins. All gone. All will be for nothing if you wait long enough. It has always been for nothing. That's why we have spent centuries making each other miserable. There's no escaping it. It's all been for nothing at all. It won't do you any good to stand by the door, she shook her head. I've already tried that. It won't make them come back any faster.

This was not the Madonna. This was a fat woman in a sweater talking to me in a hot, damp cellar surrounded by the fingers and hair curls of saints. Expounding on the delicacies of existence. Reasons for not waiting.

It's true, I almost told her. There are times when I am quiet and seem to be waiting for some organ to explode. Say my stomach bursts open and breaks the skin. Or a lung rips open my chest with a pop, and a hen comes out flapping her wings. Landing on the floor with a wet thud and squawking away into the night. My body will betray me. Someday it will betray me. My heart will stop or some part of me will welcome my killer. A bone welcomes cancer. Please come in, sir. Yes, make yourself at home. And its only reason for living is to take over and kill you. A threat from without, finding a home deep within.

There have always been strange vibrations. Odd connections. A point at the back of my hand pinched and the same pain travels into my shoulder in a straight line. We eat and maul the world. The water we drink was once water in the cup of the pharaohs. Poured. Drunk. Pissed out. Mingling with the river. Watering the bank. Evaporating into the sky. Raining down from clouds. Collected in the stream. Poured. Drunk. Pissed out. Like breath. The same water that once passed through the guts of the Huns. The amount of water is finite in the world. It has never changed. The same with pain. There is only a finite amount of pain in the world because pain cannot attack what doesn't exist.

I may have said this in response to her. I can't remember. But her hands remained on her hips and she shook her head like a disappointed teacher. It made me feel as though I'd failed her. I came away from the door and went to her side. She was twice my width.

What is her name, she wanted to know.

Alice, I was almost embarrassed to say. Her name is... her name was Alice.

There was a brown spot that grew on the bag and then one day lights emitted from between the loosened fibers.

I don't know the specifics of how it worked, but yes. There were lights. Somehow.

She put a hand on my shoulder and led me to the darkest corner of that cellar. In the milky bleak it was almost impossible to make it out until we were on top of it, but we came to a door. A door in the dark and, again, something I hadn't seen before. Because it was in the darkest corner. Now that we stood so close I could hear voices on the other side. But we did nothing. Her hand had crept up toward my neck and she was squeezing me there until it felt as if my head was in a vise.

What are we doing, she asked as if a professor before a board.

Until I answered I didn't realize she was holding me so tight. My mouth and lips disfigured by the pressure. I answered as best I could. Nothing. We are standing by the door.

And is the door opening because we are standing by it?

No, I fumbled.

Is anyone coming to open it because we are standing here?

No, I tried to say it better.

So why would going back again and again to the other door make that one open faster? Is it working here?

No. I managed to say it clearer that time. But her grip was loosening, so it might not have been my effort at all that fixed the mispronunciation.

No. Of course not. How do we get this door to open up for us?

We could knock, I said. But this was not the answer she wanted. Once more she squeezed my neck against her with her iron hand and made a tsk noise with her tongue.

You knock what happens? You knock and you are still waiting, aren't you?

I saw the knife approach my face, held in her other hand. A large knife in a meaty hand balled up into a fist around the hilt.

What happens when you knock?

I'm… I began. But she made a thrust and the knife stopped an inch from my left eye.

What?

Still waiting. We could knock and we'd still be waiting.

Her head jutted out in mock approval. That's right, little one. There you have it.

She took the knife from my face.

So, what do we do when we come to a door?

We open it.

Yes, she cocked her head and hissed like a happy snake. We turn the handle and we open it, don't we?

196

At this she released me and pushed me with one hand into the door.

Then open it.

It felt as if my lower back was about to freeze on me. I was glad she didn't ask me to bend over to pick something up from the floor. My back would have not been cooperative with that. I felt stiff and slow. My kidneys ready to burst on either side of my spine and send animals jumping out of the open skin. There was a sick pain in my head. Somewhere in my head. I reached out and searched for the unseen door-knob. I couldn't make it out in the dark. As I struggled I felt an urgency to find it welling up in me. I had to find it quick to escape her torture. I could hear her breathing in the dark.

Just at the moment I think she began to move her arm to pound on me I found the doorknob. I shuddered with relief and turned it.

There was another large room on the other side. But this one was not filled with relics and boxes and crates. There were people. Dozens of them. People sitting against the walls. People walking back and forth with their hands behind their backs. People standing with arms folded talking to one an-other. People looking at the ceiling with a hand in the air, talking to whatever it was they saw above them.

One of these people was closest to me. I heard him say in a weak, pitiful squeal. Officer. Officer you must find her. It's cold out and she doesn't have a coat.

But everyone just kept walking. They ignored him. They paid him no mind whatsoever. Everyone was going about his or her business. But what that business could be was beyond me.

The room itself was barren. There was not so much as a chair or a stool. There were no beds. No windows. It was lit by four light fixtures hanging from the ceiling. One was flickering, near death.

Everyone seemed dressed in the same faded clothes. They may have been black at some point, but now they just faded to gray. There wasn't any sign of anyone having any possessions. There were no books or papers. No phones. Nothing. They were all empty-handed. Only the woman and I had something. I had my cross. She had her knife.

56.

You must remember what happened next. I, Edju as a small child, buried the toy under the grass. I kept it safe under the turf. Pulled out a patch and covered it. But when I went back when the danger was over I couldn't find it. The clump of sod would not release. The dirt healed itself. I pulled at the blades but never found the patch. Fifty years later they dig up the lot to build a new house. The toy is dug up by a witch and poured into a truck with all the unwanted boards. All the useless canvas and concrete in the way of the grand new foundation. The toy lost forever. You remember. It was a toy like any other. Its memory is there amid the leaps of flame. The candles burn. Is it five or three I must place as a perfect row in the red sand? I can never do it. I remember and am nostalgic for the future. All the ones in the room know me. They heard this story. The woman with the muscles and the knife takes me to a side room. Three women are there. They try to pull me into the bathroom but I won't go. I fight them. It disgusts me, I scream.

Yes, I hear the doctor whisper to the nurse. This is one. Put him in detention on the hard brick line. The beaked bird and its paltry song with the dancing strongmen strong-arming me into a chamber. I know my name and say it.

In a corner I go to sleep and dream of short mowed lawns in green patches stretching down the comfortable lane. A happy house in a common tone. Each house the same color. It is like a nightmare and I can't wait to return to the bare, spare room with the dozens of others.

What was the name of the one in your bag, someone asks.

I don't know how to answer. What could he know to ask this question?

He shakes his head and closes his eyes, feigning impatience with my naivety. I had my Mary in my bag. But when the brown spot appeared the soldiers brought me here. What was the name of the one in your bag, he repeated.

Alice, I said.

Ah yes, he smiled. The noble weed, in the ancient tongue. Spoken this way, I think, among the Frisians. Alice, Alias. Otherwise hidden. The noble flower otherwise hidden. The purple flowers on the bluff. What are they called? I can't remember.

I don't know what you're talking about, I said.

Etymology. Empiricism. Epistemology. All the good words. There's a great value to knowing things. I know things. He pointed to his temple. I know things and the government will reward me for it one day. You'll see. He pointed.

I became convinced in my heart that this was the wrong place for me. That I was here by mistake. I looked for the woman with the knife but she had already dissipated into the general crowd. She melted with the rest. I could no longer tell the difference between these people except what were men and what were women. Everyone wore the same gray clothes. I do not recall when they dressed me in the same.

But these suspicions abated the longer I stayed in this room. Whereas the man with the big words seemed crazy the people I met after were normal. They said prayers to the wall. They saluted the flag in the corner. They didn't ask questions. If they couldn't align the candles in the red sand in a perfect row then they didn't deserve favor. That's how the world worked. It is how life is. Stay quiet. Don't trouble yourself with a lot of possessions. Be simple. It was a great relief to find normal people again.

We sang songs sometimes and asked the guards beyond the door if we could go to church. They never answered. This was an odd thing for a religious organization not to do, I felt. But we took it in stride. We hadn't done anything to warrant the privilege.

Once in a while the door would open and a name would get called. Sometimes when the person called would step up he or she would get taken away. Other times they got their sack and the guards told them to leave the premises at once. The people who were there the longest explained to me that those taken away were the lucky ones. They would be in the church's care and would go with their saint all over the world. Their saint would be set in a glass coffin. Or it would get cut up into tiny pieces and placed in walnut boxes or burned to ashes and kept in a vase. And they would travel with the relic forever as a mission of the holy church. They were living proof of a miracle. It made me think of Marta Vansimmerant. I never knew such a thing existed, or how it got started. It was clear to me now.

But the ones who had their sack handed back to them were not so lucky. The body they'd carried all that time was declared inauthentic. Most of the time they were just put out into the street. But once in a while, the veterans told me, if the case was fraud there was another fate. They would get their bag and soon whisked out of the room so as not to instill suspicion among those who remained. But these people got themselves thrown into a lake of fire somewhere beyond the breakers. Thrown into the fire bag and all. No chance for appeal. No pity. The people who told me this said they had it on the highest authority.

And one always believed what the old inmates told you.

This made me afraid. Not because I knew I was a fraud, but because I knew I was innocent of such a plot. I was innocent but how can anyone be sure that others would be able to tell that? How many people are in jail by mistake? How many prisoners executed because the work of the investigators was incomplete? Or lazy? Or sloppy? It is one thing to know you are innocent, but another to find others to believe the same of you by mere chance. And it was all mere chance.

Of course, the worst did not happen to me. You can tell that I was not thrown into the lake of fire beyond the breakers because I am relating the story to you now. But you must see how my mind began to make acrobatic spins as I worried about what was going to happen to me.

In the meantime, while I waited, I don't recall ever eating anything in all the days I spent there. I don't recall washing or needing a toilet. I was in some kind of suspension with everybody else. I had my usual headaches, but there was always the buzzing from my cross that cured me. I would place it upon my temple, or wherever on my head the pain was, and it would make the pain go away. There was a power. A vibration I could not understand. Some celestial power from another dimension. I would say my names in incantations. Pray for me Babbashar and Formildahyde. Save me Oshabell and Yoshakrantz. And the pain would go. It would run out the door like a thief.

Others would look at my cross and scowl. Someone whispered I should be more careful with it. That it wasn't allowed. That if the wrong person saw me they would report me to the guards and I would be in trouble. There were jealous stares. And people talked about me behind my back. There were some who wanted to kill me.

There were those who wanted to kill me and take my cross for their own. I kept my guard up. I did not sleep for weeks. But, in the end, the plotters couldn't agree on which one of them would own the cross after I was dead. So, all the coalitions and alliances broke down before they could act. One group even began fighting among themselves before they ever took it from me. The news reported that two of them died in the struggle.

And many times, I looked around for a way to bury my cross until the danger was over. But there was no grass growing in the great room.

57.

The excuse they used was that it was a matter of nature. One could not keep these urges bottled up forever. They'd kept people in this room too long. How long are we expected to go without it? This was their reasoning. Justifications in quarter time. It was a natural thing to do. Never mind the centuries of decorum established to protect the needy. No one cared about the holiday season. Never mind those easy to amuse. Forget about people like me who consider the act disgusting and vile. Animalistic. Horrid and ugly. But there they were.

It started in dark corners. It shocked many, at first. But the more it happened the more it became acceptable. Until it happened with regularity. Every morning. In the rain of the afternoon. And always in the night. The clutching and moaning. Bodies slapping against one another. It turned my stomach and made me wish for the coming of the End. The Captain of my Soul.

Everyone looked for partners. And all to their own lights. Men and women. Men and men. Women with women. Gatherings of three or more. Naked asses in the air pumping away. Smells of sweat and feet and unwashed parts. It didn't seem to matter. Fingers fumbling. Squeezing. Sucking sounds. A wretched symphony of the worst the human body can do in service to its own base and callous lusts.

I spent some nights with my hands over my ears. Eyes tight shut. Curled up facing the wall. And I told those approaching me to be their partner that I would never do such a foul and hideous thing. That I was through with such repulsive behavior. That people were for higher, grander orders. Not to be like dogs in a yard, not caring who saw them rut and tongue each other between their legs.

The worst of it, there was no one to appeal to. No one to demand they stop it. The guards enjoyed it. They took pictures and seemed to make bets about things I did not understand.

I prayed to St. Anthony the Abbot, patron of those alone. I begged him to cast down a shimmering scythe and cut down these venal monsters. But it was no use. All I got was Willibrord. And though only a sad comfort in my age, he would have to do.

I found him on a staircase, half way up. The staircase didn't go anywhere. It moved up from the floor and went straight up to the ceiling, where it ended against the plaster. No exit. No floor above. Just a dark stair running up the wall to the ceiling and then nothing. Willibrord sat with his hands rubbing his head and face and the back of his neck. Over and over. Writhing as if trying to find some internal ache or festering wound lost in his head somewhere. Trying to find it and squeeze it out. Or catch it and strangle it. He said it was like a buzzing weevil boring around into the marrow of his skull. But I said I didn't think there was marrow in the bone structure of the skull. We could not reach an agreement. There was one person standing at the foot of the stairs, hands in pockets in the shade of the bad light. He said Willibrord's affliction was that he believed he was Edgar Allen Poe in a past life.

I looked up at him, suffering crazy with whatever torment it was burrowing into his brain. His sleeves and pants were too big. He was swimming in these ill-fitting clothes. This only made him look all the more pathetic.

It could have been true. He had the aura of the mysterious about him. The air around him seemed tortured and mystical. It both repelled and attracted me as if macabre. Everything around him was dark. From the circles under his eyes to the air he expelled from his lungs.

But he was of the same mind as me when it came to the activities of our fellow lodgers.

How can they do it in public and not care about their dignity, he cried. That action is a private world for those who love. It is for roses and wine and more wine thereafter. Not for public viewing like gladiators spilling each other's blood before the gawking crowd.

There were moments when it seemed one could not escape the sight and the sounds of it. We would walk along the walls with our collars up. Our collars up and heads down. Eyes to our feet as we weaved through the ecstatic maelstrom. We talked about the planets and the cities on the sun. We talked about the great philosophers and the meaning of the occult regions of Earth. The Druids. The Carthaginians. Beekeepers. Elephants. The uses of motor oil in a dwindling economy. Anything to distract us from the carnage.

Promise me one thing Edju, he pleaded with me one day, desperate for some kind of relief from his agony. Promise me when we get out of here we'll meet up and have coffee. I would love nothing better than a coffee right now.

I promise, I said in a hush. I said it as quiet as possible because I didn't want anyone to think we were arranging some illicit meeting. That's all that was on anyone's mind anymore. I did not want to associate myself with the act in any possible form. We'll have coffee, I assured him. Where will we meet?

This question sent him into a dark place. His brows seemed to double in size and hang over his eyes like new anacondas. His face wanted to eat itself. I could see the veins in his temples begin to pound. Expanding and contracting with the pressure of my question. I wished I'd have kept quiet. He brooded that way for hours. Only once saying it was impossible to know, wasn't it?

Willibrord wanted to escape his past. The demons that haunted him ever since he was Poe. There was a woman in a bag that he loved but being so long ago and in such a faraway country it wasn't like it is now. Now, he cried, it's acceptable to walk around with someone in a bag. Back then the authorities would put you in jail. They would fill you full of opiates and the next thing you know you're a Captain in the Southern army. It was terrible.

I, not being from that country, did not understand these details about Willibrord's past. I didn't trust the talk of past lives. I wasn't even a believer in such things as reincarnation, but this man was the only friend I had at the time. To humor him seemed just the thing a friend would do. Reincarnation is a wish. A way to maintain the ego. I had always awaited eternal bliss in heaven. That was reality and in no way a lie or just a hope. But I humored him in his misconceptions because he said poetical things. Dark and funny and clever things. But I couldn't help thinking that he had a terrific talent for making the wrong choices at almost every turn. His own dumb worst enemy. Bazookas in shops of fine crystal. Ignorant comments before a crowd weighing you in the balance. The wrong turn. The meeting not taken. Too much wine the night before the drugs. This was Willibrord all over. There was nothing I could do.

Do you know the alabaster bridge in the city of Astranloth, I asked.

I have heard of this place he said, as if at the bottom of a black well.

We'll meet there.

Do they have coffee?

His question pounded back at me and made me stupid. I don't know, I stammered. I suppose there may be a shop nearby. Somewhere.

At this he grabbed both sides of his head. His whole body shook like a tree and his eyes bugged out as he shouted it's no use. It's never any use. All my plans ruined. Nothing ever works for me. I can never arrange anything without everything falling apart.

He stomped around the room and the martial noise he made attracted everyone's attention. The lovers stopped their pumping and turned to see what the marching sound was. The guards gathered by the door, wondering if an army of insurrection was forming. A bus driver from the street came up the stairs and wanted to know if there was anyone going to the Feather District. No, one of the guards said. They are getting all the feathering they need here.

But the bus driver didn't care for this answer. He began to shout at the guards. They were taking too much on themselves, thinking they were running the country. He threatened them with the end of their reign of terror and that the fascists would be back in power one day. That the king would lose his throne and his head. At which point the priests in the hall ran into the room and fell on him with clubs and fists and the guards joined in to help.

There was a great battle after this. The bus driver was a man of considerable strength and seemed capable of taking a lot of punishment. He never seemed to feel the pain the holy fathers were serving him with. He bled. I saw welts growing on his arms as he fought back. But never did he wince. He kept swinging his arms and pounding with his fists. And one by one the people making love on the floor began to put their clothes back on. Willibrord looked up from his monstrous pounding head. Everyone began to move toward the door.

One priest was down and unconscious. Two guards with bloodied faces avoided the fight. They wanted no more of it. Another priest was vomiting in a blue corner after the bus driver kicked him in the stomach. It would, we heard later, be a ruptured appendix that he died of, even God's plan for that organ gone for nothing. Getting in the way.

Everyone watched, amazed and speechless. In twenty minutes the bus driver had slaughtered all the fifth graders. Despite having a broken arm that hung like a jungle vine and skin hanging down the left side of his face, he'd won. He jumped around singing a taunt. The fifth graders are slaughtered, the fifth graders are slaughtered.

You could see the truth. Even if any of the guards and priests were still able to fight, they were laying on the floor in surrender. Unwilling to rejoin the battle.

A great roar came up from deep in the guts of our fellow inmates if that's what we were. Fists went into the air. Fingers pointed at the door.

Évitez les faux, they shouted. Libérez nos bébés, they called. N'accepte pas les substituts. It seemed like a full-scale rebellion was at hand. I had no idea if those phrases were in any way grammatical and correct. But in times of revolution even the commas get misplaced.

There would be ramparts in some rue or another. But first we must find our sacks.

58.

We scattered through the cathedral. There was a lot of killing one way or the other. I couldn't take part in the rituals. I opened a door and jumped into a dark room. The windows all shuttered and an organ played. Behind a white marble altar an old priest emerged and put a finger to my lips and spoke of the holy triumvirate. Not a salvation this time, he said. But a doctrine often misplaced for a hat. There is one face but three expressions, yet each expression is distinct. They are distinct and separate from each other but are the same one. Transitional substantiation comingled with the trireme. One face, three persons, and a lexicon created for the occasion. And if you deny the madness we will skewer the throat out of your neck and invade all manner of forbidden kingdoms.

I'm looking for Alice, I said as his hands gripped my collar. His fingers were exploring. His thumbs trying to find my larynx. He wanted to push it into my esophagus and strangle me.

They are three faces on one person. Three natures in the single body of the dove and the lamb and the fish and the crook and the ring or the crown. It changes, you know.

I struggled to get away, grasping his wrists and pushing his hands back into his old face.

Leave me alone. I'm looking for Alice.

There were gunshots in the street. A siren went off in the courtyard. The priest abandoned his attack on me and ran to one of the narrow stained glass windows. He undid a latch and opened it. The sunlight pushed in like a savior.

I clutched my cross and scrambled to my feet as he watched the commotion in the courtyard below. A bell went off. A school bell high-pitched and abrasive. Meant to martial the children out of the building. But the sounds of fighting and the sight of chairs thrown overpowered the bell. Nuns raced about slapping the inmates on their backsides with books. Boney fingers pointed at ripped clothes. There was scolding in the washrooms. Long noses and longer hanging beads, black as ice dangling from the waists of the monks.

It was a melee. Doors flew open and throats were slit with makeshift blades. All regard for holy orders thrown aside for the imperative of finding our beloveds. It was the end of order. The end of faith. There would be nothing but questions from now on. Questions planted like pepper seeds by the gigas demon. Meant to befuddle. Meant to confuse. Meant to erode the strength of belief and observance.

I found a dark corner in a dangerous stairwell and hid my face in my hands. What have I done, I cried. What's happened to my country and how did I get myself into this? I became obsessed with the fear that I would be forever seen as a rioter now. That I would face excommunication or worse. I'd heard the brothers of St. Schuppenboer resumed the practice of burning at the stake. Just in the last few months three women with bowl haircuts had been so punished. I didn't want to be on that list.

And so, the first question was how to find Alice. The first need was to remove myself from this horror without there being a record of my being here.

I'd had enough of all this. Every page of my life was now filled with some kind of violence I no longer understood. Leftist Agrarian Front. Rightist National Unity. Holy Orders of the Fist of God. The Liberal Party. The Conservative Party. Liberal Conservatives and Conservative Liberals. The Armed Hand of the Nation. Nuns. All armed. All vying for power. And what was it all for? Control of a small island nation on a wayward channel off the continent? We were once wise enough to thwart invaders, but as the world ignored us we turned on each other. What is it that breaks the bonds of brotherhood inside a nation? You think your land will live forever but difference is the only thing that doesn't change. Here were the footprints of Hannibal. Then, Hannibal forgotten, city-states dwell. The walls of the urban centers fall, and a foreign hand shadows the vineyards. In this swirling record little men hammer nails and babies get suckled into poverty. What lasts is the eternal worker and the never-ending boss. I wanted to get as far away from this as possible. Find a warm climate that never suffered from the wind. Retreat to a haven from the ravings of dogma. I yearned for the toy globe I once had as Edju the young student. I could find such a place on my globe. It had bumps where the mountains are.

I huddled in that stairwell with the lapping flames crawling up to my heels. I knew I would have to evacuate or get swallowed by the rising fire. I heard the trucks clanging outside in the street. The entire building was burning. I went to the window,

A wild-eyed man in a green and gold cape came running down the stairs above me. He wanted to pour holy water on my head. Snipers were shooting at the firemen trying to organize below me. I had no other choice. So I jumped.

59.

The updraft blew me into the soup. The soup – the smoke. The smoke from the fire and the burning cathedral. What good is that, a passing bird may have said. Instead of down I was going up. Up and around. Around the eaves and high windows of our ornate architecture, pride of our nation. Our nation, about to fall into the sea somewhere near the Dogger Bank where the first people used to be.

I flew above city streets and was able, somehow, to turn and bend my path between buildings. Right arm down and left arm up would bank me to the right. Left arm down and right arm up and I would veer to the left. I had to keep my eyes open unless I wanted to crash into the billboards. But the wind sucked the wet from them and they burned with a fury from the lack of moisture.

It was an amazing act. A hand of magic across the sky. A feeling of power few men have ever experienced before. The idea that I was flying. I rejoiced over this, somehow. But the question remained; how do I land?

Going at this speed, achieving these certain angles. How do I settle again onto the ground? It was a perplexing question. I began to scout around for something soft to fall into. A pile of hay or a stack of mattresses. A deep pool of water. Anything. But the recent fighting and unrest that ruled our homeland made such items impossible to find. Instead I saw the results of battles pass below my all-seeing eyes.

Houses turned to rubble. Places where the scavengers had yet to retrieve the dead bodies and mop up the blood. There were decaying mules in dark puddles. Here and there a solitary shoe. Garbage bins knocked over and picked through by the starving. Empty milk bottles waiting for the mail delivery. Bags of peanuts someone hoarded behind a train station.

Old men trying on coats. Here and there wild pigs feeding on the wounded. And so much of this.

I'd found a terrible talent. A monstrous ability. I soared above the passing crowds all that day. I lamented the wreckage. And in my imaginings, a longing in my chest to return to the cathedral where I was, of late, a prisoner. Because I'd left Alice behind. In my need to escape, the urge to save myself from fire or baptism, I abandoned her. I flew above the bleeding river, tracing its meandering line in the dusk by the use of my masterful arms. Dreamy in the solid air. Thinking of her. Her sack. Her stain. I did not want to imagine what became of her. I didn't want to think of the consuming fire. I wanted to believe the firemen were able to thwart the snipers and save the old church. And, by saving it, keeping her from burning.

I could see a room filled with soiled sacks. All piled up on top of each other like the dead on the Mountain, making a structure. And the flames rising and the heat building until the burlap began to smoke and smolder. And then, when the room gets to 250°, the sacks ignite. I didn't want to think about it further than that. In books the thinker closes his eyes and shakes his head at this point. Tries to clear the imagery from his thoughts. But if I closed my eyes I would fly into a building and kill myself. I lived with the image instead. It stayed in that theater two inches behind my forehead all the rest of the day and into the night.

When the sun set there were campfires on the horizons. I saw fireflies in the distance. But as I approached I heard guns and realized this innocent vision was a skirmish. A firefight between the forces that were ripping my country apart. What I'd viewed as a sign of summer beauty turned into the cold sense of killing steel. I could hear men scream as I passed over the fighting and I wondered about the sounds we make.

One knows it is pain and pain is pain but we still cry out.

For what? It won't change the fact that there is such a thing as pain. My father, when I was the boy Edju, berated me for crying in pain. I learned to keep it inside always. No one ever knew I suffered. And I grew into a sweatered man of few possessions and simple wants.

In the deep horizon near the curve of the Earth I saw the water reflect the glow of twelve moons. The reflections bounced and wobbled in the unsettled sea. These were the memories of all those who had been with me in my life. The ones who left town and abandoned me. The ones who knew I would amount to nothing. The ones who knew they could take advantage of me. The ones who tortured me in my Edju school days. School days smelling of piss and unwashed clothes. The haggard, skinny boy they threw rocks at and pounded in the back. Dragged and muddied in the yards. Left crying in the muck and rats of the alley. My friends. The ones who gave me what I deserved.

I drifted on the wind and approached the edge of the water and had a choice. Fly away to the Frisians or circle back and stay where I was born. There, beyond the waves, they drank coffee in smart shops. They ate overpriced dollops of foliage with gold tinted forks. They made wise conversation and smirked a great deal. Their clothes were only of the finest material. They made love with perfect bodies perfumed and spotless clean. Their teeth were like ivory. Lithe and trim. Like Alice when we were students.

But below me, amid the rubble and disgrace of country-man killing countryman, it was not that way. We searched for clear water. Hated each other. Disbelieved anything told to us by anyone tainted with the smell of opposition. We didn't trust the papers. We despised anyone with money. Viewed passing strangers with abject suspicion. Our food was mean and old. We ate warmed grease from twice used foil with our fingers. Our children huddled behind barbed wire. They shivered when the north wind pushed through the coastline heather. Ran for cover when the weather threatened even the whales with extinction. We'd eaten all our pets. Killed all our teachers. We separated into Agrarian Militias and Urban Planners. Lost among ourselves, having forgotten those national things we once all loved. Determined our brother enemies would never enjoy them again unless they bent to our will. I glided between the clouds all the night through. Lost in the reverie of these brutal raids and computations.

The sun came up from Norway to relight the fuse. I saw to the north-northeast a dot of land unattached to my aching country. An island I did not know of. I filed through all my memories of my, Edju's, schooldays. I tried to remember the forms and shapes on the map of our island nation lost in the sea beyond Europe and Mars. But I couldn't remember an island this shape and in this location from any of my lessons.

I put my right arm down and lifted my left arm to the west and set that course for the north-northeast.

Crossing above sharks and the reflections of old ships gone to the bottom I came to the island and circled. Around and around I flew, for the island was a rough circle. No sign of life but for birds. No houses. No huts. No piers or boats. No chimneys or churches. No roads. No plastic bags blowing in the wind. And no sign that any of those things had ever been there.

Which is when it came to mind how to land. As I circled around and around I drew closer to the land. The lower I went the slower my rate of speed. Slower and slower until by a mere turning of my body and pointing my feet to the ground I landed as if an angel in disguise.

60.

I do not know the names of old birds so I call them myself. They stare with steel black eyes and they run in the hundreds against the gray sky. A swirl of feather and smell of red wind. From high above, the island had the look of unpolished amber. But on the ground beside a dead tree like bent fork tines I saw the up and down of the land. Rises and dry gullies. A bluff on the southern end, faking cliffs. Here and there small, quick beaches. Short groves created hidden places. A rubble of boulders pinpointing almost the island center. There were trees and razor grass. Heather and sometimes purple thistle. It was an unopened book. I walked a wide arch and saw no sign of human spoil.

If I could find a way to live here this would be my home. From here, I reasoned, I could plot my recapture of Alice.

My first mission was to construct a shrine. The need to sanctify took hold of me like a bear. You cannot change the habits of saints. I ventured amid the hornet brambles and northern sage. I skimmed my hand over the smooth caps of the golden sprigs. Thinking. Thinking. Thinking and praying to St. Anthony of Padua. The patron saint of lost toys in the sod. Wondering.

In the burst of usual miracle, I came upon a field of stones and began at once. The mundane cosmos of the holiest of spirits. You see how the great manna arrives, I told myself. It would be backbreaking work but imagine the flow of bliss once the pain stops.

For two days I marked every inch of that island in my mind. I found a small, flat plain between three fresh water ponds and decided at once that this was the place. Water and flat. The two basic requirements of civilization. How the invisible hand of the holiest of spirits is always present.

After falling on my knees and scraping myself on the thorns of a berry tree I took a stick. With this I scratched an outline of my future dwelling in perfect order between the ponds.

A long beaked bird with even longer blue legs circled above me and came to wade in one of the ponds. But I killed it because this water was mine now and I wanted no competition for it. And I believe word got around among the bird groups that this was the way it was going to be from now on. I never saw another in my water. God is praised.

From then on, my days passed with digging out the larger stones and lugging them to the building site. I made fourteen separate piles. Each pile containing stones of similar size so I could see what resources I had at hand. I must build with a mind to what is available, I said aloud. And the heather agreed.

Each day after my collecting stones I rested by walking the whole edge of the island, all along its shore. The world's use creates plastic and rags. Things would wash ashore and I was certain I could find uses for things. In almost every case, things came out of the sea at the tides, but then pulled back on their return. It was essential that I time my excursion with the tides to retrieve what I could before the sea sucked it back.

After a week or so I collected empty plastic jugs, old shirts, picnic forks, and many shoes. There were dozens of sundry things I couldn't recognize. For all that I collected I stored in a grove just down a hillside from what I called the Bent Fork Tree. I spread everything across the ground to dry out and had hundreds of items in my nature's storehouse.

In my mornings I watched the freighters on the horizon. How many decades, I wondered, have ships passed in this vicinity and never found this island?

The building work began with serious intent once I

217

moved all the stones I deemed usable into my work zone. I plunged my stick into the ground along the outline I drew and chopped open the turf. When I completed the entire outline this way I went to my knees and dug out a channel in the muck with my bare hands. I made sure to make it wide and deep. In this I would place my largest stones to build a foundation for the other stones that would follow.

In the evenings I tore useless limbs from dead trees. I separated and piled these things as well. It was in my mind to use them, somehow, as supports for the walls. I needed to balance and hold where the weight of the stones would be problematic. I admit I was inventing the process as I went along, using only what was at hand.

There was always the stink of the fish headed night. That's when the monster isolation of the island crept all around me like snakes and waited in ambush. I prayed. I prayed with hands so hard my knuckles locked in place and my lips froze purple together. For the most part I prayed in thanksgiving. Thankful there was nothing to eat on the island, but it hadn't mattered in all this time. I took that as a sign of approval. A stamp on my actions from the hand of the High Holy.

I learned to ignore the human long shadows. The black columns across the ground with misshapen heads balanced on top. I got weary of looking for who or what was casting them. Even as they moved. I kept myself busy. I told myself that I have dominion if I had no live oil.

But even as I worked to build my temple and learned the proper method by trial and error, there were moments. Moments that haunted me like the memory of moonlight on overcast nights revealing nothing. Nothing and no one. The way Alice would look at me from her shoulder and laugh. Wanting me to enjoy the joke as well. Thinking of me. Desirous of seeing me happy. She would move her head when reading. A sudden but smooth jerk to force her long hair out of her face. Then a hand without a thought folding the strands behind her ear like curtains. The slowest thing, the most common move a woman makes with a hand or an arm or an eye can be devastation to a man.

On the days following such thoughts and phantoms, I returned to my work and tried to forget. But her face was in the stones. Her natural song was in the wattle. The way she moved from tree to tree. The rocks she threw. I got little work done on those days.

And though I could see the growth of my handiwork I was certain these ticks of the brain slowed my progress. The sound of her voice. The regret I held onto as if it was my mother and I walked into the door of school. If only I had never taken the mushrooms. If only I was not exhausted that morning. If only I was able to take a little joke about myself. One should curse the young male ego. It is worth no more than the spit of a skunk. All men are dogs.

When these weights jangled on ropes above my head so that I couldn't work, I went to my knees. I went to my knees and begged forgiveness from whatever saint was at hand. Passing angels. Or just a hint of incense. Always the Psalms of mayhem brought me back. To slay my enemies and use them to feed foxes. Justice to the oppressive memories of my youth. How I longed to finish my sanctuary. It meant more to me that food itself, which was something I discovered I could do without.

All my living has been in darkness. My hands held together as tight as electric, magnetic vises. This is how earnest I prayed for the power to forget and erase all the terrible things I had done. The ego. The backtalk. The telling of tales one to another. The many faces and the outright thefts. I stole a toy. A book. Glass bottles. Something treasured by someone else. Is it any wonder my life has been a mistake?

I struggled to complete my shelter, or my sanctuary, or whatever the original intent for it was. I couldn't remember. I kept my hands away from my body. All urges suppressed. I did not eat. I did not sleep on softness. I drank only to loosen the dust from my throat. I learned to work with a hanging beard that was often in the way.

And this, plus being alone, was how I lived for a long time.

61.

I had no news from the country. It was hard to see it, even on the clearest of days. And there were few of those in this part of the sea. I tried to make plans for a return but there was nothing at hand to help me get there. There were trees but I had no tools to fashion a boat. And each time I tried to imagine how I could do it a voice came and told me to stay. It was Alice I wanted to know about. Damn the country. To hell with the country. What of the country I knew remained?

Sometimes I worried that Jacinto and Hazel were still waiting in a car for me in front of the hall of justice. Wondered if Marta Vansimmerant still accompanied her mother's remains to churches across the land. And what of me, Edju? Where is Edju's place in this?

I can't begin to explain how many times it came to me that I should never have left the room with the others. That I should have waited. Waited and found out the verdict. Was Alice the thing of saints or not? I regretted my rebellion and yet – what if she burned in the fire? What if the seeping brown stain acted as an accelerant and hurried the flames to cover her?

These are the thoughts that haunted me as I bundled the long grass to make the roof of my gray sanctuary. Or whatever I had intended it to be when I began. They beleaguered me like an unwanted cousin bent on telling stupid jokes all night long. I was so blinded by them that I didn't even realize when I finished.

It took my walking from my stack of thatch with a new bundle and realizing I had no place to weave it into. That was how I knew it was over. I'd finished.

I went inside and sat in the coldest corner as penance for my evil ways. And the visions that came were vivid red.

Orange as the desert. Blue as the mineral stain that forms around the necks of the dead.

I came to realize that the Ark was possible because the continents were one landmass in those days. That all the water that killed the world sunk into the core in the final days. And no rainbows had ever appeared before the great sailor saw the waters recede. I was near death and lit the lanterns in the long halls of death. In these halls I watched souls on the verge called in and sent back to finish their lives. Mules spoke. Water changed to blood. Cold loaves spoke like humans. That fear is to be reverent, like the woman of Norwich said. That you sing praises at all hours because the maker is not steady. Its brain is filled with sorrow over all the versions that have failed. It was clear. I spoke the word that meant the thing for which we may not say the word. And there was a storm in return.

I came to know my limits. I did not think of women and had no desire to join their bodies to mine. I did not know hunger. I did not wash. I held conversations with the walls. The stones told of great adventures they'd had below the surface of the Earth and laughed at how short the lives of humans were. Sand weaving spellbinding tales of hanging caverns and oceans men know nothing of.

I spend hours staring at the cold gray sea and never blink. I take to my ablutions. Keep my clothes clean. Sweep out my home, or whatever it is, with religious care. I need nothing, glad to be rid of humans. In short, a full life.

This was my life for little more than a year. Since I'd not spoken in most of that time I no longer knew what my voice sounded like. All the talking was in my head. The constant chill of the Sea turned my skin into rustic callous. Windburn. Brittle. Hard. The scales more common to fish and particular monks. I had long ago overcome the physical yearning for companionship, talk, contact, and sex. I forced my will upon these natural but evil imperatives until they surrendered to me. I did a jig one time when I realized I'd won. I hopped around the total circumference of the island, not caring what the birds thought. The little orange beaked blackbirds. The red tongue miniscules. The white hooded assassin birds. I put my thumb to my nose and wiggled my fingers at them. And I enjoyed their complaining squawks with the gleam of a little boy. I was pure in the eyes of all the saints and, for the first time, I knew I was clean.

My celebration put me in mind of cantaloupes. The fresh juices from the slicing. The succulent flavor. But I recognized this as the work of the demon. I took a stick to a wounded bird and smashed its head in as a sacrifice to the all-knowing. By this was I granted a reprieve from the temptation of hunger. And afterward I meditated on the goodness of the masters in heaven.

After this I was ill for a time. There was a fever. I dreamed of having a normal job in the real world again. The kind I had when I kept rooms in the city and sat with Alice by the radiator. A nightmare, I reasoned. Going through these strange visions did not allay my fever or my nausea. Instead I came to believe I was and had always been Jacinto instead of Edju.

Then I fell asleep and dreamed of high walls and church bells, which calmed me considerable.

I recited the short version of *Revelations of Divine Love*, though I did not know where I'd learned it. I considered this a gift from God itself. I came to believe that the liberal spirit of Julian doctored me for all the rest of the days I spent on the island. In my blissful solitude. My studied fortress against the sins of the world. So that even when the motorboat full of soldiers arrived I stared at them in peaceful regalia. Sitting with arms folded across my almost disintegrated body.

62.

They didn't think I'd recognize them, but I saw what they were from the start. The ruff collars extending over their shoulders like Elizabethan clowns. Their small feet in delicate slippers. The coins they flipped to one another as they progressed toward my small hovel from the shore. These were the king's men and no mistaking.

I watched them scan the island. I knew they were looking for me and to determine my situation. By some mechanical spiritualism, I knew. What possible interest did I hold for them and their mortal king I couldn't say. They were deliverymen in plain sunlight. Complete with wide brimmed hats worn in the times of those painters infatuated with feet. Their bodkins and tights and jellied hair. They couldn't fool me. When the body is new the skin is fresh and clean. Then the accumulated dirt of almost a century pounds creases and sense into you. I saw their intent from the start. It did not sway me.

They came into my sanctuary of stone without a word. I, sitting by my collection of feathers from which I planned to make a garment. They, looking at each other and the meagerness of my home with amused faces. On the verge of making a joke at my expense. Just as it was in school. The tall one fingered a coin, back and forth with one hand. The short one kept looking at the thatch above his head, afraid it may all fall in. The lean one stared at me like a man looking into a mirror, trying to determine what part of himself to amputate.

What type of fire do you use here, he asked in a still, deep voice.

I don't know what you mean.

Fire. You must use some kind of fire here. Are you sure the kind you use is legal?

I don't use fire.

I don't mean fire in a metaphysical sense. I mean fire. As in some element that turns flesh to hot wax.

I have no need for either one.

But what kind do you use, when you use it?

I don't use any. I have nothing here to build a fire with.

You eat your food raw?

I do not eat.

This made the shortest one laugh. It also served to remind him of something he had stashed in his pouch, and he hurried to take it out. I was unclear what was inside the oily white wrapper. It looked like a delicate cake. The kind only made by the most talented of bakers. He set the wrapped marvel on his lap. Careful in his unwrapping so as not to disturb the artistic frosting that adorned it. The sound of the crackling paper made what was inside seem precious and delectable. It gave the feeling that the confection within was rare. Artistic and beautiful. To disturb the decoration, to open the package too fast and careless, would diminish it. He kept pulling the paper away from the cake. This way and that way. But he was being so deliberate he never seemed to reveal the contents to our unworthy eyes. He kept unwrapping and manipulating the paper as if he were cracking a safe.

We're watching you, you know, offered the tall one. We know everything you do here.

Then you know whether I use fire or not.

Don't be impertinent, came a charge from the lean face.

Am I under arrest?

We'll let you know, the tall one threatened. In the meantime, we'll ask the questions and you answer them.

What need have I to answer if you've been watching everything I do?

There was no answer. The tall one glared at me as if he was on the verge of losing all restraint. Trying to put fear into my head. He looked around to see if he could upturn a piece of furniture to goad me into violence. But my sanctuary was empty. I had no furniture. All I had was a pile of feathers. And this was too sacred even for my new enemy to upturn. There was only the man seated with crossed legs, still unwrapping his delicate confection. Never finishing the job. Unwrapping and pulling at the paper forever. Always trying to separate it from what was inside without upsetting its beauty.

We stared at him for a long while. Not knowing, I imagine, where else to go with such a ridiculous conversation. It was obvious to me they were new at this. We leaned and squinted, trying to get a glimpse of what the white paper was hiding. But either the cold dim of my abode or the meticulous nature of his operation kept us from seeing anything.

There were birds squawking outside the doorway. And besides that, the waves from the sea. Otherwise we sat together without any obvious purpose. The short man's work took him far away from our concerns. He kept at it, licking his lips in anticipation.

Did you ever hear of tea, the lean man said, unable to hide his sarcasm.

I've heard of tea.

What kind do you have, spat the tall one who hated me.

And have you ever heard of offering tea to company when they visit?

I shook my head. I have no tea.

No tea. No tea and no fire. My enemy walked to within inches of me. He smelled of creosote and dead fish. He was doing all he could to incite me to strike at him so they could arrest me or beat me or transport me to the kennels.

And you expect us to believe this, he growled.

I shrugged my shoulders. And it occurred to me I did it in the manner of a man who was trying to hide something. So, I did it again with a more convincing flair. This was better.

But I decided to quit trying as it began to look like the twitch of a madman. You can look around, I said. Search the whole island. You'll find no tea and no fire. You'll find nothing to make fire with.

The lean man pointed to a makeshift ledge I'd built on a casual day. This was where I put the cross I'd taken with me from the big room before the building caught fire. A look of recognition, and even satisfaction, came to his expression. He couldn't hide it from me. He glanced over to my enemy, breathing hard in my face, and waved a hand.

I'm satisfied with this one, he said. He put his hand on the tall man's shoulder and patted him. Come on. We're done here. Leave him alone. He doesn't have any fire.

They turned from me without another word. Everyone was moving out. That is except for the short man still sitting against the wall trying to unwrap his cake.

Put that away. Come on. We're going.

The short man hurried to close up the work he'd begun and stuffed his parcel back into his pouch. I was somewhat surprised that he wasn't more upset or disappointed. He gave up on his quest with such ease and simplicity he reminded me of a compliant child. He was quick to his feet and following them down to their boat.

I spent the rest of the day listening to them try to start their stubborn, uncompromising engine. Arguing about how to pull the cord. This angle. That angle. Prime the pump first. Get out of the way and let me do it. Put that cake away and pay attention. And more of this until the engine at last cooperated and they were off.

I watched them cut through the gray, choppy water like a knife. I had a feeling it wasn't going to be the last time I saw them.

63.

You will, I think, allow me to attempt to explain how slow time passed on my island. After the interrogators returned to their homes I returned to my own world. The duties I gave myself meant nothing more than the passing of time. I had no connection to the zeitgeist beyond my hands and the ground. In time I regained my natural hunger and had to find food. For this I used some of the plants I found growing there. This was a dangerous business, because I knew nothing of biology or horticulture. Mowing grass was something I'd never done, being a city dweller and renting rooms. What I learned I learned by hand.

I was much like those intrepid pioneers from the infancy of our species. For someone somewhere, a long time ago, had to be the first one to try a mushroom or a piece of fruit. Someone had to be the first one to taste greens and find what does and does not make a salad. The first to taste the bitter. The first to discover sweet. During these discoveries someone noticed that fruit fermented into juice. Someone found it became a wicked thing to drink. Someone had to crack open the first egg. Someone had to discern what was poison and what was safe. No one knows who worked out the process to manufacture bread and all its complex steps. Whoever came to this understanding doesn't even have a statue or a plaque in her name. And those who found the poison waiting paid for all this knowledge with their lives.

Generations of accumulated intelligence saved in the collective brain of all humanity. Each region of the planet putting their own ideas into the same basic foods. This is the start of culture. And culture, the cause of all wars. When you ponder the process, you can almost die from the magnificence of the effort and the results.

But I had no way to access this knowledge. Beyond an occasional trip to a grocery stand in my life I knew nothing of this process. For me, on that island, it was a matter of putting a leaf or flower under my nose and onto my tongue.

One day under horsehead skies I writhed in a dreamlike agony from something I ate. I was certain I was going to die, but I was wrong. Another day I found a leafy plant low to the ground that grew in colonies. The taste was uncomfortable at first but I noticed an increase in my spirit and well-being when I ate it. In short, I got by. I learned. I taught myself. I invented names for the plants I found.

The rain refilled the ponds and water was never an issue. My stone sanctuary protected me from the North Sea winds. I was never sick in all the time I spent there. And I grew a happy, great long beard down to my chest and further on.

I had eradicated the need for sexual gratification. My tryst with Marta Vansimmerant was the last time I had such a feeling in my body. Since then I have been void of the urge and the sin.

But I need to explain the trick of time.

There is a great lesson in glass. We cannot see it, I am told, but the glass in our windows and in our hands when we drink, is not something solid. It has, they told me in my school days, a viscous property. And if we waited long enough – that is to say if we grew old as oaks and quiet as the stones – we would see it for what it is. Glass, not being solid, changed by gravity from all the shapes we gave it, back to its nature. If we waited long enough it would lay on the ground as flat as a shirt. But here is that trick of time. It is happening so slow that, in our lifetimes, we cannot see it. It would take generations to recognize the effect. And as the generations come and go we build and tear down and rebuild again. We scrap old material and don't allow it to live long enough to get to the point of changing its shape. This is why, on those rare times as a boy I dug up old bottles from the ground, they were misshapen and queer looking.

That is what time felt like on my island. But I had no glass there. I could not prove the theory.

The days went past my sight as if on the backs of dead turtles on rough ice with a slow breeze at their tails. If there had been glass on my island I would have been able to watch its viscous nature. Standing windows would be flat like pancakes on the sill in my universe.

One night while I sat in the cool damp of my stone sanctuary I heard a kind of buzzing between the rushes of wind. A mechanical sound. Human made. Not any sound of nature like air or water. From time to time it changed pitch. Sometimes it rang. Other times it was like the inside of a clock. Hissing voices coming from the end of a long wire. Tickling the quiet I'd grown so used to. It did not come from any of the handmade objects I'd saved and stored. My digging tools. My smooth hammer made of rock. But it was constant, and after a while I could make out the voices at the other end.

He must be sleeping. I don't hear anything. Yeah, he's good for the night. Shut down the surveillance and get some sleep. Goodnight.

After this, a static hum as if from a radio left between channels.

I walked the room like a cat, listening. I caught the direction and followed.

And get some sleep. Goodnight.

After this, a static hum as if from a radio left between channels.

I walked the room like a cat, listening. I caught the direction and followed.

It was the cross. The enameled and jeweled cross I'd taken from the church before I escaped. They'd been listening to me through it all this time.

64.

I stood outside and screamed at the rocks I'd used to build my home. Betrayed again. Every friend gone. Every item of comfort taken away. I dreamed of Alice as I stood there, awake, shouting at the stones. Each one of them a liar and an enemy. I dreamed I saw her standing in a crowd. The crowd is talking and laughing and attuned to its own dynamic. I stand outside of it, somewhere near the curb. And instead of joining in, she turns to look at me and smile. A quiet smile. Given only at special times. But only a dream. Alice is far from me now and I will never find her again.

Resolution beats in my chest like a bellows filled with syrup. I begin to walk to the shore. The edge of my island. There are no boats there. I should have known. I, Edju the younger, when a boy, drew castles. I would swallow the drugs we bought on the street. I would put my nose two inches from the paper and draw. Starting with the keyhole in the Great Door. Then on to the keep. The notches in the walls for the archers to man. But at no time did I ever think far ahead enough to put boats on my island for when I needed them. My inconsistencies. My paint splattering on the good carpet. I can escape none of it. Wood nailed crooked. Measurements off. Spots on walls left uncoated. No boats on the island I would live on thirty years later. A miserable failure to all mankind.

Watching the golden waves like buckets of piss I yearn for a beer. No one is listening. I cannot fathom the miasma caused by the sudden stream. I sit in the rushes, tired of shouting. The stones do not care. Once, I remember, certain stones gave young men the power to take over the world. My stones taunt me in my misery.

I lay within the reeds, tired of sitting. Two hands behind

my head as I stare at the catholic clouds that fog my memory of the sky. They talk to me but I don't understand. At first.

Common sense, they seem to say. The stones are not your enemy.

Then what is, I ask from inside the ground.

Not the stones.

It makes me think. I detest that which makes me think, but here I am, thinking. The psychosis of yelling at stones was untenable. Even a blind man could understand that. But what was it there that betrayed me? And how do my betrayals of friends and relatives and sounds compare to it? I watched a white hooded moon monkey scrawl across the sky, looking for fish near the surface of the sea. It circled. Circled. Paused. And dove into the water. Up with a fish then I saw it.

The cross.

The cross was my betrayer. A listening device with horns that was all innocent when I was in my prayers and hopes. Betraying me. But for an anomaly of atmosphere I would have never heard them on the other side. It was fortune to me. This was the enemy. Not the entire cheese box but enough of the shelter to swing a cat in. I stood.

I walked.

I went back in my sanctuary and picked up the sparkling instrument. Red and blue gems just playing with the dim. The gold that separated the colors into fields of plowed jewels. Putting it to my ear, I wanted to hear them talking about me. I wanted to hear them planning to copy my life in their books. I wanted to hear them sleeping at their control panels. And when I threw this vile thing into the sea they would start and drown in their own phlegm.

This became my entire intent. So, I marched that thing, that vile thing, out the door and stormed down to the sand. With all my might I flung the monster into the soaring waves and rejoiced. The next thing they would hear would be the kissing ecstasy of lesbian squids. Let them decipher that code. Let them confer with each other on the meaning of the deep-sea lovers. Let them form an army or a navy to root out the evil they would imagine. I, Edju, would have none of it.

I watched the enameled and jeweled cross twirl arm after base after arm after head. The wind caught it for just a moment and carried it for a time. Then it became too heavy for the invisible air and plummeted straight down into the drink. And when it broke the surface and entered the nether sea the wind slowed on the water.

The sun pushed clouds aside. A ray from that orb of dancing fire brushed the top of my head. I heard the birds for the first time in days. They sang my name in a happy dance of feathers that would otherwise ruin the playa. But this was the sea so there were no concerns for it. A gentle, hushed calm came over the land. The light from above turned the sage and heather a grand purple. All the reeds stood straight as soldiers.

I returned to my abode. Stood in the brooding door of my prodigal sanctuary. I accepted the apology given to me by the space inside and went in. Resuming my usual place against my favorite wall, I put my knees up to my nose. I clasped my weathered hands around my legs, drawing them against me, and leaned into myself. My true bed.

Here I slept the dream of kings. Unencumbered by the cares of holy orders for the first time in my entire life. The memories of May parades dressed in white, marching around the church in jackboots. The memories of the sweet, scented fragrances of death incense in the chapels. The memories of thimble-fingered nuns flicking hard metal into your temple. The memories of huddling in a corner of the cloakroom praying for safety while the flames closed in. The memories of the priest's maggot fingers probing and touching. The memories of the taste of God itself in your mouth and the difficulty of scraping it off the roof of your mouth. The memories of its unforgettable taste. The memories of lying to the priest in the box behind the screen, telling him an easier sin to hide the harder one. The memories of forgetting the exact words. All the memories that refused to limit the sentence of guilt. Gone.

They were gone along with the gem clustered listening device called a cross. Sinking to the bottom of the sea. Soon buried and forgotten.

They will only find it when the tectonics shift and the cities fall. And a scientist unearths the old cross and pronounces his discovery. Look, he will say, these ancient civilizations had gears and wheels and could listen to waves in the air. They were more advanced than we knew.

And they will give him a million American dollars and a prize to hang around his neck and he will be a great man. But all the while it will be me. What I did this day, a thousand years before. The scholars will present him with the Edju International Prize. But he will not know why.

In this searing kind of peace, I slept, once and for all.

We can escape the past. We can drown it out. Smoke it out of the trees. Wipe the brain clean in the mountains and start over. We can escape it. Don't let anyone tell you we can't. I am determined to become the master of forgetting.

It came to me in that sleep. All my bleeding worship. All my belief and faith in red sand. The perfect rows of candles you must buy from the rectory. Or the nun who hides them in her drawer and has the children come up one by one, money in hand. You may not take too long. You may look quick. And you live in that dull world, with its green walls and brown floors and everyone in black or blue. The only light there is comes from the paintings of angels and crowns of eternal bouquets. You choose your candle and your candy like a wise man and the nun takes your money and slams the door. Keep your fingers away. She keeps the money for cigarettes later. And no one can believe it's true.

It is much like a suicide attempt that is based on a mistaken perception. The bottle of aspirin only does enough to reduce the headache. But the perceived underhanded action by the person identified as the reason he must kill himself clouds everything. And the failed attempt leads to changing your entire life in opposite reaction and manufactured hatred of the mistaken culprit. The culprit who, in reality, did nothing to you. Imagine what it must be like to have attempted to kill yourself based on an error of perception. Then spend a lifetime ridiculing the person who did nothing to you but is the convenient scapegoat for all your failures. Even to the point of contemplating his murder to absolve you of your stupidity.

It is a convenient way to treat an imaginary rival. Join the army and become a bitter, unquenched artist of the first degree.

65.

At one with the unattended mind, I developed, in dreams, the method of escape. Perhaps I conjured the solution. But by whatever method or correspondence... what happened, happened. I can or cannot take credit for it. This I cannot answer. That the world would perceive me as a holy man from this point on did not ever occur to me at any point during my captivity. I was without anticipation for what was about to happen.

Boats appeared out of the invisible night. A stream of pilgrims rushed about the heather and thistle calling my name. How the word of my solitude came to them remains a mystery. Even I, old Edju, who will get chased by children in a future am helpless to explain. Perhaps I will never know. What trick of fate or mystery of chance brought them to my door in heavy breathing wonder? Faces wet with sweat. Chests going. Hands gripping the doorframe in anticipation of a brilliant star. They paused there and whispered the question. Are you Edju?

Consideration of their journey to this place was not a question. That they were here was obvious. It was the method and perception that haunted them that brought me to an empty room. Who knows who has cultivated a hatred for you from the untrue poison spread about your name? You may be speaking to one who heard the lie, and believes in it, and smiles wicked in your face. Hiding their true feelings.

Dancing around my stone cottage pub in blue boots, the crowd rejoiced at their discovery.

Enough, I shouted. And the sound of my voice froze them like curious ants feeling the boulder ahead.

For you, said a trembling girl holding a bouquet of flowers. Red and yellow and golden ochre. She placed them at my feet, as the boatman called up from the shore.

Get going up there, he said. The soldiers are following.

Heavy hands took me by the sleeves and collar and tore me out of my dwelling. Despite my protests they persisted. They couldn't or wouldn't hear me. They were saving me, they said, from the approaching murderers who wanted my neck.

I don't know what you people are talking about, I tried to say. But their shouts to one another and the urging of the boatman drowned my voice into a buzz of welling nonsense.

Just before the heavy waves of the evening tide came at us they secured me into one of the boats with ropes and leather. Out into the sea we went with no more than two common yellow oars. A flotilla of rowboats in the open sea like the currachs of another age in black and white and desperate fish.

Keep your head down, they told me.

Lights from towers swept the surface. Searching.

My face down in the boat. An inch of seawater just there.

Never before this have I been so close to the sea.

Open the gates, someone cried. I lifted my head and saw the boats making way for a secret entrance beneath a wooden pier. The beams from the towers always only just missing us. From another universe not connected to our motion.

Please tell me what you're doing, I tried to say. Where are you taking me? And what is this all about?

Quiet master please, a woman said. We will get you through to safety. But you must trust us. You must do as we say so we can get you past the guards.

Reaching an oar high over his head as we passed beneath a bridge one of the men hit a small bell. The tin sound was hard to hear, but those who needed to hear it responded in time. I heard the wooden gate close behind us, swishing the water aside. Making an echo under the pier that hid our transit from the world.

Someone told me to lower my head. We all did as we went into a tunnel. Soup black water and dull, fetid air inside.

The boats came to a thumping stop against a stone and brick ledge built into the water. A single torch lit the cavern. It was a man-made thing. Perhaps once a sewer. Perhaps a hideaway for pirates since the days of Napoleon. The privateers who ran illegal goods through the blockade to England. Perhaps just a ledge with no meaning at all.

Under the single torch stood three men. They waited for all the boats to come to a stop. Three men in important hats standing with arms crossed. They were patient in manner but their faces confessed to ragged lives and jutted out of black hoods. The welcoming committee, I guessed. The leadership of this odd seafaring troupe, I supposed.

Vile smells came out of the water as the crews bumped against the ledge. Dead fish and the bodies of a hundred lost waifs never to rise again. They secured the boats to rotting posts with wet ropes. They helped me from my hiding place and lifted me to the ledge. The three men approached and one shook my hand.

Wise Man of the Heather, they called me.

Xenolith of the Island, they cheered.

Yellow oars waving in the torchlight. The muffled cheers bounced harmless off the wet unseen walls.

Zaratite rocks placed in my hands were cold to the touch. They led me to a narrow doorway that went to a stairway bathed in bright orange light. As I ascended, the green of the stones in my hands turned blue in that light. And when they saw this some began to cry.

66.

When I cross the street of fire I cannot see the trees for the smoke. If the street lamps sang the widow's song justice would be in league with nightmares. I am given coffee and it doesn't matter what time it is. A young woman in a school uniform and short hair sits at my knee and tells me what has happened.

The country is in ruins. There is no central government, and the radio station changes hands every other week. Everyone is in hiding. Everyone armed. The hatred that exists between what were once countrymen keeps coffins neutral to gender.

How did this happen, I ask. Will it ever come right again?

There is a saying all through the country, she replies. When the far moon pales the living hand children will point to nothing at all.

But what does this mean?

No one knows. Yet everyone knows. Men argue and fight over rotting food behind the alleys. There are militias protecting men who say they are gods, returning for their children. Two of this kind pop up every month.

What of the church?

They switch allegiance to whoever seems to be winning and have lost the faith of the workers. They have a penchant for fascists anyway.

This was the worst of all news to me. First the radio cross and now this. How can I explain the torture and betrayal I felt at this news? The saints were the one thing, the only thing, that brought me to peace in the world. And now they were no better than cheap Italian dictators who force trains down into silk bags.

Many of their buildings are on fire. But they are still powerful because of their connections.

Of course, I nodded. International connections.

The secret societies and private donors are still behind them. But they have lost their amber relics to the socialists who have melted them down for butter. Such is the level of starvation in the countryside.

Are there no relief agencies? Nothing from the nations?

Some. But food trucks are hijacked. Medicines always find their way to the black market. There is a move afoot to cut off all aid until they find someone to negotiate with. But there has been no one powerful enough to do that for some time now.

It was at this point that it occurred to me I had been away longer than I suspected. So much happened since I made my way to my island. And yet now I understood why the men who came for me once never came back. They were all dead or scattered or powerless by now. How long have I been away, I asked her. I only half wanted to hear the answer.

The party estimates you were on that uncharted island for six years. Anyway, by the length of your beard I would suggest closer to three though.

My hand reached up to my mouth and I felt my beard for the first time. I knew I was growing one because I did not have provision to shave in all that time. But I did not consider that it had grown so long. And I did not realize I was gone for such a time.

Is there a way I can shave this off, I asked her.

They have been looking for scissors for you for the last hour. We have shaving equipment. I think we stole it from a French relief truck. But scissors are another matter. You can't always shave with a razor until you get rid of the long ones first.

Yes, of course. I understand.

She took my hand and led me outside. The air was acrid.

Yellow. Filled with the stink of triple based propellants and a hint of sulfur. From where we walked I could see before me the roofs of buildings ahead of us. Small buildings in a gully or a hollow that we went down a hillside to get to.

Surrounded by higher ground on every horizon, the houses and buildings ragged and unpainted. They looked abandoned and uncared for. Like a mining town in the coalfields, appearing from another age. Old and dirty. Wooden planks for sidewalks. Pitiful piles of junk and refuse everywhere. But these places were not abandoned. They are filled with people waiting for the next idea. Wondering where to go. Refugees picked up by the same people who rescued me from the island. Two little boys were fighting over a cigarette. It was obvious the only clothes owned by most of the people were the clothes they were wearing.

She gave out a deep sigh as she led me down the dusty street. When the prattle of past lives haunts you like a face from the window, she said. All magic breaks down into unmatched pairs.

I understood her lament. But what are you, I asked. There are factions and militias fighting each other in the streets and the hillsides?

Yes.

And what is your faction? Who are you?

She shook her head. She stopped and tried to smooth out the wrinkles of her plaid skirt. Then she pushed her hands into the pockets of her dark blue sweater with another sigh. A hurting sigh. A sigh from the tops of the bridges you jump from. If I could only change my shirt, she answered. God would reveal the true purpose of squid.

I could tell by the field of lament that occupied the energy around her I should be quiet. There was no point in asking.

We are the next to disappear, she whispered. We, ourselves, are almost out of ammunition. What funds we got from the UN have stopped coming in. There is no way to feed anyone beyond Thursday. We have been rationing for months now, and everyone here is starving or dying. Only one doctor remains. The rest have gone to Belgium. The beer the monks make there is a tremendous lure once the water in your own country turns brown.

Brown?

The water supply. It's all polluted by the leavings of worms. Sometime in the last year or so foreign worms came in with some relief supplies. They found our little island perfect for them. Too perfect. They've even taken to eating some of the birds' eggs.

I didn't want to admit it, but when she told me this I couldn't help but think this would make Jacinto proud.

No, she continued. Whoever we were the fight is over for us. The best we can say is we've rescued thousands. As you see. But you will all be on your own again soon enough. I'm going back to Baltimore in a few days myself.

But who are you working for? The UN? Relief agencies?

I don't know. They collect money on television in America and send a little of it here. We don't know who gets the rest.

She was not giving me the answer I wanted. Her effort to not give me a direct answer made me suspicious and angry. But I couldn't continue with my questions. We turned into a house that had no doors. Inside were a hundred mothers and their babies. Crying. Distended bellies. Hairless. Bug eyed. And the children were no better.

A man in blue nurses' scrubs came running from a back room. He had a pair of scissors working in his hand, held over his head. Found one, he shouted over the racket with a grin. Without pausing he ran to me and began stretching my beard to set it into the scissors and began to cut away.

It was uncomfortable for me. An intrusion. An invasion of my privacy. But it made some of the children stop crying and start to smile. Some even began to laugh. And the mothers of the children who were thus distracted looked relieved.

I allowed him to carry on. The generosity in my soul revealed itself and overtook the insult of his invasion of my privacy, I told myself. I was like a clown in a circus. Only a friendly one, without the makeup of someone who ate children behind the freak tent.

But when one little boy crawled up to the droppings of gray hair on the floor and tried to eat it, the joy was over. I was lucky he finished cutting my beard so quick. I knew, in my head, I couldn't stand to stay in there too much longer.

Back in the street, which had somehow turned from dust to mud without so much as a drop of rain, my guide handed me a small box.

There is a razor blade and handle in here. We scrounged it from the communists. They went through here the other day looking for deserters. We stole it while they weren't looking Take it.

Are you sure?

If we can't eat it, it is of no matter to us.

I took it with gratitude.

You will have to use water in the stream beyond the graves over there, she pointed. But don't drink the water. I'm sorry. I have no shaving cream.

I will manage, I began. I wanted to thank her for all they'd done for me. I wanted to offer my help even though I couldn't think of any possible way to help. I would be another mouth to feed, in the end. I said nothing more.

I have something else for you, she smiled. Follow me.

It was a few short steps to a dugout where two scrawny men with rifles were eating berries one at a time. They smiled, almost toothless when I came close. They were smiling at her.

Tonight, Ingrid? One tried to nudge her arm.

Never. You're filthy. Where is it? She looked around on the ground by their feet.

The second soldier bent over and picked a small satchel up from the shadows. Here, he said, unable to hide his disapproval. But I still say we should keep it. We need it more than he does.

It isn't ours, she scolded. She took it from him with a pull and handed it over to me.

I don't understand, I shrugged.

Your gun and ammunition. We found it among the burned books. No one knows how it ended up there. It's your property. Take it. The satchel too. It's fake leather, not the kind you can cook.

It was the Nagant M1895 and an unopened box of ammunition for it. I cried.

I'd forgotten about it, I stammered in gratitude. I didn't think of it for a long time. I can't believe this.

I still say we should keep it, snarled the soldier.

Be quiet, she ordered and touched my arm. Go now. Before this one loses his mind.

I looked around, wiping away tears. Which direction back to the old capitol?

Their faces turned to white stone. My question sent them into the mortified shock of discovered thieves.

Why would you want to go there? She asked in a hush.

It's where my rooms are. I just want to see if my rooms still exist and are empty. All I want is to live in them again.

The men shook their heads and laughed.

It isn't recommended. There are at least seven militias fighting each other there now. It is a hole of hell.

Different from anywhere else?

She frowned and looked at her shoes. I see your point. There, she pointed. To the southwest. You'll see the blood red smoke over two more hills. It will be coming from the city you call home.

This way, I asked, pointing in the same direction. Just to be sure.

Yes. But for a few kilometers you will go through Lothan County. I would recommend going around. In Lothan, when they catch people from other counties, they eat them.

67.

I walked into the cold alley hoping no one would see me. As I slipped along the grime blackened bricks there was music in a window.

Wait. I've been here before. Once I escaped into an alley and there was music. They must not know I am going or they will want me to pay them money. They will call my family even before I reach my rooms and threaten them. This is not the same, except in places where it is. Did she say west or east?

I crawled beneath a mirror used as a ceiling for a tunnel. I swam through waist-high water. I startled dogs in the weeds. And always, at every moment, I expected snipers. Or to get stopped by a guard. Or kidnapped by cannibals. And it began to snow.

If I was making tracks in the street, would the snow cover or reveal them? This and a hundred other questions came as I made my way between the trashcans and broken alley gates of the old city.

The song I heard from the windows was a lover's lament. Or an expression of unbearable affection for an unattainable woman. It made me yearn to have Alice beside me again. But as I slithered in the gutter with the sound of searchlights burning my shirt, I knew the truth. I will never see Alice again. I retraced the sorry events in my mind. How could she escape being burned to ashes in a fire? Or lost in a mountain of like sacks and forgotten. Even if they declared her a saint and show the colors of her holy banner to the world I've lost her. Far away from this sad country and lost beyond the waves. Cared for by the castrating hands of the high holy panjandrums. The insolvent guitars. The last few violins. Holy water and red silk cake.

As snow will do, I and the rest of the world became deaf to the air. If I wanted to take advantage of this and run I would have to do it at once. But if I stood to run the watchers would shoot me blind. So it was hands and knees. My rolls of fat wobbling beneath my tattered clothes. I tried to hold in my stomach in case someone was taking a picture. And by twelve o'clock, according to the clock tower ahead, I had no idea what was left and what was south.

I should have stayed in the protection of those that saved me. In a cold corner by a broken fence post I leaned and rested, the night that close. The snow building on the top of my head. When I regain my breath, I decided, I will make a dash down the street. Run in a zigzag pattern from curb to curb. Singing a hymn and flapping my arms like some extinct bird. It was my only hope.

Which is what I did when my chest stopped hurting and breathing returned. I looked out into the shining darkness of the deserted street in a winter night. Soundless. Nothing moving. All the windows blacked out. Doors blown from hinges or boarded shut. The slow drip of oil from an overturned car still smoldering from a battle I never heard.

I tromped across to the other sidewalk. Staggered back to the starting side. Advancing one hydrant, one broken tree, one low sill to the next. I could sense someone waiting for the perfect opportunity to shoot me. I felt the heat of gun sights on my back and my head. On my neck and my legs. I kept running. Across the street and ahead. Back again, gaining a few feet each time. My shoe caught something on the upward. The force and weight of my body flew out into the open. I landed on the frosted cobbles face first, scraping both hands.

I was out in the open. The middle of the street. And beneath the one last lamppost still lit in the entire city, a willing target on a merciless stage. Full lit so the performers cannot be mistaken. I kept my eyes shut tight. This was a theory that children had. A theory they believed in. If they shut their eyes no one could see them. A sane man's nature forces him to say this is absurd. But no one was shooting.

I crawled out of the light and back into the dark armor gleam of the wet street. Still nothing. Looking back, I can't explain what madness led me to stand straight and erect. Eyes still closed, I turned my unseeing face toward the sky and taunted them.

No one shot at me. I stood long enough to catch my breath. Even put both arms out, away from my body. Christ about to ascend into the abyss.

Nothing happened. I was neither carried to the sky by angels nor pelted with angry bullets from the anxious guns of madmen. My eyes opened without my consent. Everything came back into focus. Still nothing.

It wasn't that I was invisible, it was just a deserted street with nobody in it. I'd been dodging no one for an unknown amount of time.

I walked along the sidewalk, telling myself to stay safe anyway. Close to the buildings and stopping only once. Only once did I stop my progress. Once, when I saw my reflection in the only shop window still in place in all these storefronts.

I had not realized what I looked like. I took out the razor the young schoolgirl gave me out of her scrounging kindness and finished the job. It was a good job, considering the low light and the lack of soap or water.

At the edge of the city, blustering snow pounded at the vineyards. I could see the war machines hidden among the vines. But rusted now. Out of ammo. Left there. Never to get used again. Lost and solid with rust. Permanent relics of our displeasure and hatred for one another. The fangs and the jowls of the eater. The studded rolling pin of the grinder.

Once there were summer mornings. Garden dew on the

fresh petals. Now there are only the broken industrial hulks of extinction chemistry littering a field. I rested my head against the wheels of a half-buried half-track. If I listened hard enough I could hear fighting from almost every direction. It's lightning threatened a storm of sores. Houses were no longer safe from what falls from that kind of sky.

Dissatisfaction is everywhere here. Everyone has a grudge. Everyone is certain someone is oppressing him or her. And no two ideas seem to match. Compromise is impossible. Everyone else is at fault. The luxury of self-critique is out of the question. People wouldn't mind if their political enemies died by the bucketful. Compassion is so rare one must remind people there is still such a thing. That it still exists. Catch a picture of it and show the world. And yet most of the populace is in hiding. Partial to neither side. Just wanting tomorrow's sugar. They have no part of it. Are the ones who have no stake in the fighting stupid or wiser than the combatants?

We sing the curse of history. Something easy to hold to the heart instead of reason. The ancestors of the races stood upon the rock and spoke...

These generations of hatred have we established for your benefit. Whether you see yourself as the progeny of the oppressor or the oppressed. It gives a comfortable score to settle. A happy argument to help avoid the truth of thy own failures. The security of a ready-made point of view. Your handy excuse. Your identity you need not forge yourself. A convenient vendetta. Something to say for yourself. Press the automatic button and get your bag of chips. Let's hope it doesn't get caught on the other fellow's wiring.

This is my country. In the snow. Beside the dead rhinoceros. Flares to my right and left. A nation of cannibals waiting up ahead.

68.

As I am abandoned and at the mercy of the weather, I can't remember my geography of silence. My silent days. Studious with unwrapped pencils. And how do I know? How am I supposed to know the shape of Lothan as it is today? Three bedroom real estate, lines on the measured lot. A murderer behind every bush. Old men plagued by gout. Knives in their teeth. Do I go at night when the maudlin green monsters, afraid of the light, travel? Or wait for day and let the brainless sweet berries of children help me eat weeds and curry favor?

I finger my Nagant. A blessing to the hand. Some will say an ill chosen thing. But I am not a bird. I have to traverse the ground wary. Looking always left and right. Am I stepping in a trap or a goal? There is one last cigarette left in the country and I wish I had it.

What if I decide to shoot everything that moves? No one is innocent anymore, you know. Everyone has his or her game. Their argument. Their hobby. All the prophets I have met say the country is already apart at the seams. At the seams and into the fabric. Food shortages. Hate mongers. The oppressed masses in ironed shirts and slippers, riled by the pig faced blubber on the radio. And the pig face changes every other day, they say. One totem killed beneath the next. An exchange of gunfire and the degrees of influence spin the compass.

I wish I had a blanket but the snow must suffice. I allow it to cover me and lay motionless. It is wet as it clings but if you allow enough inches it will be the mantle to my planetary core.

But I am not allowed the patience.

Something is moving down by a broken fence. Low to the ground. Sunken into the snow. Just visible above the drifts. It is either aware of me and therefore ready to pounce, or oblivious altogether. I sneak my Nagant out of my belt. My hand is cold red shaking. I don't know if there is a moon tonight. I don't know if this is an eater or something to eat. I follow the rustle and undulation with the tip of the pistol.

The thing comes to the end of the fence in the middle of a field. It is a fence without a true reason to be there. If the thing stands it will be a threat and I will kill it. If it sees me it will reveal my presence and I will kill it. If it keeps still it is plotting to attack me and I will kill it. I fire the Nagant. The bolt feeling pushes my fist back to my face. The suppressor action mitigates the sound to the vicious spit. The mean pop sweeps across the snow. Bounces off an unseen farmhouse. Returns to me as a complaint.

Don't shoot, comes a voice from out a mound of snow. Don't shoot. I'm going to put up my hands. Put my hands in the air. And I will stand up. I am not armed. Don't shoot me. I have no weapon and there is no food for you. Do you hear me?

If I speak I could pinpoint my location for an accomplice. If I reveal myself this one's cohort could put a bullet through my ear. Their elaborate trap sprung. I say nothing but scan the grounds all around for a hint of anyone hiding. The second person. The shooter in the window. I see nothing, but that doesn't mean he isn't there.

Then comes a spark of light from my left. I can trace the path of the bullet in the night snow. But it isn't headed for me or the one I shot at. It goes off in another direction. And when it lands, another spark answers it in worse anger. I can make out other flashes too. Far down the lane. Across the fields. Guns are going off everywhere. But it is not a pitched battle, one side against another. The bullets are flying in seventeen different directions from points all around me. I look back to the end of the fence where I'd sent my bullet just in time to see a spark of light from where the voice came. An unseen hornet of a thing flings into the ground beside me. He is shooting back at me after all.

I dive to my stomach as bullets start flying across the air in crisscross tracks. I see the undeniable form of a man with a rifle not ten yards from me. He is shooting at someone beyond the fence. But as he fires he is also hit by a bullet from his other side. And he sprawls as his wound waters the snow dank red.

In seconds there are no pauses between shots. I see movement behind me and shoot at it. Bullets from across the way land near me. It's mass hysteria. Everyone is trying to kill everyone else. There is no rhyme or reason. I don't know how it came to be or how I got in the middle of this. Each shooter belongs to himself, under his own flag. Any target a hated thing. It is the Mountain again. The Mountain. Only played out across a snow covered prairie in the middle of nowhere instead of a hill like when we were young.

This is the thing I escaped so many years ago. Only here it is guns. It is how the Mountain of Flesh began. But we used hand weapons then. Swords and knives. Daggers and halberds. Armor and chain. Not this. This is madness. There can be no winners here.

My only need was to get out. But to move is to die. I stay on my belly. Still as a watching spider. I let the snow cover me complete. The sound of gunfire becomes a lullaby. The cries and screams of those getting killed are white noise. The moaning of the wounded like cool evening air through the window at night. I am rocked in a pleasant swing of the spinning planet. Comfort and peace in my stillness. Let them fight it out. Let them kill each other. There will be those who will say I am a coward because I don't join in. There are those who will say doing nothing is the same as agreement. But I have long ago refused to abide in their worlds.

The snow covers me and warms by bed. The sweet lilac of sleep douses my head with quiet syrup. I dream of childhood toys and rocking horses. A pleasant mother calling my name. A father taking pictures. A painted fence with no barbed wire. The gunfire falls far away.

I cuddle in the arms of the elements as the rest of the world kills itself over nothing.

69.

In the morning when I rise one eye scans the field from beneath a pillbox of heavy snow. The killing zone is quiet. I can just make out bodies scattered across the open land, all half covered in snow and blood. I listen for voices. For footsteps. For the telltale sign of the humans. Ready to spring up and do murder to someone before they can do it to me. This is no way to make breakfast. If you are a beast, your life is a tragic nothing. And when you die there is rejoicing.

Panic sores welt up in my hair. I clutch at the dead grass beneath the snow, wishing I could dig a tunnel. But the constant silence leads me to believe this horrid landscape is dead fish I need not fear. What if I was a rat? What if I ate pigeons? You see how the mind plays tricks in terror.

I watch for a long time. The melting snow forces my hand. I put my Nagant inside my coat and wipe it dry, being careful not to shoot myself in the nipple. My hands are beet red and twitch with blains. I fear returning to the human race. No one is your friend. Your dreams mean nothing at all. You fight for food. You step over the weak. These hands shake half from frost and half from fear. They will not understand if I raise my hands and beg them not to shoot. They will just kill me, these humans. But I can't stay here or I will die in the ground.

And thus, I stand. Crouched at first, straightening my back with caution. One step begs another. I am moving across the expanse. Half mud and half snow. There are two suns. The one we know and the larger, halo sun behind it. It is a terrible day to have a taste for bread and honey.

I find a stand of birch trees waiting like patient giraffes. I walk in and out of their legs, touching. Safe in here. But what of the cannibals, I wonder. There is no one feeding on the bodies sprawled about from last night's battle. No one is collecting meat on that field. If there were cannibals in Lothan wouldn't they smell the kill by now? Wouldn't they be planning a feast?

I cannot live in this country anymore. It is not the country I was born in. Just a few days ago there were angels rescuing me. Now everyone I see is trying to kill me.

There is a long trek ahead of me. I scratch the white bark from the trees and break a piece into something that will fit into my mouth. It is not food. But it will keep me from being hungry.

70.

I remember the devil's face on the boy who threatened to kill me in school. Kill Young Edju. Childlike boy. We are only eight years old and I cried like a pitiful goat. Frightened and weak. I was certain I was going to die, though he hadn't put a hand on me. It was a magic spell. He threatened with a wave and an evil eye and I cowered. I saw the realization of power in his face. He did not know he possessed such power before. And he gloried in it. And, like a prince, allowed my pardon. I ran from that room to the sound of flushing toilets. In three seconds I forgot about it all. When I sat in my chair I was proud of myself. I'd found something that worked. It would be a shameless lifetime practice. In time I would codify it. Send money to the starving waifs. Pronounce my placid, flaccid philosophy to the world. No violence. Begging for my water and my safety. It was an act. In private I beat everyone who threatened me. Shouted horrible words into their ears, turning them sour and deaf. Victory over all. Locked behind my door. A cult-like king.

These are the thoughts that plague my head as I made my way through the lands of the cannibals. Though I hadn't seen any. I thought they must have all eaten one another, seeing not one living soul for such a long time. But I saw inside. I knew. I judged myself and was stern with my own velocity. Remember, I told myself. Overconfidence leads to errors. And I stayed wary until the next nightfall.

Naked fortune gave me a place to stay under the wind. Though the snow kept falling I was not uncommon cold. It was a large raft made from some type of siding from a building just lying in among the trees. I propped it up like a lean-to with old branches and faced the flat side against the wind. It was more comfortable as it had any right to be. The soft carpet of old leaves and moss made a perfect floor. I sat inside that shelter on crossed legs. Hands on my knees. Waiting for the familiar tug that comes at the edges of sleep.

In my Roman days I would have here made prayers. But I couldn't do it. What death came close to me over the last few years came at the hand of tarrying for the saints. What safety I found I found on my own accord. No pronouncer rubbing fat fingers together as he goes on about the word of the cross led me here. No readings. No candles. No flying chariots and fire-rimmed winged wonders carrying golden pitchforks in the sky. No one threw the wide black book around against the devil's face. There was no savior in the bathroom when I was a boy and about to die. There were my own wiles. My own acting. My own pull, a fast one.

And if these were gifts of God given to me to help me survive, what is the game I am forced to live through? And if I stumble, was it foretold? How many times must the master planner start over before he gets it right?

I did not notice, in my wayward trance, that my body began to glow. I realized it later, after the pilgrims arrived in a modest single file. Putting bowls of soup and plates of bread before me.

I do not know where these people came from. Perhaps attracted by the glow I emanated from afar. It was a wonder to me until I saw the glow coming from my arms and legs, lighting up my impromptu shelter. The pilgrims gave their gifts and knelt like sheep around my prophet's circle. Waited for the wisdom or some miracle to come out of my face.

The savory scent of the foods they brought made me understand just how crazy with hunger I was. I held up a hand and said now my children wait for me to restore myself and I must tell you the universe. After I eat. I am thankful for your loyalties, I said as I lifted the closest bowl to my mouth. There was a warm spoon in that bowl and I splattered the soup down my throat with it like a licking cat. Then the breads. Some were light colored, others dark. There were slices of onion and thick, Slavic lard. With the bread, the onion, and the lard I made a monstrous sandwich that I ate in six bites or seven.

They waited with hands folded in perfect points. Like little children in a school bathroom waiting for the flames to find them. I ate my fill while they murmured their prayers. I did not care how long I made them wait. Nor did I trouble myself to try to make up some gibberish to pronounce when I'd finished. I trusted it would come to me. My filling stomach and satisfied mouth gateways to a self-assurance I did not earn.

There were two other bowls of soup. One with a mushroom flavor and the other a nondescript broth thick with rye dumplings and salt.

I wasted nothing. Not one crumb fell to the ground for the ants. I hated ants and wished them to starve. All bowls were empty. The mugs of beer and cups of water drained. I licked the spoons and the butter knife with which I spread the lard. One last, lone slice of black bread remained on a pretty yellow plate. I wondered if that was the gift of the thin little African girl praying so earnest in the snow. I closed my eyes in anticipation. Put the slice deep into my mouth and chewed.

It was bitter. Rancid and queer. It broke apart like old paper, crinkling into black shards. I spat out a mouthful of old dead leaves. My worshipers were gone or, more to the truth, never were. I sat beneath my shabby lean-to having feasted on leaves, mud and snow melt. And the rending pain that stabbed through my stomach and into my head made me wretch it all back out again.

When I emptied all I'd put in, I fell to my side in a crumpled ball. I had lost the last bit of mind that wasn't cut out of me. A momentary act of treason.

Madness. At last.

71.

And yet welcomed. Now I see said I, I said, aloud. Talking in the third person to the fourth nearby. Fourth minus distance and a staggering stare into the steel clouds and brass fixtures of the day. The day resumed and so did I, says I. I, Edju, at this age in particular. Not the running, hiding little boy. Not the stiff monster in the snowy streets as the ancient one. But I. I myself. The invisible I. The all-seeing I. I on board my own ship of state. I took up a twisted branch as walking stick and carried on, Nagant at the ready anyway. In spite of the I that I am today.

I had never noticed the dirty world as it is before then. The poets see beauty and I see filth. Slime trails and vapor stains. The organic beauty of the hole. Channels for water when it runs. In or out. My right leg is numb and the left one is dowdy. But as many men and women greater than I have reported – even the birds have left this country. This battered country killing itself. The birds took one look and twitched into the air. There are other trees. There are other streams. The people here are mad and will eat even little starlings out of chance desperation.

The skies, which I look to when I can think of nothing else, are empty of these things. And birdsong no longer exists. The result being the proliferation of worms and all the other things birds consume. A bird's nest from three years ago rolls across the bog like an escapee.

But why does it matter, in the end? I say to the stoic tree whistling in my rear ear. In years to come, far away, the sun will expand into a giant red ball. And it will consume the inner planets before collapsing on itself. The Earth and its memories, its books and its great names, will be a cinder in the star gas left behind. There will be no one to remember Napoleon or Einstein. The discovery of the simple cell. The music that ever was. The hatreds and loves you had as a young human. The roads we built. The cities we inhabited. The vaunting structures and the smite of natural wonder. And Alice too. As well as myself, of course. And you. And everything we've known. The fire from the red sun will consume it. The billowing fire from the red sun. The red sun as it eats Mercury and Venus and comes for us like death comes for us all. And there will be no mention of us in the cosmic stream. No mention of us, or anything we've done. All accomplishments. All the petty killings. The larger wars. The paintings. The arguments between this and that. Proof will come that it had all been for nothing. That greatest thing of all time. Gone. Along with time itself, for only humans count time. It can go on without us. The universe is not there to care about your leg cramp or hiccup. It cares nothing for starving children. It only eats us and we die, forgotten forever. As if none of this ever existed. There will not even be anyone left to forget us.

A man may go one of two ways, the rabbit hiding from my careless feet whispered. Knowing this end, he can begrudge the cosmos and indulge his vices. Or he can live in small rooms with few possessions and be simple. With Alice in a bag and the freak of holy relics always near.

I took the gun from my belt to kill the creature. But it already burrowed into the network of tunnels that have laughed at mere men for ages.

Yesterday I would have avoided it, you see. But today, with the red giant sun almost ready to devour everything that was ever known, I did not. Down in a dry gulley mixed amid a hazard of trees and shrubs, people huddled around a fire. They were not singing and I was unafraid. I called from above and they turned to watch me speak from the ridge.

May I come near you, I called with a hand beside my open

mouth. May I come share your fire?

They spoke to one another as I came down the slope toward them. One shook his head, but the others were calm and waved me on.

As I approached their shabby camp I became conscious of my need for a bath. A man can go two ways when the sun is turning the Earth to a cinder. Wild debauchery or quiet rooms. I still preferred the latter.

Four faces around the fire. The blue face wanted to believe something spectacular was about to happen. The red face had already seen the hopelessness in that kind of expectation. The green one only wanted one chance to have a clean shirt on and smell like cologne again. The yellow face wasn't taking any chances and stared at me the whole time. What color face was I, I wondered. A dark face? The dark face was looking for a mirror in their faces.

And still more stories of the troubles came out. I shared parts of my story. But they told me things I, again, could never have imagined. My country, the birthplace of my music, had seen men reduced to living in burrows. People wore what clothes they could scrounge or take from the bodies of the dead. There was a rise in diseases that hadn't been in our country for more than a generation.

People are eating leaves, the blue face frowned. They are eating leaves and thinking they are cheese sandwiches.

The laughter this generated among the others made me uncomfortable. I did not taste a cheese sandwich. But the thought of the flavors of specific foods began to dance in my mouth and my memory.

When was the last time we celebrated a holiday in this country, I asked. It was a general question addressed to no one. Spoken as I stared into the fire so hard the center seemed bright green. My face, the dark face, must have resembled a man hypnotized. Or lost in memory. There was a long period of silence before green face responded.

Do you know, green face said, there has not been a bowtie worn here in two years? And there are no more red tablecloths, he sighed. Do you recall the red tablecloths our mothers used for Christmas?

There was a collective sigh from everyone, as I remained silent in the fire.

They are all gone for flags now, yellow face said. Just like the green ones.

Well, there was the war, blue face said. Remember? I think four years ago? The one fought over what color tablecloth to use for which holiday. Remember?

Red face nodded and gave a sick smile. I'd almost forgotten. The greens won it, didn't they? Green tablecloths became the standard for Christmas tables all over the land for a year.

Yes, said blue face. And then there were no more Christmases be bright.

All those people died, yellow face shook his head. For nothing.

Seems to me that's what's been happening all along, red face was angry. A lot of people killing and dead, for nothing. I mean what's it all for? He stood up from the circle and put his hands out. About to engage in a soliloquy worthy of capes, skulls and Yoric. But yellow face shouted at him.

Sit down and shut up. We all know what we've lost.

Red face obeyed as if a bleating sheep and went back to staring into the fire like everyone else.

I used to follow the football matches in Astranloth, green face sighed. Every Sunday my Dad and I would get the paper and his cigarettes. We'd bring it home and spread all the sections out on the carpet. He'd smoke his head off and we'd recite the scores to each other from the previous week. Skaarheather has a good team this year but they're not getting it done, I'd say. Oh, Skaarheather has a loser for a coach. They got shutout three matches in a row. What kind of professional team has that? I used to miss those days.

Have you seen the news about Skaarheather, yellow face asked as he poked a stick at the ground.

No? What place are they in, green face allowed a burst of childish excitement out onto the surface.

Don't be ridiculous, yellow face threw his stick down. Skaarheather is three hovels and a mule nowadays. That's what I was going to say. The rivalry that existed for ages between the east and west sides of town finally got resolved. They ended up burning the city to the ground and killing anything that moved. I think there is a cow there, but I wouldn't doubt somebody killed and ate by now.

I used to love a good steak. Ever since I went to America one summer as I was between lessons.

Red face looked at green and made a ticking sound with his tongue. That's what we need to hear anymore. American steaks and football. And here we are starving to death in a frozen stand of birch trees.

From there on no one had anything to say. And a sullen silence put the camp under a spell. We sat a long time. I stared into the green of the inner flame until it changed to hot orange.

Two of my hosts disappeared for a time, and around dawn the snow returned. The flakes were large and fat and seemed more like fairies than crystals, the way they floated. Somewhere behind me there was a sound of a someone sharpening a knife on a stone.

My instincts told me to move on. I thanked them for their company and made my way toward a telephone booth some seven miles off.

The sound of their arguing and recriminations accompanied me all the way over the first ridge.

72.

The bat hung in the high willows like an omen on the day of departure. There were no cannibals here. Only metaphors. Something not understood called something else. There was thunder in the high places, far outside my ability to believe in what I can't see. It exists, you see. It is. Taken for granted. Since there were no longer birds anywhere in the land the bat had grown to five feet in height. This is how it works.

What was the point of it, after all this? A person wants to live their life under the threat of storms so long as the storms kill someone else. There are men and women too who count up the scores. People keep score. Why didn't you come to my party? Why didn't the bat attack you like thunder instead of me? People add the unfairness in long columns down the page. All ciphers they sum up.

With me, as I ducked beneath the shreds of boughs from the ruined trees, I was free. The only free man left in the world.

I sat near a frozen brook where the water had turned orange sometime in the night. Fish were stuck in it like ancient insects in the amber. Never to return. I don't know what you want from me, I said to the sky. The children will chase the stiff old man who threw away the only woman he loved. Whose friends kept the secret of their hatred for him but smiled with pretty faces when he was near.

I stood in the perfect dark. The national grid switched off. All our lights out. Our island, at war with itself, a blank spot in the sea. What is it you want from me, I asked the sky. There was no answer. Only the red moons of the Milky Way and American spy planes hiding in the star grist.

I waited for the snow to return. It would cover me in

warmth again.

I dreaded the call of the work mills. I wondered how the fighting would stop. I was afraid I'd get killed for no reason. Jailed for suspicion of something I didn't do. Kidnapped by the thieves that roamed the land. Eaten by the starving. Bought and sold like a slave. Hit by lightning. Killed by an avalanche. Snared in a trap meant for a bear. Falling into quicksand. Having a meteor land on me. Having someone mistake me for an escaped convict. Shot by hunters. Ambushed by creatures from another planet. Turned into a stone at the flick of a magic wand. Having the blood sucked out the top of my head by that gigantic bat in the willows. Or someone saw and knew that the phantoms that danced in my head were only made of sticks.

The sound of a vehicle broke the trance. I saw the rays of the headlights sweep across the moor. Another vehicle. And another. Three trucks silhouetted against the common horizon. That line between the ground and falling off the planet.

They formed a haphazard semicircle and stopped. But they kept their lights on as if they didn't care about the possibility of snipers. It was a revelation to me since everyone else took this precaution. Weren't they afraid of getting shot at? I took my Nagant out of my belt in case I had to save their careless lives.

But I need not have worried about their safety so much. Men jumped out of the trucks in a stream of hate. Rifles. Grim faces in the starlight. And from the cab of the first truck I'd seen, a man in an officer's cap came out and clapped his hands.

The men formed a few ragged but vicious looking rows. They stood somewhat at attention but were not rigid. Some were smoking cigarettes. Their delicious blue smoke made the bat in the willows stretch its black cape wings and look about. I heard them move like flexed leather.

The officer spoke in a low voice and I could not hear the words. Only the drone of a man in command. You will. We will. We must not. They might be. It was all I could imagine from the sounds he made. The men applauded. An odd thing for soldiers to be doing.

But in an instant, they formed one long skirmish line facing to my right. Then, on a command, began to advance toward a distant hill. They crouched as they went on, hid by the tall grass as well as the darkness. But someone saw them.

Ahead, on the ridge they were heading for, small flashes of smeared light went off. Seconds later I heard gunshots and the men crouched lower but kept advancing. They were in some sort of an attack on those heights. I covered my face with my hands and moaned.

Everywhere I go my countrymen are killing each other. Fighting each other. All the time. Every day. And still, after all this time, there was nothing to show for it. Nothing but orphans and corpses. And no sense of who was fighting whom.

After a while, the advancing men quickened their pace. Still they did not return fire lest they give their enemies the range and location of their advance. I did not see anyone fall. The more steps they took, I supposed, the more successful the assault. This seemed to be a reasonable assumption and I was somewhat proud of my military acumen.

There was a series of heavy thuds, like more thunder, from over my left shoulder. I turned in that direction but could only make out low flashes from far away. When I turned back to look at the assault I saw explosions erupting on the ridge they were attacking.

Artillery. These men had artillery supporting their attack. This was news. I'd heard the artillery used early on by the forces that fought one another. It'd been years since there were any active artillery units in our country.

But think about it, says I. If all that was the case, where are these coming from now? It was a question I toyed with as I watched the last image of those soldiers disappearing into the distance. It was obvious that new money had entered the game for control of the country. It was a matter of where it was coming from, and who was getting it.

The bat in the willows had flown away at some point during the fighting. I did not see it go, but it must have been a majestic thing to see.

73.

I did not stop to see who won the battle. Nor did I, at that moment, even understand who was fighting. For all I knew we were still torn into a multitude of factions and militias. Stranded, with no possibility of knowing who was who. Especially not in a field of faceless flags and dirty banners from the mud.

I struggled past the fighting and only had to pull my pistol out once. But I did not have to use it as the dog died without the mercy I intended to issue it. So you see, there was at least one person with a heart of compassion left in the country. The poor creature did not deserve to face the madness of the killer species it had decided to take up with. I walked from that spot hoping it did not suffer too long before it perished.

My city came to me, as I walked, in a dream of alabaster and crimson. And I saw what looked like a pair of pants wedged deep into a pool of mud. I had seen the lone shoe in the field and the underwear on the street, but never such a thing as this. Being a victim of my times, I admit I looked at the pants pocket to see if there was a wallet. I had no money and I admit I wondered for a second, but I saw nothing like it. Instead I noticed the pants moving. A pulling motion, ever so slight. Odd in that the mud looked solid and did not have a current or a flow of any kind. In fact, it looked ready to dry. But there was an unmistakable movement. And when that movement seemed to be repeating itself it dawned on me. Someone was stuck in this mud and was struggling to free himself. As I watched I wondered how anyone could breathe in that. And how does one fall in? And sink so far down in what looks almost solid.

I sat beside the dark brown pool and watched the pants try to wiggle and pull. There was a legitimate question about whether the poor fellow would make it. To be honest, the movement stopped a few times and each time I thought it was over. But there was still life in there. I came to own a great deal of respect for the brave soul trying to save himself down there.

After watching for some time, I decided to help him. Otherwise he wouldn't have made it, in the end. It was obvious that at some point he would be out of breath and drown in a sea of mud as if he never had a name. I braced myself across the mud, both feet on dry ground, and stooped to pull him out.

I think to this day that when he felt someone helping his spirits rose and his struggle became more animated. I believe bending over to give him a hand ended up being the right thing to do. Though I cannot now say what became of the man after he departed.

But when at last he was free I sat him on dry grass. He worked to dig the mud from his ears and nose. Somehow his mouth did not fill up. I attributed that to the talents of amphibians. The blood and knowledge they gave us, coursing through our veins from primordial days.

I thank you, he panted, wiping and flicking the mud from his face.

Did you almost die, you think, I asked him.

He didn't respond to this with words but stared at me with wide eyes as he continued cleaning himself. It was not a pleasant look he gave. More like a disapproving nun about to hit me with a book. After that the modern era came and a few killings changed those things.

We lay on our backs chewing the ends of hay strands and watching the morning come up. The sun kicking up a cloud of red dust on the horizon, or so I thought. When I mentioned this, he shook his head. No, he was sad to say, not dust. The blood of the ancestors. The blood of all our ancestors. Because nothing gets settled in this country of ours anymore. And the ancestors are rending their clothes like wolves.

I didn't want to explain that wolves never wore clothes and told myself he was only trying to be poetic. But it became obvious he saw this as a literal truth like arks in a wilderness of oceans.

His introduced himself as Spieglith. He said he was from an old Frisian stock, even before the Dogger Bank sunk into the sea. He boasted, my family has been here since the osteolepiforms roamed these waters. They were everywhere. Those were the days. We, that is my family, predate old Canute giving this island as a land grant to the Daalbans. That was the original ruling family, you know.

I did not want to appear stupid, so I nodded and made a sound somewhere between an amused hum and a knowing moan. He did not seem to appreciate what sounded like a medieval grunt. But I suspected he didn't want to seem too disapproving of me since I'd just saved his life.

I am headed back to Astranloth to find my old lodgings, I explained.

He smiled. That's where I was going, he grinned and slapped my arm. You have family there too?

No. I'm trying to find Alice.

Oh, he blushed. You've got a girl.

No, she's dead. I had her in a sack. She was either incinerated in a fire or pronounced a relic. I can't be sure. I don't have any idea what's become of her.

I understand, he nodded. That's a wide angle of possibilities. Incinerated or made a saint. I saw plenty of sacks burned because of the fighting. The bastards didn't care what they set on fire. Come on, he stood up on his tiny feet. And tapped me on the knee as he rose. It'll be easier if we go together. What's your name, by the way?

I am Edju.

Edju the young man or Edju the old man the children will hit with rocks and snowballs someday?

Somewhere near. Yes.

Ah. The Edju looking for his dead lover in a bag. I understand.

He helped me to my feet. I could not understand how his tiny feet supported such great weight and roundness. But since he seemed willing to help me I put that out of my mind. His was the face of a friend. And we went on.

There was a stretch of road the color of glass passing between a sad forest of dead trees. We walked to it from the mud pools and he pointed in the direction of the smog on the horizon.

It's there, he pointed. We just follow this road, as far as we can, and we'll get there.

We went free and easy. The first time I'd felt so calm and so good in ages. There were gigantic bats in all the dead trees. But even they seemed to whistle.

74.

Vulgar plumbing all the way down the bridges. Bridges after bridges across a series of rivers. Some frozen, some flowing. I did not understand.

It is because each place has a different temperature, Spieglith droned. He had the manner of a bearded lizard.

What is, I asked.

The reason some rivers are wet and some are solid. Do you think the air is all one temperature? Don't be ridiculous. It is a certain amount of degrees to my left and a certain other amount of degrees to my rear. He pointed at a tree. The temperature beside that tree is not the same as the temperature of the river we just crossed over. Simple.

I don't remember there being so many bridges, I shrugged. That's all.

No, you were thinking about the rivers. But never mind. Never mind. There are still a few more to cross.

But where did all the bridges come from? I don't recall there being all these rivers here. Were they always here? I've lived in this district all my life and I don't recall so many bridges. How many have we crossed? Four? Five? And still more ahead. I don't understand.

There are reasons we go the way we go, he replied in a cryptic voice something like a razor. You were gone a long time on your island. Much has changed.

And there you go, I challenged. How do you know this? Have I ever told you I lived on an island? Have I ever mentioned how long I lived there? No, I did not. How do you know this?

He answered my questions with the common drone of the mere matter of fact. When a man dies all in a rush, he explained, they say his entire life passes before his eyes. When the same man dies a slow, laborious death, the visions of his life come in chapters. They drip as if from an upturned bucket going dry. The memories torment him. They torture him. He lays in his bed, dying, and reviewing all the terrible things he's done to others. And I might add you've done plenty of that. But when a man gets swallowed by mud and struggles to free himself he gains power. The power to see into other men's hearts and minds. I know what you're going to say before you say it. Yes, I do.

No, you don't.

I already told you I do. You see? I said yes, I do before you could say No you don't. I knew what you were going to say before you said it. No, it isn't a rhetorical trick.

It's a trick.

See? I did it again. You're not listening. I already told you it isn't. You may think being stuck in a mud puddle doesn't give a person special power. I can't top you. But you'd still be wrong. I could fall in a hole and shoot straight to hell. You could push me and kill me that way. But that wouldn't make you right. Only a murderer.

We walked onto yet another bridge. The fifth or sixth since we'd started. I kept quiet until I could regain my own composure. It was impossible for people to read other people's minds.

I know a parlor trick when I see one, I said at last. Being stuck at the bottom of a pool of mud didn't give you super powers. It's ridiculous.

You see? I already answered this comment before you said it. Yes, I did.

No, you didn't.

I already said I did before you said I didn't.

We took a few more steps.

So, what am I thinking now?

It doesn't matter. It only matters what you are thinking

now. Or, rather, now. He gave a heavy sigh, as if burdened with a monstrous kind of knowledge. You see? Now is a series of things that become what once were just a moment ago. One can never know now because as soon as you have it, it isn't now anymore. It's a terrible responsibility. I have had to teach myself to use it with caution lest it makes me mad.

He put a lizard's hand on my shoulder as we walked. I could feel he needed my strength to support him. He continued to explain.

I have had to learn when to stop talking. When I keep going I always answer a question or reply to a comment before you say it. It's a curse. It's hard work trying to stop.

But wait a minute, I complained. You were only in the mud a little while ago. Did you learn all this just now?

Spieglith made a sorry smile at me. As if an apology. My boy, he said. I have been in the mud many times in my life. This was not the first time.

This struck me as even more ridiculous, but I didn't say anything. All I wanted to do was get back home, and he seemed to know the way. It was obvious I was unfamiliar with this route. Or, if I was familiar with it at one time, too much had changed by now.

It seemed to me that roads that accommodated two cars were now all widened to take four or even six. Stop signs replaced with efficient lights. And where once I could see my uncle's house from the top of a hill, now there were too many other houses in the way. The sight lines of my youth thus obliterated, I turned my thoughts back to my Alice. I dreamed of her the other night, I realized. She was alive and we spoke. We had plans to make love when everyone left, but there were people who saw what we were doing. They would not leave. Out of spite for us. I do not know the meaning of stupid dreams. Only the ones that make sense. I'd forgotten the dream, but I don't know what triggered the suppressed memory.

Spieglith looked at me from the side, trying not to draw attention to his watching me. But I saw him. And I could tell he knew what I was thinking. I hated him more than the bridge after bridge nonsense we had to endure.

We were silent for a long while. Days, I think, after that. I can't remember the details. Since I was sure he was sucking the images straight out of my brain I tried not to think at all. And, doing this, I think I did some permanent damage to myself. For there have been long lapses in my memory ever since. Plus, sometimes I have spots within my field of vision. When they come on I cannot see beyond some strange, ethereal blockage. It comes and goes for I, Edju, the older man.

And we came to a bridge that was splitting in the middle. Hard metallic cranks and squeals came from the gears and pulleys. The sources of these noises hidden somewhere in the apparatus. They were raising the bridge for a boat to pass.

What you cry into the sea becomes rivers of heavy water running under the waves. In all this time I thought there was no joy in my country. I believed deep in my heart all was sadness and misery. And yet here approaching us was a boat filled with laughter. Dancing. Strung haphazard with bright lights. Couples kissing in private corners. Bottles breaking underfoot on some unseen deck. Men and women arm in arm in a line, kicking their feet crooked into the air.

Spieglith stretched back, hands on his mammoth hips, taking it all in. Look at that, would you, he shook his head. Starving children in the gullies of all the shires and here they are, boozing it up. They ought to feel ashamed at how they're acting.

I agreed. I said something pious. Something chaste. Something responsible and haughty as if we knew best. We two homeless drifters. He covered in dried mud and I, Edju, getting older every day.

Some of the revelers waved and pointed in our direction. I could not make out what they said. It didn't matter. Spieglith said they were all going to hell. If not for their callous behavior in the midst of our demise, then for their drinking. Drinking and sex. And noise. What a waste. I don't like this modern music, he said as the boat passed between the lifted bridge halves.

Music.

I haven't heard music in a long time, I said.

You call that music? That's just somebody repeating the same few words over and over. Plus, a drum. They force all their rhymes. It's ridiculous.

I didn't say it, but to me it sounded like magic. Music, I thought, listening, is the sound the mind makes when it's working. Not like a clock. Not like a machine. But music is the gears. I didn't know what the song on board the vessel was about, but it captivated me. Then and there. I wanted to jump in and swim out to the boat. I wanted to shout for them to wait for me. To take me with them. Like three older cousins heading off to the lake but I must stay behind because I am too little, Edju. Or the moment they tell you that you are dying. And it isn't the dying you mind as much as the things you will be unaware of from then on. The smiles you will miss. The something going on without you. Death makes everyone an outcast. Your social life destroyed once and for all.

Spieglith and I watched the boat move down the river, taking its noise with it in its wake. A lone woman just at the stern, bare brown arms on the white steel railing. Looking at me. So much like Alice. Green eyes, I imagined. Hair the color of clean washed sand. Staring into my face.

The bridge began to crank and rattle, ungreased, back into place.

75.

But yes, she sang the exact words you thought she sang. I see it. These same streets. In olden times the horse drawn vegetables and electric power streetcars. You have no idea. And now we throw snap grenades over the heads of little boys walking. A world of wickedness and cruelty. It's what we are good at. This was my city. I loved it and hated it in turns. It bore me but wanted nothing to do with me. I left and gave up all authenticity. Accepted nowhere. Outcast in my own home. Now the smoldering dog piles, the pockets of bricks. Holes in the walls. The earwax that jumps from your head as if escaping. Hard arms and withering muscles. The end of an era. Once this place ripped the teeth out of pigs and ate them. Now it is a quarter of hiding apes and a lock on every mouth.

I stopped talking to Spieglith. I wanted him to die or slip or go his own way. Every few minutes he would say something and leave his words in the air like a dangling rope. It was a noose I walked into time and time again, until I shut up. I shut myself up in my own empty head where there were no prayers. My own private reliquary echoing between my ears.

I go on for a taste of cake. The memory of cream. In days of revolution no one bakes the pastries that kept the poets alive. And there is nothing to eat and the poets become soldiers like the rest. There is no more talk of the existential threat. There is only mayhem and killing one way or another. Poets talk in tortured pairings anyway. Few people care how many turned into murderers.

The charred walls black as rotted fruit. Many windows busted open. Shop displays empty. The friendly corner store pocked with bullet holes and dead snakes. Rags and small boxes amid the newspapers strewn useless. My grandfather would want the evening edition to see about his horses. There were strange smelling ornaments on the tree at Christmas. There were wayward toy figures separated from their set. The neighbor throws a plastic doll at my head. A man lifts a rope to my neck as I run by and I fall on my back. The driver asks if I hear what men do to men sometimes. I tell no one and disappear into my books.

Now here I am again, grown, without Alice. A son of a city that doesn't know me. No longer little boy Edju who receives the blows of cruel strangers and stays quiet. But larger now. A man without his blessed saints and the comfort of the confessional booth. The world stripped everything from me.

Spieglith stops and points down a broken street. There, he says. Three blocks down and turn left.

I bend my neck to follow where he points. There is nothing but ragged hulks. Here and there rough, demure buildings hiding in the shadows. We go on a few more steps.

I wonder where my house is from here, I scratch my head.

Spieglith stops and puts his hands on his hips. He turns to me as if I am a lost child with half a brain. Perhaps I am.

He lifts his hand and points behind us. There. Are you stupid? Three blocks down and turn left. Do you want me to take you there by the hand?

I do not know why people treat me this way. The entire world? A whole planet of such? No matter where you turn? Every last soul of us?

Then good-bye at last, I tell him. He waves me off with his bruised hand, limp and dismissive. As if I am a useless dog he would be grateful to be rid of. And good riddance too, I think. There is a brief moment when I think of taking out my Nagant M1895 and shooting him in the head. As I walk away from him I even put my palm on the butt of the stock. I can count the serrations with the cool skin of my palm. And

I want to feel the smooth blue trigger under my finger. I want to kill him. I admit it. I hear him hurry away.

This would be my chance. Who is watching? Who would stop me? Who would arrest me, there being no law anywhere? We are free to do it. If anyone was watching from a splintered sill what could they do? I fought with myself as I walked. I always let the abuse others hand me fester and linger. I never take it out. It lives in there and travels to every point of my compass. And when I do fight back it is too hard, too much, too much out of context. What if I let it go once?

I pulled the Nagant out and, in one motion, turned on my toes toward Spieglith. On one knee to steady my hand. Ready to fire. Ready to kill him. Ready to let myself go, just as she wanted. At last.

He was gone.

That's right. I heard him start to run while I was still debating, didn't I? Yes, I did. He'd read my mind again and was off, the bastard.

I should have figured it out. I hated his powers and fired anyway, into nothing. Across the dead street. My anger echoed along the old walls and hollowed rooms opened to the air by bombs during the fighting. My bullet ricocheted from brick to concrete and landed at last, killing a wooden door.

I returned the pistol to my belt, stood, and turned away. I was alone in my city again. Yes. She sang the exact words you thought she sang. Profane. Hidden from polite company. Words women do not say in public.

But that was long ago. This is now. And here I am.

76.

It was the ripping spikes of constant memory. Those things remembered that move of their own volition. The block became ten miles. The street became a thief. Watching. The eyes that watch from hidden placebos. The mind of the other, blaming you. Everything is wrong. Everything is my sweepings. Even past the buildings shorn and tattered, I keep my eyes on all horizons. I wait for the clank of reason. Or the fizz of attack. The extinct volcano of hate. Extinct in nature but casting a long shadow. And there are shadows on the Moon.

Something is watching me. Following from window to window as I go. As if there are no walls between the buildings. The buildings one long, constant place. The eyes swimming in and out of the window frames. Bigger. Smaller. A globular ball. Its paranoid wine tastes the sea.

There are no roses on the Moon. There are only eyes like daggers waiting for me to become vulnerable. To pounce and eat my face out. Do I remember the carnage of my nation? My people out in the hinterlands, far from abandoned cities like this? We burrow into hillsides to escape the concussion bombs. Obscure the openings to our dens with foliage. Escape the fighting, that is all we say we know.

We've neglected the country and the bulls. Forgotten the buildings and the yellow line. The land and the water, miscreant. It's the dangerous muddle we're in. We've made for ourselves. Remember the taste of candy and gum and your sweet summer chocolate. The favors given by drunken uncles. These things fade beneath the threat of the squat monsters in the hills, sending shells to kill you.

Every step reminds me that I am watched. Always watched. Watched all the time. There are machines that need human flesh for fuel, they say. I know I saw them at St. Bibiana, on the road.

I could hear the clanking muse. Metallic wings. Gears and hinges squeaking. A low moan of a rumble aching to dig into my cage and devour me. Somewhere near an open lot, gravel crunching beneath my boots, I pulled my gun.

There was an expulsion of gas. A blue vapor from behind a building. An old factory with all its windows broken out like bad teeth. Jaw hanging out into the air, dislocated and in pain. I turned three times to noises that taunted me. Fingered the trigger and vowed to kill whatever was stalking me. And I shouted as much.

Whatever is stalking me I will kill you, I shouted. Do you hear me? But it ignored me as if I were a little snit. Insignificant in the middle of the day despite my talents.

I heard the footfall. The iron heels. The ground rumbled at each step. I threw myself behind a rusted mailbox tipped over on its side. The rust, like orange mold, gripping it like a claw. Little by little I raised my head above the protection of the metal rim. I saw it approaching from the other side of the lot. A heavy-handed creature with teeth already dripping of blood from its last meal.

I aimed my pistol at an eye. The left one I think. The right one as I looked at it, but the left one as it looked out at me. And I squeezed the trigger ever so calm and careful. Jerking it makes you miss, especially at this distance. It was as if I could see the bullet like a black bee arching toward its face. But it did no damage. It was as if the monster was a pool of plasm that sucked in bullets like energy or food. Sustenance for a death coated breed. It waved two giant arms like Edju. Stiff and rigid and useless in the main. But threatening nonetheless. And it did not stop.

I held my gun hand with my free hand. Steady, steady, I demanded, and fired.

A round hit the beast in its face. It roared a little, bothered by wasps, but kept coming. Coming for me. Calling my name. Edju.

I stumbled from behind my cover and sprawled out in the street. I turned and fired twice more without aiming at all. Turn in fear, I hoped. Run in fear. But it was useless. My chance of frightening this scale and fire was next to nil. I ducked into a storefront, abandoned and empty of all things but ugly dust. I imagined I was in the dark there, but it was as if it saw me. I fired again and again out of that dark. I think I hit it once again, but all it did was make it angrier.

Now it stepped on the open shells of beaten buildings and crushed them. One foot. Giant and iron. Came the other, knocking over a car and a truck like toys. I heard my name again. Edju.

I ran a little way ahead and reloaded, because I didn't know how many I'd fired. This was mortal war. Edju, it kept calling.

Twenty. Thirty. Forty times until the monster's jaw set pockmarked in its mouth from my lead handiwork. But from the unseen quantum mystery to my left something slapped my face and called my name.

Edju for God's sake stop it.

I didn't recognize the face. But the face knew me somehow. I was famous as a child. Everyone knew my name. Then came the ages when no one remembered. But a few stalwart believers kept thinking of me. Somehow, I was a star to them. I don't know why. After the age of no one in my life came the ones I didn't care about. Then I had a job. Then I forgot everything. Then Alice. Then all this. Now an old man whose pig face meant nothing to me, pointing behind him at a building. His fat body obscuring my paltry vision.

Look what you've done, he moaned, pointing.

I stretched my neck to look around his massive self and saw a high white steeple in the sun above the clouds.

You've shot up the belltower. Why? Don't you understand people need these things? That's an important part of historical architecture. It's on a tour they give to people from the continent. Now look what you've done.

I thought it was a monster, I whispered.

Enough of your ridiculous memoir. He shook his head. Why I waited for you to be someone, to make something of your life I don't know. Now look at you. Laying filthy dirty on a street and shooting up a church for no good reason.

I thought I saw someone up there. Someone trying to kill me. Shoot at me. It was a story. I invented it on the spot to save myself. Save face. What dream was I having? I looked up and saw a clanking iron machine bearing down on me. I did what all reasonable men do when attacked by killer robots. They take out their guns and try to kill it. It's only natural. But, seeing the truth of it, I had to think fast so this person wouldn't think ill of me. I don't want anyone to think ill of me, so everything I do has to have a reason. Even when I am caught doing something stupid. I must make it seem brilliant somehow. I repeat my story. The parenthesis of belief stand around his eyes. I can see he wants to believe my explanation.

To be honest, I go on, I think I got him. He was green. A Green Man I think. Up by the angels. Didn't you see the nun point up there and say – oh yes, there's a Green Man in the statuary?

No.

That must have been before you arrived. But I got him. I saved her life and now everything is back to normal. If it hadn't been for you I would have never snapped out of it. Thank you. It is so good to see you again.

I could tell by the snap of my feigned recognition that he was proud I remembered him.

No. I couldn't remember his name or from where I knew

him. But he knew me. He straightened his tie and released a great, gray smile.

It's alright, he began to sweat. I'd have done it for anyone.

I stood up and dusted off my backside, forcing a fake, self-deprecating laugh. Well I appreciate your help. I looked up again at the tower, riddled from my bullets like a tattered pillow. Yes, I think we got him. That's one less Green Man to worry about.

I tapped him on the arm as he stood there with a stupid smile. I put my pistol back in my belt and turned away.

Thank you again, I told him over my shoulder. Earnest eyes. Serious demeanor. A slight military wave as I went.

He twiddled his fingers. I rushed into the smoke.

77.

I could rest in the sleep of the medication all night. The fog like a notion from ethereal days, weeping. I am a pure warrior. What I will put into my body from now on will be holy. I will shave at regular intervals. I will spray cologne on my ass. I will avoid all physical contact with all other human things. No written word will pass the portal of my eyes and stain my brain again.

This was the answer I determined as I walked away from that episode. My mistake back there embarrassed me, and the gun was still hot in my pants. I recognized that I had lost my head and it must never happen again.

Perhaps if I never speak to anyone beyond necessity again. Never offer a quick opinion. Never talk to anyone about anyone else. Stop myself from trying to be funny. Being clean. A blank slate. An open book. A ruined dominion. A soft acorn on the radiator of life. A slice of onion with that lemonade. From now on. From this day forward. Here and forever. Closed. Tight. Fit. Quiet. Stoic. A mystery all to itself.

I made my way through the smoke. The residue of battle. The battles of hate and slime. Making countless lives useless for the glory of the open dirt maw. The cavern that eats the flesh of dead men who never return. And the same men, for whom I am nothing but a joke, are dead in it. They created it. Let them wallow in it. Posing for pictures. Making sure they are richer. Better. Smarter. More handsome than I. I am the pure warrior. I kill churches and never fail. I eat rice and have sweaters. I use towels and wash my hands. I do not piss in the bed.

As if estranged and then reunited, I see the shattered gates. I remember the broken sidewalks and the forever weed that grew in the cracks. There was a bakery here. An old woman made cakes for children. There was a wild girl who lived in a black house. A common man wearing socks with his sandals. A world of people with old names and uneducated habits. Taverns. Movie houses. Shops of varied kinds. Newspapers. Catalogs. And the detritus of heaven. I began to recognize the bricks. I was getting closer to my home.

And seventeen steps from the door beyond the iron-railing fence came the first few signs of normalcy.

A perfect pile of dog shit with an absolute blanket of shimmering flies. Green eyed and black skinned. Red beady heads and festering hands at the ends of hair thin legs. I had found my way back into civilization at last.

A bodiless head of an old rubber doll that was once thrown at me from the neighboring yard as I ran, a boy.

The once dead body of a nameless animal. Hit by a car and rolled over by a hundred thousand tires until it was flat as a plate.

Half a penny whistle. Crumpled paper from failed tests. The glow of past moons kept in a jar the shape of a bell. Shards of things broken from other things that no one could describe. I was close. I could smell the old urine in the hallway of my building. Whether this was all in my imagination or the saints had preserved a touch of home for me I could not tell.

And Alice?

Well, I said as I saw my building again for the first time in ages. Time goes. There will be days I will sit at the window and wonder what might have been. What trails would I have taken if I had kept her by my side. What smoke from my pipe would color the ceilings of recollection. It would need a cold look and a heart full of dust. But this is how all people survive a loss. She's on her own, as she wanted to be. And perhaps, in the end, I made too much of her reaction. Maybe, on her leaving, she forgot me two days later.

If that long.

78.

Stand in front and yell the moon the moon yells back, you hear it through a tin ear. what noise you ignore. go in you cannot. walk away, thou art a pointless pilgrim.

Before my house I swear to you it was spring and the moons rode horses out of the Pleiades. This can't be right, I said. The Pleiades are only in the winter, I thought. But the moons saddled the star horses and rode the grist way trail anyway. Through the orange stars and the blue stars and the red ones too. Young lovers made animal things, it being spring. And I told Alice to go. She called me back in three days and I said no again and three days after that she was with another man. She looked over her thin shoulder as they walked away and gave me a sad, sick smile, Victory. She'd already moved on.

Before my house I stood thinking of this. Wondering how I'd forgotten the scene. She moved on. I flatter myself to say I ruined her life. She walked away with his arm around her waist and she looked over her shoulder and saw me. Now the whole country lies wrecked and the Scarecrow she made love to started it all, so the fault is mine.

Before my house with its scars and burns. Its busted windows and dirty paper curtains fluttering out into the open air. Breeze coming in from a shell hole in the back wall.

If I told you I stood before my house that once was and was near to tears you would believe me but it would be a lie. There are no more tears anywhere in the country. If I told you I stood before my house and wasn't afraid to go in you would not believe me but it would be the truth. The last time I was here – what – ten years ago – strangers had taken over. There were children in boxes and the scent of ammonia from the urine in the hall. I think there was a woman with a gun but it is foggy.

Before my house I stood scanning the places where green grass once grew. The trees changed colors in the fall and the winter air was fine. They are brown patches and dead limbs and the winter will never be as before. It will only mean starvation now. Now even the seasons need reforming.

If I told you as I stood there that I questioned myself on why and how it wouldn't matter what you believed. I saw her dead on the street and a string played from a golden bow like a violin of sodden twigs. I rushed to the Mountain and retrieved the bag. I stuffed her in it to protect her from the grudges men hold on the street at night. If I told you why you would listen but I would not convince even myself. Everything changed when I sent Alice away.

I'd forgotten her before I lived in this house. I went ahead with my life too. Maybe there was always a twinge. Because she was so beautiful and so unlike the others. I hated the idea that she would be like a bauble. A thing I could parade. A captured thing. Look what I snared. Look how beautiful she is and how ugly I am yet here she is. Look. But I'd forgotten it all and went on with my life too. Other things were important. So why did I bring her off the street?

Now I stood before my house without her body supported by my shoulder. No longer a weight I must carry. Vanished from me again. If I told you I thought about that growing stain in the last days I had her you would think I was a madman. But it worried me.

It worried me then in the same way I worried about what was next as I stood before my house. Who was in there? Was anyone left at all? Is there still running water and electricity for my spare light bulbs at night. I am a man of simple wants and few possessions. I don't need much. But water and light I still required.

If I told you I hesitated before my house you would understand. But I could wait no longer. The acid rain was forming green clouds in the sky and they began to boil and churn like angry priests. The first drops began to burn the top of my head and my shoulders. I would have to get inside and deal with whatever I found. I pulled the Nagant from my belt and kicked open the gate.

I wish I didn't feel I had to kill everybody I meet. If there is a dark glass in the world I am it.

My pistol pointed to the sky, I opened what remained of the door and scurried into the hall. Many of the small red and white tiles that made up the floor muddied or missing. Used for teeth I'd imagine. There was mail in my slot. I fumbled for my key. When I finally opened the little brass door, I could see hundreds of pieces of mail jammed in tight. So tight I couldn't pull it all out with one hand. I shut the little door and looked up the stairs to the first landing. I vowed to return for my mail once I was sure the room and the building were clear. I was alone now. The country had gone crazy. It was kill or die. The supplies were short everywhere. And it was my mail. It didn't belong to anyone but me.

One step at a time I worked my way to the first landing, keeping on my toes for silence. Stepping as light as I could with the weight of the Nagant I carried, I also listened for creaking floors. Doors closing. Muffled voices. I heard the mice and the rats scurrying inside the walls. They were no threat but, instead, may be a clue that there is some food around.

There are two doors on each landing. My room was behind one and, for a brief moment, I'd forgotten which one it was. It didn't matter, I decided. All these rooms would need clearing out. And, if there was no one in the whole building, I would pick the best. Maybe at the top floor where I can keep an eye out for patrols and the dragons that often flew in midsummer. It didn't matter one bit. I opened the door to the room on the left. I was certain this was mine.

There was no glass in the windows in this apartment. I could feel the rush of wet air blowing through the front room. It came through the broken windows, over the useless radiator where Alice once rested. Yes, it was mine. I recognized the carpet. The spare, plain, furniture.

There was a man sitting in the recliner that never worked. He smiled, watching my every move. I held the gun at the ready, but he was not armed and did not look like a threat.

I'm waiting for you, he said. I am next.

What do you mean, next, I asked, stretching the pistol toward him just to make a point. But he didn't have to answer. He looked familiar. Like my poor old father. But my father died long ago. And when he died, he was younger than this man.

It's an Argentine trick, he laughed. The prizewinner does it all the time.

I don't understand what you mean.

It doesn't matter, he waved me off and started to get up.

Don't make any fast moves or I'll plug you. Do you hear me?

He grew agitated with me for this. Put your stupid gun down you ignoramus. I'm not going to hurt you. He pointed at the coat rack beside me. I was still in the doorway during all this. I want my coat is all, he grumbled, shuffling his way toward the rack and me.

I sidestepped him and stood in the middle of the room, still keeping the Nagant pointed at him. It didn't seem to bother him. It took him quite a while to reach the coat rack and when he got there he worked at catching his breath.

See me out the door will you, he asked in a feeble whisper as he slipped on his winter coat. I can get down the stairs alright, but I'm always a little light headed by the time I reach the street. Okay?

I nodded, still waiting for him to whip a weapon out of his coat and start blasting at me. I expected it at any second and was more than ready. The second I saw blue steel, or silver, or dark brown, or cobalt, or whatever color his gun was, I was going to kill him.

But his hands never went inside his coat or in its pockets. Instead he went out the door and started down the stairs.

He went slow. One step for two feet. Step and join. Step and join. The way old men always descend in the films. Both hands on the rail, sliding along as he struggled. I returned to the doorway to watch. All the way down and shuffling across the broken tiles. He didn't wave. He didn't speak. He opened the remnant of green door and a bell tinkled, like the ones the old city shops used to have. Funny, I thought, I didn't hear it when I came in. It made me jealous. Like cartoons on soda bottles. I never got those coveted bottles. They always gave them to my younger lies.

It had been snowing since I'd come inside. There was a beautiful white edging growing on all the busted parts of the city. I could see the flakes billowing down from above just outside the open door he was going through.

Watch I don't fall, would you, he looked back at me, pitiful and spent.

Alright, I assured him and went back inside to take a position at one of the broken windows. The snow was getting in, but I had no way of stopping it.

Down the quick-crusting sidewalk he went, dragging his left leg and shuffling the right. Wherever he was going, I imagined, it would take him a year to get there. Funny though, I thought as I looked at the snow. I thought it was spring.

I heard voices. Young voices. Boys. A kind of giggle. A couple of mean squeals, and a snowball hit the old man square in the back of his old coat. And another hit him in the back of the head.

He stopped and turned, trying to wave his futile, stiff arms to shoo them away. And the grunts coming from his throat were those of a Frankenstein's monster. A sad, pathetic, growl. More hurt than angry.

When he took a step toward them the boys stopped throwing and screamed. Run, they yelled, run. Edju is coming. Edju is going to eat us. And they disappeared down the sidewalk, squealing, heading for hiding places I couldn't imagine.

The old man turned back to his intended direction. As things turned out, he would never return.

So, I said aloud, there is a future for the country after all this. I felt a strange sense of relief in having seen it.

79.

I heard the bells of St. Thorfinn.

I heard the bells of St. Thorfinn through the collected blood in my ears. They replaced the shining war thunder in the distance as if by magic decree. There had been no fighting anywhere for days. The birds were returning from the Frisians. Though the air was still cold the constant sun melted the packed snow. It turned the ice brown. But I suppressed the notion of going to the cathedral. It might be a trap. Our summers are so cold now. Like the sun at midnight in these high parts of the world. The yellow borealis. The doll heads we fish up from under the sea.

I heard the bells of St. Thorfinn over the days and weeks after my return. I collected many things inside my fortress. There were spools of twine and spatulas. I found white rocks in the alley and put them in a yellow box. One never knows what will pass for currency in the coming days of chaos. And these stones were so clear white and undimmed by the war. They will be worth something someday, I believed.

I heard the bells of St. Thorfinn as my hoard of goods filled the front room. There was so much, I had to clear a path to the window if I wanted to see the convulsions the world was making. I made a careful study of my possessions. I was cautious with my plastic lids and precise in the stacking of my cans. I kept a tally of left shoes and right shoes and spent many an enjoyable evening trying to find and create matching sets.

I heard the bells of St. Thorfinn but I stayed careful. I did not allow anyone to see me while I foraged, even though my range increased each week. Most of the time I went out when it was dark as the electricity was still out. Except for that EAT sign on the corner the world was black. Maybe once in a while you could squint at what were low candles in an occasional window. But the EAT sign was always on. The neon in the sign was clicking and buzzing as the illumination sometimes flickered. I assumed it was about to die at last, and I vowed to keep an eye on it so I could take it later. The dead glass tubing might be useful for something. One never knew.

I heard the bells of St. Thorfinn. But it did not hold the same magic as before. What the world has done to my simple trust. If faith can move the little cup then why are there disasters? Strange how we return to the playground of our captors. But return we did.

I saw the spire of St. Thorfinn in the evolving orange mist. The metallic haze of war parted by the natural wind. Replaced by brown whiffs of the dead river. The river down the same steps the boys took ages ago. To eat the ancient rocks and rub themselves against the old maze stones.

I watched as days became the calendar, frozen in our eyes. Ballistic expertise replaced by the more common things of daylight. There was water more often, and shops opened up. Men and women with medieval brooms and jackets made from sheep hides. Steel helmets as worn in the first war, a hundred years ago on the dank continent to the south. Different voices. New ways to say old words, I heard. And tenants in the rooms upstairs. I wondered what became of the landlord.

I heard the bells of St. Thorfinn on the day the electricity returned. It was as if sullen mannequins, half dead with dirty neglect, came alive as little monsters. Arms moving and heads rotating, soaking in the power from the cord in the wall. One never notices that all lights buzz as they shine. When the world was in darkness there was silence. With light comes noise. The choice is yours.

I watched my street return to life itself. Color and voices. Flags and trappings. A peddler pushing an ancient fruit cart, as if I had returned to my childhood. It took days to get used to it. I sat by my window, watching, my blue steel pistol at hand, careful. Searching for targets, avoiding becoming one. I am the oldest man in the country, it seems. These young people think themselves the center of the universe. Matching and measuring sticks to holes. Their parents brought on the times of troubles. Everything before last year was bad. Wrong. And yet they rely on the time-honored nakedness just like any generation before them they could name. I no longer saw the draw of it. I no longer looked at women's skirts. I was the pure warrior, sitting by my broken window beneath the power of my gun.

I remember the bells of St. Thorfinn. Their belltower and the calendar betrayed my whereabouts before. Who is to say they wouldn't betray me again? This was my thinking in those days I watched. And I would have been content to patch my life through this way until the end. But a man must eat. They took away the EAT sign on the corner and I felt my stomach cut with hunger and wretch with sourness at the same time. The thought of food drawing and disgusting me in the same moment. An awful line to dwell in.

More and more the young people in blue uniforms milled around. They walked in pairs, brisk and curt. Shirts and pants, skirts and shoes. Caps. Ties. Socks. Handkerchiefs. All the same color blue. Bright yet dull blue. Clean yet menacing, in a certain way. One color. That same mechanical blue on the same mechanical men and women. Always young. Always with a frozen smile. Always in pairs. Always pointing and talking and directing. Passing out pamphlets. Answering questions. They were never there, but they were always around. They appeared as if by some communal magic.

What troubled me from time to time were their faces as the bells rang. Within days of first seeing them, they began to look alike. The same open eyes. The same perfect nose. The only difference in the lips was that the women colored theirs. But it was as if one queen toad let loose a million eggs and each one the same. Pink glob, circle center, black eye gliding. Morphed and shaped as protrusions stir and there you are. A million perfect siblings. Even their voices carried the same lilt. And, dressed in their repairman blue, all blue, they carried themselves straight and official. But as a friend, you see, answering impatient questions by phone.

I heard the bells of St. Thorfinn on the morning of the parade. I'd forgotten what time it was. I heard the drums and saw the jugglers turn the corner. A crowd on both sidewalks, waving hands and laughing. Happy to see the glass coffin held high above the heads of weeping monks. Followed by the regal gait of Marta Vansimmerant. The daughter of the molding saint aloft.

I heard the music from the marchers. The bells in the distance. My chest became a lockbox. Seizing up with adrenalin and fear. A vacant, sizzling feeling behind my eyes. The spire of the belltower. The river down the steps. My old world returned. Complete with pairs of blue clad helpers.

They hid in deep corners, the story goes. Candlelight again. It's always candlelight by secret things. Plotting on garage floors, smell of dirty cement. But these were not the holy kind. They were not the watchman ships that sail the darkened night. Whispers teased the candle flames in planning innuendo.

If I could but remove the stain of sickness that follows me. Absolve all my demons. Will the cut of memory reduce by the use of time? I blame myself for not watching how it happened. If I'd paid attention maybe the world would be moonlight vistas promised. Until then we nod our heads at every oath.

The young people in blue are everywhere. Bells of St. Thorfinn or no. The sight of the dead saint's daughter stirred something inside my guts. I could not tell if it was lust or disgust. Can one exist without help from the other?

All these things flooded my head as I saw the moving platform that bore a nondescript sack. Gray or brown, I couldn't tell. With one spot of something like grease, as large as a quarter of the whole, to one side. I did not have to be told. I recognized it in one instant flame. The shock of genius and the new theory of chance. It was Alice. She was alive, though dead, after all.

80.

My hands shake. Nervous energy the master of my eyes. There is another kind of storm. I finger my pistol because it is safe. But it is not thunder there. The fighting draws nearer in real time and there is no avoiding it.

A boy runs under my window, mad crazy arms, a desperate race for safety somewhere.

You there, I call. And it works. He stops his hard shoes on a skid and turns his face up to my call. You there. Who is fighting whom out there? I shout my question over the rolling black noise.

It's a grave matter sir, he calls up with a hand to his mouth. The government is cancelled again because the Blues want a law against sepulchers and the greens say they're daft.

What do you mean the government is cancelled?

They were getting along but for... He didn't want to stay and answer my questions. His feet started to move and he began to walk sideways, not wanting to stay but being too polite to up and leave. Then there was a thing about graves and the Blues said that burial vaults need removal. That started the fight. Mister I have to go. My father is expecting his chowder.

Alright, get on then, I waved a hand. I waved my hand like a stiff old man. And I recognized what was happening. The onset of old Edju had already begun. In the next year or so that boy will taunt me on the street. And how you are buried won't mean a thing again. Like in the old days.

I busy myself with work to rebuild my life, such as it is.

I spend my days inspecting each room in the building. The top floors are the worst. More unsafe than the other floors. The rooftop is gone and the walls crumble at the touch. The further from the top you go, the more stable the structure. I take the time to gather simple things of necessity and return them to my rooms. My old rooms, just above the first floor, are the safest.

The back door, from the kitchen, goes out onto a gray porch. Someone barricaded the porch with wood, broken wagons and chairs. This would provide adequate protection from an assault launched from the alley. Of them all, only the solitary window in the kitchen above the sink remains intact. There is running water, but I found you cannot run it for long. And the longer you don't run it, the more collects in the pipes. There is no electricity, but this is no disadvantage. There is no electricity anywhere except for the neon sign at the corner buzzing the word EAT again. I make a note to find out how this is possible, hoping to tap into the source some way.

I have collected shirts left behind in closets. A tin box of band-aids. An empty cigar box. Three forks. A dry fountain pen. A pack of unused manila envelopes. A man's thin necklace that looks like mottled gold. A picture frame. Towels. An unopened package of batteries. A coatrack. A butter dish. Rubber bands.

These things I gathered in a hurry because of the sounds outside. There were no specific ideas what I would do with these things. But it seemed they might be useful somehow, as I did not have any of these things in my rooms. The construction qualities of the human mind are endless. Ever since the Babylonians built a tower to God and he told them to get down. This was in ancient times, before the war.

I did not take pillows or bed sheets, as there are rumors of human skin spawning dangerous creatures in them.

Sunk deep in my fear I watched the street from end to end. You see what you have done to me? Standing in piss puddles I turn to you and say, the noise from the jets overhead is like a breath of air in all this waste. How did we get from rubbing magic stones on our bodies to ordnance from 2,000 feet? I can't hear your answer, but the hidden message pulsates with venom.

And the sun remains the sun no matter how many times we use it. It is not yet the red giant that will render dictators unremembered. But a flame to candle out measurements of energy for want of a fleeting idea.

Voices from windows up and down the street still haunt me. I hear a lone clarinet in the deep dark. I know there are still people here, but no one shows their faces. They poke at reason as if it is a dead rat stiff in the dirt. Young Edju lifted a dead rat by its hard tail once and never got the plague. But the memory in my fingers was never the same.

There was heat in the smell of familiar houses, comfortable and old. Wet boards drying and edible mushrooms waiting for fingers. Life was better then, when the old boys built things. We always say we will make a better world but never seem to do better than the one we leave behind. Somehow there are still sailing boats on the water. Women in impossible jewels. Despite the eroding rain. After the fighting. The shouting. Beyond the fumbled hatreds of war. Children persist. They keep arriving. They construct fairy castles out of pounded rubble. They play stick figures marching inside the busted walls they call home. We do it again and again. We've become quite good at it.

I think entropy at the sound of the nearest turning page. The desire to see over the next hill is not the warmonger's payroll. But a tainted windmill tilted at the purveyor's grave tells all secrets. We knew it was coming. All the time.

I sat before the statues of the old saints and defied all reason. We raise the holy host and announce the security of prayer far and wide. We say good tidings to one another. Help feed the handless. Turn the clock in times of need and want. Yet we pound the pulpit bloody with the dripping fangs of vengeance when the wars come again. They will come again.

They are always lurking. It is energy spent so that the rest of history gets lived in quiet corners.

Count all the leaves that brush by before the winter comes in full. A million or a billion. The same beady eyes watch from coven shadows waiting to do their duty on your carcass when you can no longer look.

And we walk in piss puddles beneath the spy planes. Ready to kill the next thing that moves. Both we and our victims are kind to animals in the meanwhile.

Tell me where you've hidden the other bodies. Tell me my saints cannot hear me. Tell me the illusions of freedom are the means of control. Tell me what to see. What to hear. Tell me comforting tales that explain why I am favored above the naked native. Tell me all these things so I am never a bother to your plans. Never a bother to your conscience if ever some light shines on your brooding truths.

We kill each other over the kind of graves to be allowed. We kill for this.

I wait at the window for Alice to return. Gun in hand. I will run the gauntlet of hate the boys will spew when I am old. She will find her new lover unfit. Wait and see. I wait.

I am already moving slower than before. An easy target in the making. If I didn't need to eat I would never trust your world again, and I would stay in these rooms till the spiders wept.

RW Spryszak's recent work has appeared in *Peculiar Mormyrid, A-Minor Magazine*, and *Novelty* (UK), among others. His early work is archived in the John M Bennett Avant Writing Collection at the Ohio State University Libraries. He is editor at Thrice Publishing and Thrice Fiction Magazine where he recently produced *I Wagered Deep On The Run Of Six Rats To See Which Would Catch The First Fire*, a collection of contemporary surrealist and outsider writing for 2018.

Made in the USA
Monee, IL
26 March 2022

93585982R00178